ST. MARTIN'S PAPERBACKS TITLES BY

RELENTLESS AARON

SUGAR DADDY
RELENTLESS AARON

St. Martin's Paperbacks

If you've ever felt deceived and alone, abandoned by life and all of its heavy promises, then this book is dedicated to you.

Also, thank you, Tiny, Julie, Wataani, Shetalia, Alese, and all of "Team Relentless." The army of men and women who believe in me and my dream.

Sincerely, Relentless Aaron

This is a work of fiction. All of the characters, organizations, and events portrayed in this novel are either products of the author's imagination or are used fictitiously.

Relentless Aaron, Relentless Content, and Relentless are trademarks of Relentless Content, Inc.

SUGAR DADDY

Copyright © 2005 by Relentless Aaron. Excerpt from *Seems Like You're Ready* copyright © 2008 by Relentless Aaron. Cover photo © Barry David Marcus.

All rights reserved. For information address St. Martin's Press, 175 Fifth Avenue, New York, NY 10010.

ISBN: 0-312-94964-2
EAN: 978-0-312-94964-8

Printed in the United States of America

Relentless Content, Inc. edition published 2005
St. Martin's Paperbacks edition / June 2008

St. Martin's Paperbacks are published by St. Martin's Press, 175 Fifth Avenue, New York, NY 10010.

10 9 8 7 6 5 4 3 2 1

CHAPTER

1

Vince Reed was full of himself, his ego peaking at 99 (on a scale of 1 to 100). He and Toy cruised along River Road, a stretch along the New Jersey side of the Hudson River. It was a clear, starry night, one where you could imagine a wolf howling—or perhaps you wouldn't mind pulling over to lie on the hood of your car to stare up and out into the distance.

But that's not what Vince Reed had in mind. Reed was thinking of something more sinister, as usual. This occasion was personal; one of those rocky periods in his short relationship with Toy. The two weren't talking at the moment, and that further encouraged his mind to wander; that instant when the evil crept up from his heart so that the evidence was there in his eyes. Reed could melt steel with that evil gaze of his. Either that, or make a woman cry.

Toy was just the woman he could do that to. At present, she was focused on River Road's winding pavement. She wouldn't have any idea what made him act this way—this attitude of his—and that was perfectly fine with him. Better to keep this trick in the dark about his thoughts.

Keep her confused, was Reed's motto.

Despite the gray area between them, the two had no choice but to be absorbed in the glove leather seats of Reed's Lexus GS, a late model that had cost him well over 50 grand. He could've easily bought the Jag or even the Bentley Continental T that some other playas sported on the set. But he settled for the lesser-priced vehicle instead, tricking it out with all things digital and plush and gratifying. Those other vehicles, $75,000 luxury cars and trucks, would attract too much attention—way too much for a counterfeiter like Vince Reed.

"Pull over," Reed said, his voice breaking the silence oh-so-suddenly. Toy's head jerked slightly, and she gave that shy eyeballing that was (and wasn't) meant to be scornful. As usual, Reed irritated her with his abrasive commands.

Reed normally had Toy drive his car, taxiing him around, to duck and dodge the whole "profiling" epidemic in New Jersey: many state troopers targeted black males with expensive whips. A black woman, however, usually got treated differently. She might be a business owner, or the wife of some white executive. She could even be a churchgoer. The main thing was, Toy fit that perception of a black woman (at least in this day and age) who did not threaten the authorities and that macho male libido, nothing challenging. Just show them a woman who had her shit together, and they'd likely think that she was maybe deserving of such luxury. True to form, Toy McNight Williams fit that stereotype well. At least, as far as the eye could see, she did.

"Huh?" Toy said, accompanying that naive roll of her eyes. She figured Reed was trippin' as usual.

"I said, pull over. Whaddo I speak, French or somethin'?"

Toy barely sucked her teeth—no sense firing up his salty manner any more than it was. Then, as was her reflex from the day she met Vince Reed, she obeyed.

What does he want now? Here on this dark road?

They had been heading back to Fort Lee where Reed had a duplex condominium near the toll plaza, just next to the George Washington Bridge. They'd seen a movie featuring Queen Latifah, and then had dinner with Kitty, a new friend of Toy's. Generally, it felt natural to do as Reed asked. But something seemed threatening now, and Toy was suddenly frightened by the absence of light, the seclusion amidst the trees on this off-road spot. She didn't recognize the area, had only passed by now and again, but she realized that it made for a good lover's lane. And love was not what was in the air right now.

This must be about the money, Toy told herself. Even though they had discussed the incident—how she caused him to lose more than a half million in funny money—and it seemed she was forgiven, from the tone of his voice, the way he looked at her, it must still be on his mind.

Toy sank some in the driver's seat as Reed hopped out of the passenger's side of the Lexus, slamming the door with that "thud" that new cars make. She watched him as he walked around the front of the car, breaking the beams of the headlights as if by magic, until his steel-eyed expression eventually confronted her. Toy's heartbeat quickened. She could hear her own breathing and how nervously it seeped between her lips. And now she was trembling, like the last time.

The last time Toy felt fear like this it was too late, Reed had already smacked her. There had been no time to anticipate or feel threatened since she didn't know it was coming. The trembling, the fear and the choked-back sobs were late, but they were responses nonetheless. She never forgot that day, or the sting that Reed's palm left on her skin; in her mind, a sting so biting that she wanted to faint in order to avoid the throbbing pain, to avoid perhaps being hit again. She didn't faint, however; she merely submitted to the shock, knowing that she was wrong for how disrespectfully she'd spoken to him. In a strange way—not that she was a freak for pain—Toy was okay with the punishment, since it sort of marked the end of the episode. A quick bout of pain and misery, but then she could at least look forward to the after-argument sex. That was always good, a sweet n' sour sensation that felt like ice water dripping on her enflamed, confused emotions, all of it eventually soothing over the worst feelings. She felt trapped, but in a trap she could bear.

And now, here she was again, under fire. Only this time it was the anticipation of Reed's wrath that was the worst. Toy's nerves were tightening under her skin, her heart was pounding in quick-time, and a heated fear flushed her light brown skin. She was afraid, and needed to pee as she wondered what she'd done to tick him off in the middle of some dark secluded road by the riverside, nothing but the moon and Manhattan's brilliant skyline to cast some kind of hope on the situation.

The next few seconds were shortened by the flurry of sounds: the driver's side door, the annoying bell to indicate that the door was open and then, of course, Reed's voice.

"Out," he said, and he didn't wait for Toy to respond. He jerked her up and out of the driver's seat, almost causing her to bump her head. He did this, even though he'd expected her to obey his command. And Reed wasn't a small man: almost a foot taller than Toy, he weighed about 200 pounds— a tight 200, as a result of his constant movements each day, overseeing his growing counterfeit empire.

While the gravel made that familiar crunching sound beneath their footfalls, Reed led Toy toward the front of the car. And now for the face-off, where Toy would be made to confront Reed's impulsive whims again.

"Baby, I . . . I'm sorry about losing the money . . ." Toy referred to the delivery she was supposed to make earlier in the week. It wasn't specifically the *money* she'd lost as much as Reed's trust in her. And to add to the event, the car Toy drove—one of his Honda Civics with safes welded into their floors—was gone too.

Toy continued to plead for forgiveness. "I had no idea . . ."

"Listen, I don't wanna hear about you being sorry, or about your ideas—I should beat the shit outta you right here, right now—"

Toy cringed.

"You knew the fuckin' rules. I told you not to get outta the car."

"I'm so—" Toy caught herself before the shit got any deeper. She wanted to be clear about what had happened. Just to make it detailed enough: about her getting gas, and that she'd used the restroom while the attendant handled the task. *It's not all my fault.* But Reed had heard that story already.

"I don't give a fuck if you were ten months pregnant and about to give birth. If you couldn't do the job or you couldn't

follow the rules, then you shoulda stayed the fuck home.
A half mill I lost 'cause a' you . . ."

Toy wasn't 100 percent in the dark here; she at least knew
that the half million dollars that Reed was upset about would
only net him a 20 percent profit—$100,000 in legitimate
money. She'd grown accustomed to overhearing his business
calls, conversations with this n' that mid-level associate about
the points he'd expect on whatever delivery. But despite what
she knew, there was no way Toy would *dare* throw those
facts and figures around; no way she would act too smart for
her own good, especially now that she was forced to confront Reed's wrath.

With a lack of any appropriate response, Toy merely
sighed. It was a purr compared to Reed's abrasive remarks,
and there were no other sounds to compete with; no passing
traffic, no sign of other people; no one to save her in the
event things got out of hand. Toy's eyes welled with tears,
her body bracing itself for the unknown. She wanted to
speak.

"Don't say another fuckin' word." Reed had his stiff forefinger an inch from Toy's nose, as if it were a weapon; a
sword. He turned away from her for a time, his hands on his
hips, huffing and looking out across the water toward Manhattan. There was a decision he was considering, and then
one he made.

Spinning swiftly, Reed reached over Toy's shoulder,
grabbed her ponytail and swung her around until she was
standing somewhat off balance with her back to him. He
pushed her head forward until she was bent over the hood of
the Lexus, her breasts feeling the heat and vibration of the
engine's hum.

Toy's thoughts raced and tears soon fell onto the metallic
plum color of the sleek car.

"Stupid trick, you prob'ly the reason why Colin got locked
up in the first place . . ."

Reed's ranting opened up old scars but that was hardly
Toy's concern now, as her body was being manhandled, her

arms stretched out past her head toward the windshield. Toy had long erased thoughts of Colin from her mind: Colin, her long-ago husband; Colin, his federal convictions for racketeering and counterfeiting . . . Colin, her lost love. Those were painful images of the past, far from what was happening *now*; now, her only choice being to play the hand dealt to her.

Reed hooked his fingers in the waistband of Toy's blue miniskirt and snatched it south. A rip tore through the night, leaving her lower body bare against the June air. Within her web of confused thoughts, Toy wondered why Reed didn't just go ahead and say he was going to fuck her. Why didn't he just *take* her the way he had many times before? Why did he have to do it *this* way . . . so cruel . . . forcing himself like so?

Sometimes I just don't understand him.

A gasp escaped Toy's lips, and again once she heard his belt buckle and zipper come undone. By now, her every sense was consumed in this latest puzzle of Reed's actions. And besides, the combination of fear and control titillated and nerve-racked her, both. Beyond this overwhelming mania, though it was hard to believe, there was still the calm of this night, the scent of a skunk somewhere and the fragrances of trees and bushes around them.

Reed smacked Toy's bare ass and her body jolted. She let out a cry that cursed the treetops. Next, she felt his erection pressing against her, between her legs and finally inside her walls. She managed a winded wail, her semimoist opening able enough to accept his full size without tearing. Still, the friction was raw, nothing close to the bearable discomfort she had experienced one or two times before.

And now, Reed was pumping himself inside Toy without remorse. The Tiger-bone juice he'd drunk earlier kept him stiff and full-blooded as he worked his tool, pushing against Toy as though she were a challenge, however an unwilling one. His in-and-out thrusts hoisted Toy further onto the hood. His circular motions forced carnal hisses and squishing sounds from her lower regions, all while he breathed and panted as if he were busy running track.

When Reed withdrew Toy seemed to wilt, left to lie out on the slick hood—slick from her perspiration. And still, Reed wasn't done. He spread Toy's cheeks, hawked and then spat a glob of saliva into the crack of her ass. Then he entered her again, this time through her back door.

"Now I *know* you ain't gonna be difficult . . . relax that ass! Lemme get up in there!" Reed was telling Toy to do the impossible, probing her all the while. Another shriek cut into the dead of night once he made it inside. Her cries and whimpers increased with Reed's ever forceful thrusts.

Again, he smacked her ass. Another thrust. Another smack. The tension eventually loosened, allowing him in as far as he could reach, tight as a hand in glove. At this point, the air was spiced with the tweaking scent that seeped up from between them.

Sounding like a wounded animal, Toy gave and gave under Reed's weight. He grabbed her waist with proprietary command, owning her as he plunged deeper into the farthest reaches of her ass. His own husky, hell-raising holler cut through the trees with a slight echo, marking his completion. Reed propped his hand against Toy's spine to keep himself from collapsing, ignoring her whimpers, trying to regain his own composure.

Toy was numb from Reed's misuse of her body and could barely feel his throbbing dick shrink inside of her. His breathing over her back slowly returned to normal. Her skin was hot and tingling as she did her best to cope with this latest reality. *How could things have turned so sour?* From her happy home with the beginnings of a family . . . prosperity and hope . . . her life had seemed to take a spiral toward rock-bottom humiliation and abuse. She felt guilty and maybe deserving of every twinge of pain she endured.

"Pull your clothes on. Fix y'self," Reed told Toy after finally lifting himself up and away, his shriveled penis falling away from her. Toy tried to pull herself together, cutting an evil eye at Reed since his back was turned, since he was already headed for the driver's side of the Lex.

"Don't worry," Reed said as he opened the door. "I'll drive." Shutting the door behind him, he revved the motor, a cue for Toy to speed it up. She wiggled back into her miniskirt and found further issues since he'd ripped the garment earlier. Humiliated all the more, she held the skirt together and went to get into the car.

"Hurry up!" Reed's voice was muffled behind the windshield, but Toy could make out every word. *"And get in the backseat!"* Obediently, she went and lowered herself delicately onto the leather. Closing the door behind her, Toy noticed Reed adjusting the rearview mirror so as not to look at her.

I don't wanna see you either, Toy told herself, and she slumped down, defeated again. For the remainder of the drive, lying across the backseat, she eased in and out of a dreamy, tear-filled spell. She wished so hard that things could go back to the way they were.

CHAPTER

2

Toy McKnight wasn't much for traveling. She simply never aspired to expand beyond where she lived locally. Sure, she'd joined her friends on shopping romps to Delaware, to Philly, and there were one or two class trips when she was a teenager. But for the most part, Toy was a Jersey girl. A homebody for most of her young life. She grew up like most girls of the time, intoxicated by rappers, cars and clothes. After all, she never entertained things beyond those social norms . . . the impetuous trappings of a generation. Images and sounds from raptresses: Eve, Lil' Kim and Foxy Brown. They rapped about the hard-knock life and indiscreet sexual acts, and rarely reached beyond their own growing pains, while perpetuating similar trends, fads and practices among their followers.

These patterns were a fixture of the times, where lack of parental control might lead to disastrous anchors, references that weren't necessarily the best for a growing girl—sex, strip clubs and the latest clothing labels. On television, there were the sitcom comedies such as *Martin, Living Single* and *The Cosby Show*, all major productions that consistently crushed the stereotypes planted by those older dusty shows: *Good Times, The Jeffersons* and *What's Happening!!* Beyond radio and television, there were the magazines like *Essence, Right On!, Vibe* and *The Source*, all of which did little more than play on the virgin mind with what was trendy or what *should* be, pitching ideas and concepts alongside of the whos, the whats and the wheres of Black America.

For Toy and her peers, it was hard to escape suggestions of

what was "in" or what should be. She grew a desire for making her own money, being independent and making some man's dreams come true. Never mind the contradictions, Toy was a product of her environment, and so too was her thinking.

Her dreams soon progressed from having seven children (some of them white, to match her collection of dolls) to the fantasies of being a rapper's wife, most notably Nas. It was only when her buds grew into full C-cup breasts that she began to surrender to reality. And besides, her mother explained, "Thinking about having children and getting married is not the same as actually doing it."

So instead of ideas about having children and bedding a rapper, Toy's mind turned to eyeliner, formfitting outfits and the latest hairstyles. And finally, her mother guided her through the other issues such as menstruation, the use of tampons and how to best protect herself when the time came for sex—stuff a sixteen-year-old needed to know.

"I can't tell you what to do, Lord knows I've tried up until now. But you're a growing young woman, Toy. Old enough so that I can go out and party a little. Why should you have all the fun?" her mother said.

These were the local ways and means. Out of Toy's friends, Sonia, Stacy, Nicole and Erika, only Stacy made it to Howard University. The others were left to settle in as locals. If Mary J. Blige wore the flip style, if Brandy wore the braids or if Halle Berry sported an Egyptian cut, then so did Toy and friends.

Toy loved to look good. No matter that it might cost her last dollar, she had to be appealing, fly, ghetto fab. No, she couldn't afford the outfits such as the Roberto Cavalli boots, the Prada this or the Fendi that—names that the rap chicks promoted. But Toy nonetheless did the best she could with what she had, keeping her own variety of hairstyles and applying a little makeup to enhance her God-given good looks to keep on top of her flirt game. *You never can tell when a sexy thug might cross your path*, the girls used to say. And keeping her game tight meant she had to be first in line for the first come, first served deals so she could maintain her fan base—those young men who admired her captivating eyes, her delectable lips and the body that was still as fit as when she led cheers for the varsity squad back at Snyder High School. In a pair of jeans and a baby T-shirt, Toy sounded the call of the wild.

There were three types of guys that Toy knew of. There were the "squares," there were the "macks" and there were "thugs." Everyone else was in training to be one or the other. If they played ball, drove a fly ride or aspired to be a part of black entertainment, these were the only picks Toy had access to; part of that same small pond in Jersey City. Never mind that these were someone's sons, or that Toy was somebody's daughter; there was a sole objective here: flaunt your resources in order to attract hungry eyes.

Many of the nubile beauties at Snyder High, whether black, white or Latino, had a crush on Stan (The Man) Spencer, the school's quarterback. He was cute, something in the way of a soap opera star, and built like a young Hercules. He seemed to be all that Toy's mom said to look for: dashing, considerate and goal oriented. In time, Stan oozed his way into Toy's consciousness. She became infatuated with him. Even though she'd never been with a man before, or had any idea what true love (or soul mating) was about, Toy committed her all to a young man she only knew by reputation and other external characteristics.

By eighteen years young, Toy was no less than a sculptor's wet dream. Her eyes still twinkled with a certain innocence. Her smooth curves were unblemished by time, and her smile was warm with charisma.

Toy and Stan dated for a number of weeks—pizza, McDonald's, a couple of movies, a bus trip to Six Flags amusement park (a school trip)—until prom night neared. On the day Stan prepared to ask Toy to be his date, it was as though she could read his mind. Before he could get the inquiry out of his mouth, Toy said, "Of *course* I'll be your date!"

The prom was a simple occasion at a banquet hall at the river's edge. Some so-so house band played covers of popular songs, there was some mixing and matching with couples using the event to pledge their devotion or else to call it quits and there was the requisite booze that certain hotshots snuck in. Otherwise, the festivities were nothing to get excited about.

What *was* groundbreaking, and maybe historical in Toy's mind, were the post-prom events. It was on that late night/early morning, in a cheap motel at the lip of the Holland Tunnel, that Stan The Man took Toy's virginity.

Toy was upside down with anxiety and nervousness, looking forward to what "being made a woman" felt like, while Stan was up to other things. She was tipsy and he was drunk, all part of the plan (his plan) to win the bet he had going with his buddies. He'd boasted that he would hit it raw (without a condom) to prove that he could thug love Toy, one of the last virgins in town, and get her pregnant.

Stan had his own agenda, of course, since *saying* something and *doing* it seemed light-years apart. Plan A was to straight-out ask Toy. Plan B was to merely *tell* his buddies that, yes, he went up in her raw dawg. Only, he'd be lying. The truth would be to trick Toy by cutting a slit in the condom so that his semen would escape the bag. Once everyone heard about Toy missing a period, there was no doubt that Stan would be the one who did it—Stan, The Man. Plan C was to take the pussy by force and call her a liar if she opened her mouth. Whatever plan Stan decided on, the end result was to get Toy pregnant. It was nothing but a game to him. Another girl conquered. The $600 pot—his winnings— would immediately drop to $400 once he gave Toy the money to take care of *her* problem.

Although the odds were against her, Toy wasn't that stupid. She knew very well the statistics of teenage pregnancy since her friends Sonia and Nicole both got in trouble and then "solved" their dilemmas by abortion. Nicole had done it three times. Another friend, Sheree, actually went through with the birth, but then she and her baby disappeared; to where, nobody knew.

It wasn't until years later, long after prom night and the eventual breakup with Stan—and, of course, her abortion—that Toy learned the horrible truth about "Plan B." She ran into Bobby, one of Snyder High's "squares" and they talked about old times over pizza at a Broad Street establishment.

"We *watched* you, Toy. All the guys did. We knew all your business: how your pops left home when you were younger . . . how your moms was earnin' slave wages, waitin' tables at Gino's Diner . . . we even studied how you juggled time between after-school activities and necking with Tom, Dick and Harry . . ."

Toy was startled by the revelations, but she quickly protested, "It wasn't *that* many guys, Bobby. Just two— *Jesus.*"

"Okay, Toy. I can't even argue—*you're* the record-keeper. I just know that even kissing *one* dude, the *wrong* dude, gave you a rep."

"A rep?"

"Of course. You were hands off. It was bad enough that dorks like me were intimidated to approach you—then you were with this jock and that. Who's gonna compete with *Stan The Man*?" Bobby was sarcastic with the quarterback's name.

"You're so sweet. I think I woulda given you a shot, Bobby. At least you were going somewhere with your life. You had goals," Toy replied.

"Yeah. And I was so busy with 'em that I missed the boat."

"Oh, please. You can catch any girl you wanted."

"Maybe now." He smirked. "But *then*? No way, Jose." And then, while they were being so open about things, Bobby had no problem bringing up Toy's "problem."

The moment he dropped the bomb, exposing Stan and his cruel trick to win $600, Toy spit up what pizza she'd eaten right there on the table. There was a bout of coughing, and she wept some, but Bobby helped her regain her senses. In the end, Toy felt as though she'd been raped, only she hadn't known it. She felt more than betrayed. It was a revisiting of the memory of the abortion doctor sticking those damned forceps up into her uterus.

"But look at you now, Toy . . . forget the past! You gotta be the hottest butter pecan cutie in Jersey City. Scratch that . . . better make that *all* of Jersey. When I knew you when, you were a kitten that didn't know her way. Now you're a feline, girl! Infinitely marvelous."

"You're just saying that to make me feel better."

"No. I'm for real. But I *do* see your attitude changing." Bobby, with the reassuring grin.

"It still hurts somewhere deep in the pit of my stomach. But I guess I'll be all right. Just like anything else, I'll get over it . . ."

And so she did.

Despite her pains and tragedies, Toy managed to keep her sanity, maintaining hopes for brighter days. College was beyond her aspirations, so she tried following her mother's footsteps. When that job became one that brought mother and daughter too close for comfort, and that showed Toy no greater promise than what and where her mother was in life, Toy tried hostessing, and eventually bartending.

All of these attempts to earn her own substantial wages, to build her own little nest egg, were futile. Money was spent as fast as it was made. Toy helped out with expenses at home and purchased a secondhand car that was never quite right, always in the shop for one thing or another. Besides the car, Toy had to keep up with her ever-stunning image; something she believed might be her only valuable resource since she didn't have a substantial trade or a bankable career. She kept a clean credit report, but, as was her luck with men, Toy closed bank accounts one after another, unable to control her spending habits.

Hope and misery came and went like the seasons. By age 24, things changed dramatically. Demands in life caught up with Toy. There was the boyfriend she found was married—a secret he failed to share with her; one who cheated on her; and another who stole her car. She was able to lease a new ride, but the robbery left her with little money; the payments fell behind, and the finance company eventually repossessed the car.

There were many days that Toy teetered on the edge of depression, feeling as though the sand in her life's hourglass was falling away without anything to show for it. In time, Toy became desperate, fiending for a direction.

CHAPTER

3

Toy responded to a call for bartenders at a go-go club in the bowels of Jersey City know as Nuts & Screws.

"The money is real good, baby. You should try it. You sure got the body," said N'Tasha, one of the club's most popular personalities; next to Toy, that is. She was dark like a chestnut and had plain Afrocentric features under a long crinkle-curl weave. But all the coercion in the world wouldn't get Toy onstage.

Toy exhaled some built-up temptation and said, "I don't *think* so, N'Tasha. I'm not, like, an exhibitionist or anything. Plus, some of these men I've seen in the street . . . I couldn't face that . . ." She scoped out the club quickly, as if to consider the idea.

"So you think that stopped me?"

"Oh-h-h, no . . . I *know* it didn't stop you, N'Tasha. *Nothing* stops you!" Toy was thinking about the most extreme customer relations tactic her co-worker employed, such as the time she grabbed a customer's testicles while he was whispering in her ear. Although, now that she thought about it, even *that* was modest for N'Tasha. "I guess I just never . . . I'm too chicken-shit," she finally blurted.

"Mmmm . . . you ain't gotta tell *me* that," N'Tasha said, chiding her playfully. "Wanna hear a secret?" she asked.

Toy nodded, and that pretty, crooked smile crossed her lips.

"All you gotta do is put a dog's face on every man in the crowd. *Pretend* . . . use what they call mental pictures. Visualize . . ."

"No, N'Tasha."

"I mean, it ain't like you gotta go far, girl. Look at old fogy over near the VIP area—see 'im?"

"Mmm-hmm. He's one of my better tippers."

"Mine too," N'Tasha agreed. "But look at him lustin' over Samantha like she's a T-bone steak; like he ain't ate for a week . . ."

Samantha was the brunette onstage, with made-to-order breasts and a knowing seductiveness across her cute face. She had on a red lace thong and matching shoes—nothing else. Meanwhile, she was going to work, twisting her body like a pretzel in the face of the gray-haired, bespectacled patron, fogging up his glasses.

"Matter fact, I'm 'bout to get ugly with Miss Thang, cuz he's feeding her *my* money . . ." N'Tasha said with a scowl. "But, or, um . . . as I was saying, these men are soft, Toy. *Soft.* They're more fucked up than you n' I put together. Most of 'em got wives and kids at home, and still they need to get away for that thrill. They're low self-esteem–havin' dogs, Toy. Nah-mean?"

Toy's head craned into a slow nod.

"A lot of 'em are too insecure to ever go after the woman who will rock their world. *Scared.* They'd rather sneak around . . . keep us a secret . . . talk all kinds of ooh-baby-baby shit in our ears. Oh, baby, I could buy you this . . . I could put you in an apartment and take care of you for life. Blah, blah, blah. But at the same time they're conservative on the surface. They wear masks, girl. Back home it's that girl next door for Mom and Dad to meet. The girl their parents will respect."

Toy giggled at N'Tasha's witty details, how she was ghetto with it, but still managed to hit the nail right on the head. "Now that you mention it, that guy *does* look like the Marmaduke cartoon."

"Oh—*shit!* No-you-*didn't*! *Marmaduke!* Ha-ha-ha-hooooeee . . ." N'Tasha's heavy laughter drifted off as she returned to the stage. Break time was over. It was time to make money.

Toy thought about what N'Tasha said: *"Put a dog's face on every man . . . "* Of course her friend was both bitter and biased, but she also made a lot of sense. As she went to serve another drink to old fogy Marmaduke, she peeked up at N'Tasha onstage. N'Tasha, with silvery contact lenses in her eyes, stripped and tossed her brassiere so that it landed on the counter next to Toy. While Toy stood there, mouth agape, N'Tasha winked and jiggled her tits for the few dozen spectators. So proud of her gifts and talents.

Toy couldn't help thinking about the six, seven and eight hundred dollars that N'Tasha made for one day's work. No fucking the customers, and they'd never touch her, if that's what she required. A piece of cake. Toy hadn't given the idea too much consideration in the past, but suddenly, it was enough to make her reconsider being such a chicken-shit.

Being a bartender was not much different than a mother, a priest, a counselor or a disciplinarian. The only thing special about the job was that you poured drinks and exercised tolerance. Of course, a pretty woman was a target for pickup lines, bartender or not: "I'd like to kiss you, but my friend told me you were already interested in kissing *me* . . ." "Excuse me . . . I think part of your body belongs to me . . ." "I've been watching you turn down guys all night. So, can I have your phone number?"

These lame pickup lines, and dozens of others like them, were tried by all colors and sizes of men. Sometimes the mere phoniness was a turnoff, evoking memories of Stan, the ultimate trickster. At other times, Toy laughed it off, charging the man's words to his head and not his heart. There was a certain finesse she had to keep in order to save her from losing it, perhaps smacking a customer for being downright rude.

One day Mr. Harris, her boss at Nuts & Screws, made a suggestion, something that changed Toy's thinking. "Think of yourself as a living, breathing billboard. You're part of the show. I know you're a bartender, not a dancer, but that's not my point. I hired you for your charisma, but with that comes the tits and ass. Nothing more, nothing less . . ."

Toy was somewhat taken aback by how direct the boss was, but he went on explaining. "I know it sounds a bit crude, Toy, but that's life, girl. At least in the good ole USA—it's all about looking good, young and sexy. Sex sells cars, soft drinks and airplane tickets. Remember what I'm telling you, Toy. At my establishment, sex sells drinks and it keeps the customers coming back. So, sell it. Put on the show, the smile, the sunny attitude, the whole package. What you do when you're at home is your business. But while you're doing your shift behind this bar, shake that pretty ass of yours and pour long into those drinks. Tell the customer whatever he wants to hear to keep 'im buyin'. But just remember . . . don't take the job home with you."

Mr. Harris and his keep-it-real way of saying things helped to desensitize Toy to the constant flow of male and female advances. It even empowered her with confidence so that she turned up the level in her work performance.

Just when Toy figured she'd seen and heard it all, a man she guessed was in his mid-twenties approached the service bar. He was almost her complexion, a copper-gold versus her butter pecan brown. It was Toy who struck up the conversation first, wondering why he'd come to a bar for a virgin strawberry daiquiri and not something 100-proof.

"I guess I never was much for getting high," was his response. "I get high on spontaneity, music and making money."

"Oh," mouthed Toy, her eyes wide. The three-pronged testament caught her attention. "I never heard of *that* before, how music makes you high. How's that work?" She was in the mood to be humored.

"Easy. Even the *word* music tells the story. Muse-ic. Muse means inspiration."

"That so," Toy muttered, waiting for the punch line. Most of her patrons leveraged a few words, manipulating ideas to eventually get around to the subject of sex.

"Sure. You're from around here, right?"

Toy nodded, her intuition already alert and waiting for the next shift in subjects. At the same time, she was reluctant to share any more details with this stranger. "Yeah. But I want to hear more about your point . . . about music getting you high."

"That was why I asked where you live, 'cuz if you're from around here, I'm sure you're familiar with Teddy Pendergrass."

"I am."

"Good . . . good. So you know those old-school jams, like 'Turn Off the Lights' or 'Feel the Fire'?"

Toy shrugged, neither confirming or denying—the truth was, she wasn't as familiar as she pretended.

That's when the customer hit a tune for her. His voice was soft and velvety, as if he was making little effort. "Betcha by golly wow . . . you're the one that I've been waiting for, forever . . ."

Toy stared at the man. She couldn't believe he was singing to her right there at the bar, with all those other men standing around. *This is a first.* She began to feel like Juliet, warming to Romeo's pleas. "You're just too much. What, am I supposed to tip *you*?" she joked, flashing a welcoming smile.

He smiled back, and suddenly Toy was conscious of the attention they grabbed. N'Tasha gave a thumbs-up sign, embarrassing the hell out of Toy. "Okay . . . see, you need to stop this. If this is some kind of trick to spin me and get me all teary-eyed, all mushy, just 'cuz you can bust a tune, then—"

He cut in, "Then say you'll have dinner with me. Let me have the opportunity to become a part of your life." The man took her hand over the bar.

"I can't *believe* you!" Toy said. Her clenched teeth and darting eyes hinted that he was putting her on the spot. "I don't even *know* you. I don't even know your name."

"Well, thank you for asking. My name is Colin Williams, pleased to meet you." Colin bent down and kissed Toy's hand. By now the entire club seemed to be watching. The crowd gave the two a raucous standing ovation—whistles and foot stomping included. The attention made Toy shiver with delight and flattery. "And these are for you, in case you need some, ahh . . . inspiration," he said, smirking.

"Oh—my—God," Toy exclaimed, her mouth hanging open.

Colin had presented a modest bouquet of flowers, evidence that he had been interested in her all along. Toy was left with that expression on her face, how she'd been played.

"If you need a dinner break I won't be mad," Mr. Harris said. Again, Mr. Harris put Toy in a state of disbelief. *The boss, giving me a break?*

"I can't believe you did that," Toy said to Colin as they looked across the small table at each other. Having been successfully swept off of her feet, Toy was now across from Nuts & Screws at King Jia's Garden, a Chinese restaurant. It was a step above a fast-food joint, but just shy of formal seating.

"My boss even encouraged this," she continued, voicing her disbelief.

"Well, how else was I supposed to approach you? I figured you must get at least a couple hundred passes a day, everybody wantin' to get into your pants."

"And you? What do you want from me, Mr. Colin Williams?"

"You want it raw? Or sugar-coated?"

"I'm fine with raw, but don't turn into a slut," said Toy, intense sincerity in her eyes.

"Toy, to keep it real with you, there ain't no denyin' I'm a man. I'm just like other men, with much of the same wants and needs. So . . . if you're askin' if I'm interested . . ."

"No, that sounds sugar-coated. Be specific. What do you *want*?"

Colin took a deep breath, suddenly faced with all of Toy's luggage. "I want what's at the end of the rainbow, Toy. I want to know what's what, down to the very root of the blooming flower that's sitting in front of me. I want to share your joys and pains. I want to know what makes you tick . . . what makes you sad . . . whatever makes you feel complete. Are you lacking something? I want to give that to you. I want to fill in those blanks in your life."

Eventually, Toy came out of her spell—or tried to. She

started to say something but the words seemed to stick in her throat. Her nether regions quivered.

"What?" asked Colin, his curiosity virtually sucking the words from her mouth and mind.

"You . . . you can't just roll up on a person and be so open. You don't even know me. I could be a bartender by day and a murderess by night—"

"Yeah," Colin interrupted. "But you could be a closet freak too. So I'll take my chances." Toy's eyes shifted up toward the ceiling fans and she wagged her head slightly. "But the truth is, I've been by the club four times since last week. I've talked to a few people about you. I even followed you home one night . . . well, two nights."

Toy shoved back from the table. "I knew this was too good to be true. You're a friggin' stalker!" She was a wink away from getting up to go back to work. It was nice while it lasted.

"Easy. . . . easy . . . it's not like that, Toy. You usually take a cab home, right?"

"And if I do?"

"Well, on those nights, I guess, you accepted rides home from customers."

"And if I did?"

"I just wanted to see that you got home safe. I didn't peek in your windows. I didn't wait around till morning—"

"How do *I* know you didn't?"

Colin ignored that and went on to say, "I just waited till you got safely in your front door, and I left."

Toy felt the intensity of his sincerity. She stared at him through watery eyes, her emotions in a tizzy. This, she assessed, was a first. "One thing after another," she said, her lips barely moving. "The whole singing bit, the flowers, *investigating me* . . . making sure I'm getting home safe. Who—are—you?"

"Toy McKnight, I hope that you'll let me in your life . . . I hope that one day I'll be the man of your dreams."

CHAPTER

4

Toy couldn't get to sleep that night. She was ready for sleep. She was relaxed, and her body was fatigued from day-long activity. But something deep down wouldn't allow it, like a flame that refused to die out.

There was Colin's image: not too much taller than she. Short black hair, brushed forward, only a hint of a mustache over his lip, with no other facial hair to cover up his skin's glow. His lips, she recalled, were curved into a thuggish pout, and his nose coned out to a slightly arched button point. Toy could even smell Colin's natural fragrance, how it stayed with her, on the hand that he had held . . . and kissed. The same hand she swore she'd never wash, or at least for as long as she could stand it. Toy could hear his voice singing to her; that deep, velvety vibrato that soothed every fiber of her being. The words he spoke, wanting what was at the end of *her rainbow!?* Wanting to get to the root of her, the *blooming flower!?* And wanting *to be the man of her dreams!? Damn!* He knew all the right things to say.

Colin, are you the man of my dreams?

She recalled Colin's story, how he came to New Jersey from California. She saw him as that "catch" that her girl-friends (or any woman, she imagined) never got to sink their teeth into. He came here to take advantage of "certain financial opportunities," he'd explained. Toy liked the sound of that; not so much the financial theme (although that certainly was a *plus* in her ears), but that this man would travel so far across the country to pursue opportunity. It was the very urge that Toy had—to get up and leave to follow her dreams—but which Colin had acted on.

Eventually, Toy closed her eyes and dreamed of being in Colin's arms, cuddled in safety, warmed by burning logs, taking turns feeding each other cherries and champagne. The dream carried her into a deep, smiling sleep that included her clutching pillows in her arms and between her legs.

Consummating the relationship took less than a month. Colin had a friend who had a time-share cabin in Martha's Vineyard. And although black folks migrated there at certain times of the year, Colin's intentions were wholly unique, and had nothing to do with any movement by any particular group or following. This was about Colin and Toy making history together.

The cabin was simple, and left much to be desired. Once they crossed the threshold, Colin's face registered salty disappointment.

"What'd you expect? The Plaza Hotel?" Toy asked him. She spoke as if she'd visited all four corners of the earth.

"I'm all right with it if you are," he said doubtfully. Eventually he zoomed in with those soulful hazel eyes of his.

Toy could see that Colin was totally into her, his signals and intentions subtle and unimposing. She'd passed that ring of concern where she was afraid she'd lose out on having him, and now she was alone with him, more so than ever before. She was still a bit nervous about the power and influence she'd surrendered to Colin, coming all the way to Siberia (in a sense) so they could explore each other further. This was the moment of truth, when she could look past him being just another good-looking man with an impressive talk game. This was a time to expose all of her physical secrets and imperfections. No more of those clever innuendos or hints about what their "union" might be like. No more mischievous glances over dinner, coy gazes or promising remarks during their walks in the park.

Toy wanted to be realistic about her expectations during their weekend stay on Martha's Vineyard, but at the same time she wanted to be conservative. She wanted this connection to last. Colin wasn't like other men, and she didn't intend to treat him that way. But she also hungered for him, already familiar with his soft kisses and sensual touch. She wanted to let herself go . . . to show him just how hot she was for him, and how hot she could be. She wanted to get the most out of this, giving him the most of her. But what would he think of her? Would he think of her as a freak of the week?

Ultimately, Toy was caught up in a three-dimensional field of confusion where her desires fought with her righteous values, all underneath the clouds of her past experiences.

Colin, on the other hand, wanted to make this easy on both of them. He didn't want Toy to feel trapped simply because Martha's Vineyard was his idea; the cabin, the seclusion, and one "activity" to indulge in.

So he kicked off their weekend by making chicken shish kebabs, and they fed each other. For dessert, they fed each other green grapes, then graduated to bananas and whipped cream. It was messy, but also erotic the way Colin ate the sweet stuff from Toy's lips.

When the sun went down, Colin took Toy for a walk by the shore, and they walked just out of reach from the tide. Their footwear got wet and they wound up splashing each other until Toy chased Colin back to the cabin.

Back indoors, Colin started a fire in the wood-burning stove, and then took lingering leers at Toy as she dried her hair. Whether or not she was making an effort at this, Colin wasn't sure, but it was working. He was seduced.

"Here . . . lemme do that," he offered, and took the towel. It seemed so natural to have his hands on Toy, to touch her in some way. And from her hair, he graduated to a neck massage. "Mmmm . . . that feels good," purred Toy, her head turned to the side, offering him greater access. Then she blurted, "Wait, baby. Lemme step in the bedroom a minute . . . clean up a little." Colin brooded, as though those were painful words to hear. Toy emerged a short time later wearing a purple camisole, matching see-through bra and bikini panties and a pink garter belt holding up black fishnet stockings. Her hair was tied up in two pigtails, like the young high school girls wore. "You like?" Toy asked, one hand on her hip, the other on the wall.

"*Whoa!* I thought you said you were gonna clean up a lit-tle, not turn into a sex kitten."

Toy frowned and looked at Colin as if he were crazy.

Colin jumped. "No-no-no . . . I didn't mean it *that* way . . . I like, I like. I'm just surprised."

Toy's frown faded, and gave way to an embarrassed shine.

"So . . . now, can I pull out *my* surprise?" Colin suggested cleverly, although he gestured to let Toy know *It's not what you're thinking. At least, not yet it isn't.* He raised up from the bearskin rug and went for the knapsack he brought along. "Ta-dow," he said, producing a Barry White CD.

"Okay, but it's not gonna put me to sleep, is it? I'm not into old school too much, as you know."

"Please trust, baby. Barry White is more than just old school. He's the smoothest there ever was. Just sit your pretty behind down and let *me* handle the DJ work." Colin flashed his best smile as he popped the CD in place. Then he joined Toy on the cabin's only couch and snuggled up.

"I like it. Sounds real smooth."

"I told you . . . he's the smoothest of the smooths."

"Mind if I do a little entertaining?"

"Of course not. What did you . . . have . . . in . . ." Colin's words faded off with the help of Toy's fingers against his lips.

"Shhh. You just have a seat. Let me do the work," said Toy.

Colin's loins stirred as she stood before him. She bent over, teasing him as she wiggled her body. She kissed him lightly on the forehead and cheeks, and then grazed his lips. Then she whispered in his ear.

"Hey, lover . . . ever have a woman *completely* blow your mind?" Colin sniggered under his breath as Toy backed away with a devilish grin. She turned her back to him, swaying with the smooth tempo. Barry White's voice carried Toy through her motions. With her arms held high over her head, she loosened the bows that kept her pigtails in place. Her golden brown tendrils fell down onto her shoulders and back. She turned back toward him and removed her camisole, leaving Colin's mouth wide with awe.

Toy swayed back and forth, approaching Colin again, doing her best to follow moves that she'd seen N'Tasha execute at work dozens of times. Soon, Toy was on her knees smoothing lips along Colin's thigh and groin. She could imagine the length of him, since it formed an impressive bulge in his shorts. "Holy cannoli, Colin. A little excited, aren't we?"

Colin barely answered. "A little."

"Well, hold on to your seat belt . . . I see I'm gonna have my work cut out for me," said Toy. She lifted his T-shirt slowly along his torso, her fingers walking, lightly clawing his chest all the while. Instead of lifting the shirt all the way off, she left it covering his head, his arms still caught in the sleeves, obscuring any view he had.

"Now you're getting me nervous, Toy. What the hell are you doin'?"

Toy smiled to herself, knowing that she was turning Colin on, not getting him nervous like he said. She nibbled at his stomach where some of his pubic hairs reached up in a thin trail to his navel. She continued on his pectoral muscles and then to his collarbone, whispering through the T-shirt over his head. Next, she propped her foot up on Colin's thigh, smoothing her toes along until they played up under his shorts.

Colin shook as if he'd been doused with ice-cold water on the hottest summer day. "Baby! You're driving me crazy!" he growled.

"Crazy-good?" Toy asked, taking the opportunity to pause and circle the couch, where she reached over Colin, playfully clawing his abdomen with her designer fingernails. "Or, crazy-bad?"

Colin couldn't take any more. He snatched the T-shirt off of his head and used it to lasso Toy. "C'mere, woman!"

Toy let out a joyful shriek as he swept her over the arm of the couch and into his lap. He nuzzled his nose and face into her belly, tickling her mercilessly. The screams were quite real by now, turning to gasps, and then sighs as Colin zeroed in to kiss every inch of skin he could get his tongue and lips on. The kissing and licking turned to the rubbing, sucking and grasping of Toy's now unharnessed breasts and erect nipples. "Now you're . . . driving . . . *me* crazy . . . Colin Williams."

"Well, don't worry. I won't torture you like you did me. I'll satisfy every . . . single inch . . . of you . . ."

"Oh, God," Toy exalted. "Is that a promise?"

"That's a sho-nuff promise."

Colin gave Toy a deep tongue kiss, and they kept at it for a long time, breathing when they could. Slobbering all over one another until their lips grew tired.

Then Colin stood and took Toy up into his arms. He carried her into the bedroom and laid her down—his prize.

The music was distant now—

I've got . . .

Love power . . .

—an ongoing groove that fused perfectly with the emotions in the air.

Colin unhooked and unbuttoned what other clothing Toy had left, and in the glow of scented candles, the two made passionate, unbridled love. There was both fire and electricity in the way they loved each other, both of them telling the stories of their lives—things they hadn't said yet, things they'd never say—with their bodies alone, sharing everything and losing themselves all the while. The two managed to squeeze a lifetime's worth of desire and fantasies into that single encounter.

Colin woke at about one in the morning to the smell of antiseptic spray. He wondered if the night's frolic had fogged his senses so much that this familiar scent was overcoming him as a consequence. Then he realized that Toy wasn't by his side, in his embrace, as he remembered her to be when he drifted off into a peaceful, satisfied slumber.

"Wha—?" Colin made an effort to speak, but was too sleepy, too exhausted for words. He pulled himself up, much like a sleepwalker, and he ambled out into the open area of the cabin. The lights were on and the music was bumping 50 Cent raps over Dr. Dre beats. Colin might've been seeing things, but he could swear that was Toy all done up in dirty jeans, a painter's hat and an oversize T-shirt tied off just underneath her breasts. "What the *hell?*" he exclaimed.

"Oh! Baby! You scared the shit outta me."

"Okay, I guess that means we can curse in front of each other now. So, what the fuck, Toy?" Colin spread his arms, indicating Toy's appearance—and the fact that she was on her knees, with a dingy rag and a bucket.

"Oh, this? I couldn't sleep. I . . . I thought I'd clean up around here."

"Really? At—" Colin checked his watch. "One in the morning?"

Toy shrugged and made a face: that *call me crazy* look. Meanwhile, the cabin appeared to have undergone a thorough cleanup. "Guess I had some extra energy," she said, still grooving, bopping her head, biting her lip with determination, like she was the one rapping and creating the music. "What about you? You need . . . hold on . . ." Toy got up from where she was, in a corner to the left of the fireplace. She danced over to Colin and draped her hands around his neck, gyrating suggestively as she might on New Year's Eve, with the second hand closing in on midnight.

"What in the world is up with you? You doin' drugs? Is that it?" Colin could've been talking to himself, with Toy carrying on like she was. Her back was to him now, her arms doing a sort of shimmy, as she rubbed her ass against his hip.

"Yeah, baby . . . *you* are my drugs. Can I get another injection?"

"You're buggin'! I'm goin' back to bed."

"Suit yourself. But when I'm done I'll be in there butt

naked, with bells ringin'. Ain't you heard—a girl's *gotta have it*! Go on, get some sleep . . . while you can!" Toy cackled.

Colin just shook his head and went back to the bedroom.

Meanwhile, Toy was back to work, lending her voice to the music:

You can find me in the club,
bottle full a bub . . .

CHAPTER

5

Those were memorable beginnings for both. Anytime they heard songs by Barry White, 50 Cent, or Dr. Dre, Colin and Toy reminisced about Martha's Vineyard and their first intimate weekend together in that small cabin.

After that the two became tight, and making love was pure energy. For Colin, specifically, it was easy to love Toy. She was beautiful, witty and candy to his senses. Just saying her name pleasured him. Even better, he felt a security in their union, where he didn't need to play cat and mouse to find a mate. It was also liberating since he could now call himself a "committed man." Most important, they were both in love.

Toy loved Colin so much she tattooed his name on her upper thigh.

She'd do anything for him.

She cleaned his ass.

She kissed his ass.

Colin's devotion was displayed in his work. He was a man who chose to live by independent means. He didn't want a job where he'd be subjected to a desk, helping someone *else* make money. He wanted to put his 8 hours, 12 hours, even 18 hours into his own moneymaking venture—whatever that might turn out to be.

He had some banking experience, working as a teller at Bank of America after high school in LA. That was short-lived; he was conveniently laid off before he could qualify for unemployment benefits. Colin was frustrated by the cruel decision, but he wasn't stopped. He found a job with Sunset Check Exchange. SCE was a large corporation that owned and operated check-cashing centers throughout downtown LA, and in parts of San Diego and San Francisco.

A solid work ethic earned Colin a position as branch manager by the end of his nineteenth month with the company, and eventually he became the man responsible for six locations that stretched along Hollywood Boulevard. SCE's big-dog executives grew proud of Colin's three-year track record with them. He showed them how to save money, while increasing their earnings. In return, he was promised the promotion to senior branch manager, a $95,000-a-year position that would have him oversee all the SCE branches in LA.

Colin could do no wrong. At 25 years old, he was set to become the next successful black executive who'd overcome the deep-rooted racism and statistics that ended in hopelessness for many of his generation.

Then, suddenly, things went haywire.

"Mr. Williams, we have an issue that we need to discuss at once," a voice squawked over the office intercom system.

"Sure, Mr. Ade. Do you need me to bring any ledgers or records?" Colin asked, unsure of what "issue" his boss meant. Jerry Ade was in charge of all SCE's LA branches—the position that Colin had been promised.

They both worked in the same tall office building in downtown LA, so it was a cinch for Colin to hop on the elevator, and reach the executive offices within minutes.

"Go right in, Mr. Williams, they're expecting you," said the receptionist.

Colin proceeded through the glass doors and down the carpeted hall toward Jerry Ade's office. He was too focused to wonder who the receptionist meant by "they." At the far end of the hallway was another set of heavy glass doors leading to a conference room. Colin could see a small congregation of suited executives beyond the doors. Jerry Ade jumped quickly to his feet, waving Colin on to come and join the meeting.

"They" apparently included the entire SCE executive staff. Jerry Ade was the least powerful of the group. Colin braced himself when nobody stood to shake his hand or greet him as they might have otherwise. Instead, they made eyes at one another, or pretended to shuffle papers, avoiding direct eye contact with him altogether.

"Have a seat, Colin," said the company's chief operations officer, Bill Kellerman. The *way* that he said it implied that this was more than any average sit-down. His tone was condescending, as if Colin were some disruptive high school student. "As Mr. Ade here has told you, we have an issue we must discuss," he continued. The other executives present, Richard Tocci, Erik Sinclaire and Kamalin Mills, looked on with certain interest. "We've had one or two meetings before regarding this issue, so it should be nothing new to you—the problem with counterfeit money."

"Oh, sure," Colin answered, relieved that this wasn't something more serious.

Previous meetings had focused on the procedures; how tellers would check the bills they received. For the larger bills—fifties and hundreds—it was mandatory that the tellers scan the currency under the ultraviolet light. Even if they did identify the faint impressions and markings in the stock of the paper, a store manager still had to approve and sign the bill. The smaller bills, such as fives, tens and twenties, were scanned at random.

For the most part, SCE dispensed cash for checks from blue-collar workers and local businesses. But with banks being so busy and service charges shooting through the roof, it was also convenient for folks to pay their utility and phone bills. They could also purchase money orders and phone cards.

"We have here the data sheets on some of the losses we've taken over the past two months. Have you seen these figures?" Bill handed a wad of spreadsheets to Richard, who handed them to Erik, who handed them to Kamalin, who handed them to Jerry Ade. Jerry strolled over to Colin with a prosecutor's stare, an expression that Colin hadn't seen before.

Colin took the papers and reviewed them as Bill continued to speak.

"If you look closely, you'll see a pattern, the twenty-dollar bills especially. Last month alone, we took in three times as many counterfeit bills as we did in October. And that's your group of outlets, specifically. Here . . ." Bill flipped through his copy of the same spreadsheets. "On page sixty . . . this month we took in almost five times as many bills. That's an estimated eighty thousand dollars if you do the math."

Colin wasn't focused on the calculations. Instead he was busy wondering what the company could do to eradicate the problem. The troubleshooting began in his mind, but before he could utter any solutions, Bill spoke.

"Do you have any idea how extreme this problem is, Colin? We're in the business of disposing of cash, and yet, the convenience services we provide are killing us. We've been swamped with funny money."

Colin looked up from the sheets and realized that they were all watching him. He thought nothing of it and quickly went back to reviewing the data. "Mr. Kellerman, Jerry—it shows here that . . . what is it, seven hundred-dollar bills came into the Sunset branch on November second . . . Am I reading this right?"

Kellerman scanned his copy and nodded matter-of-factly.

Colin continued, "Gentlemen, that's just not possible. I mean, I know what the paperwork says, but I've been working our records for three years, and I've never seen more than three—four at the most—hundred-dollar bills come through any one branch. Maybe we have a discrepancy in the records. There's gotta be—"

"Mr. Williams, I've double-checked these records personally," Jerry interrupted. "The numbers gel in regard to the receipts, the day's count slips and affidavits from the branch managers."

"Affidavits?" asked Colin. "What affidavits?"

"Well . . . we've . . ."

"I'll explain, Jerry." Richard Tocci added his weight to the discussion. "You see, Colin, we're federally insured. I shouldn't have to explain that to you."

"No, sir, you don't."

"Okay. Then you should also know that we're accountable for every one of our thousands of transactions, just like any brick and mortar banking institution. We're obligated to provide explanations for such discrepancies . . ."

Bill Kellerman said, "Colin, the bottom line is someone has to be held accountable . . . and we've all agreed that this is just too great a loss to take on the chin—"

"Okay. I think I know why—"

"Colin, I'm sorry," said one of the others. "You're aggressive, you have a good work ethic and you're gonna go places in life . . ."

"You seemed like a good man," another added.

"Seemed?" Colin mumbled through a tight-lipped grimace.

"What we're trying to say is . . ."

Colin suddenly realized what this was. He could see through the smoke and mirrors. Jerry Ade had to be the one to fix this, to doctor things; he probably made a shitload of money too. No . . . maybe they were *all* behind it—they had to be. *Look at how they're all working against me. They won't even let me get to the bottom of this . . .*

". . . we're going to have to let you go."

There was a moment of silence that appeared to be uncomfortable for all of them—everyone but Colin. Again, the suits were avoiding eye contact. At least Erik Sinclaire flashed a compassionate expression, but even that looked like it was prepackaged and insecure. Colin concluded that this was a lynching, and regardless whether only Jerry had set him up, all of them were villains. Every one of them was an enemy.

Just like that, Colin was given the boot, after three years of hard work. An investment in time. He assessed that his effort, aggression and "work ethic" helped SCE (and all of its partners) make money—at least five or six times as much as they *claimed* to have lost in their sorry excuse for his termination. And that wasn't counting all the money they'd save or all the money they'd make in the *coming* years; all because of Colin's dedication to the company.

So to say Colin was enraged was an understatement. He was on fire! His vision, both literally and in his mind's eye, was blurred. And while he might have left the SCE corporate headquarters peacefully, his life's purpose (at least at that moment) was to seek revenge. He felt as though he'd been punched. And there was only one way to respond to a punch: punch back, but do it harder.

Colin's mind veered off wildly into the fantasies of a madman. He remembered reading somewhere about an angry boyfriend who set fire to an entire housing complex, trapping everyone inside of what became a massive incinerator. With that reference in mind, Colin thought of doing the same to the "good ole boys" up at SCE—burn their no-good asses to smithereens. He quickly turned that idea to action, even going so far as to buy gallon cans of gasoline. The gas fumes made his decision a very real choice, seducing him further into the violence playing out in his imagination. This was always the truth: how a person could easily decide one way or another to take action, to change the course of reality by following through with a step-by-step plan. For better, or for worse, the process was indeed proven. And there were always clues to show for it. This same theory—the method of making a dream come true—was one that Colin had for so long lived by. He believed in himself and his ability to achieve. And now, that same science was sucking him into the madness, the passion and the unshakable lure of revenge.

For hours Colin sat in his car across the street from SCE, psyching himself up for the task. He'd already gone through the phase of talking himself in and out of the goal—but in the end he felt betrayed and ready for war.

Whatever it was, his conscience or good old-fashioned common sense, Colin couldn't follow through with the caper, not during the daytime, anyway. But at night was a different story. It seemed as though the darkness was more suitable for such an evil deed; a deed that he felt guilty and ashamed of even conceiving.

He waited until the wee hours of the night, three weeks after his termination. Once the night watchman hobbled his way to the Dunkin' Donuts shop two storefronts away (on schedule as always), Colin ran up and tossed the heavy jug of gasoline through the street-level windows—right where he knew the company's accounting department was situated. Then he lit a Molotov cocktail—a Coke bottle filled with gas and stuffed with a rag—and tossed it into the shattered opening.

At once, a *whoosh* swept through the first floor and glowing flames immediately engulfed that portion of the building. Colin didn't stay to watch the violent spectacle he'd produced, but vanished into the night.

Hours later, before anyone could speculate on the who or the why, Colin skipped town. He took that long cross-country drive, entirely unfamiliar with what the East Coast had to offer him, but ready for the change nonetheless—New Jersey, or bust.

Meeting Vince Reed was a mere coincidence. Reed was at Club Jaguar, a spot in Jersey City where the music was thumpin' and the women were young, hot and flirtatious. Colin was at the bar waiting on a drink when he overheard an associate of Reed's asking a girl if she could tell the difference between two twenty-dollar bills. Both bills, the real one and the phony one, were laid out on the counter for the woman's perusal, and Colin was close enough to see and hear all.

"That one," the woman said, all caught up in the mystery, the suspense and the bait that money represents. She pointed to one of the bills, guessing it to be the real money.

But Colin could tell that the girl chose the wrong twenty. He wanted to say something to expose the con the guy was playing, but decided against it. After all, what did he have to prove? What would he prove by showing how clever and knowledgeable he was about currency, in a nightclub in the middle of a strange environment?

The counterfeiter told the woman, "Just when I thought I could put one over on you . . ." He dropped another line: "You're sharp as a tack, woman. I bet you can see right through a man, right down to his mismatched socks . . ."

The woman blushed and smiled, overcome by the flattery.

And then, just a few minutes later, the guy asked her to give him two $10 bills in exchange for the "real" $20.

It was only when the woman fell for the okey doke that Colin felt the urge to speak up. "Excuse me, I couldn't help overhearing . . . I got two tens for you," he said.

The fraud made a face. "Yo, man, this is an A and B conversation so C your way out of my business."

"You call trickin' this woman *your business*? Do you have any idea who this woman is?"

The trickster's head dipped to the side, and he looked at both the woman and Colin as if to say, *This, I gotta hear*.

"Well, the trick is on you, dog. Bet you don't even know her name," Colin said, guessing his way through this.

"Um . . . Marie, ain't it? Yeah. Marie . . . so you don't know what you're talking about."

Colin smirked. "Gave him our cousin's name, huh, Grace? Yo, dog, Grace is my sister. That's number one. And number two, this bill?" Colin took the money from "Grace" and slapped it on the counter in front of the dude. "It's phony. What, do you think I'm gonna stand by and let you take advantage of my sister?"

Colin played it by ear, uninterested in causing a scene. "Let's just let the issue die. You leave me and my sister alone—you never saw us. And I'll pretend you haven't spent a few of those funny bills in this club."

The fraud sucked his teeth, aggravated. "Whatever," he said. He looked at "Grace" as though she were the one losing out, before he stepped away.

"What just happened here? And who the fuck are you?" the woman asked in more of an affectionate tone.

SUGAR DADDY

Colin chuckled, realizing that there was some gratitude in
her eyes. "I'm your brother," he replied.

That night Colin experienced his first one-night stand in
Jersey City.

Colin returned to Club Jaguar for more of those one-
night stands. He was successful in a few other attempts, but
he couldn't help feeling like an investigator, as though he
worked for the government, there to detect felonious activities. It couldn't be helped, though, since all manner of criminal activity was taking place from week to week in this n'
that corner of the establishment.

Meanwhile, Colin was welcome there, keeping his rela-
tionships open with those women he befriended. It was a
home away from home in many ways, since the music, the
people and the excitement were constant and familiar. For
the new guy on the block the social scene wasn't half bad.

"W'sup," said a man's voice behind Colin.

When he turned to look there was the fraud, the one who
Colin had interrupted weeks earlier. "Yeah, w'sup. Find any
marks lately?"

"A few. And every one I meet I ask 'em if they're related
to you."

"Very funny," said Colin.

"But seriously . . . name's Bruce. No hard feelings." Bruce
put his hand out to shake Colin's, but Colin balled his fist to
exchange a pound. A handshake was inappropriate so soon,
especially since Bruce was into victimizing strangers.

"No hard feelings at all. You do what you do, and that's
what you do. It's really none of my business."

"True."

While Bruce made small talk, Colin considered the various activities he'd witnessed in Jaguar during the past
weekends. Bruce was some kind of low-level member of
Vince Reed's crew, which ran a counterfeit money ring that
dealt drugs and probably guns too. Colin learned some of
these basic tidbits during his dates with various women who

frequented Jaguar. It seemed that everyone knew about Vince Reed's enterprise, and they respected or at least feared his power and influence.

Beyond what Colin heard about Reed's organization, he also observed a great deal. More than a few times he could see across the dance floor where Reed conducted meetings and transactions in the VIP area. He'd nod to his intermediaries, who would in turn take out a fresh $20 bill. The visitors would get the currency, check it, talk amongst themselves . . . more nods . . . then a suitcase would change hands.

Colin could see that the activity was similar to how drug deals went down—on TV and the movies. Actually, with how people imitated most everything, Colin wasn't sure if this atmosphere too wasn't surreal—elements of his imagination—with how the big Willies were suited up, their egos flashing with varying forms of material wealth; meanwhile, the lower level associates acted their roles—hungry dogs, ready to perform any tricks on behalf of their masters, while the women gravitated toward indications of power and away from the wannabes.

"You work for Reed, don't you?" he asked Bruce.

"You better bet it."

"I hear he's responsible for half of the counterfeit money that's moved along the East Coast."

"It's possible. How you know that?"

"Word gets around."

"You a cop?" asked Bruce.

"I hope I don't *look* like a cop. What makes you think I'm a cop?"

"I dunno . . . I seen you in here a few times . . . you pulled my card that day with a girl I was tryin' to hustle—callin' her your sister—and now you're askin' questions about my boss."

"You want the truth?" asked Colin.

"You're not gonna pull out a badge on me, are you?"

"I ain't no cop. I used to work for a company in LA. My job, one of them, anyway, was to control the incoming currency at about three dozen check-cashing outlets."

He went on to explain (briefly) the fallout he'd had with the company's executives, and how he had to start anew, looking for a job where he could earn close to the money he'd made in LA. But when he tried to find work at a check-cashing center in downtown Jersey City, he learned he'd been blacklisted: his previous employers, the "posse" back in LA, had spread Colin's name across the country as a suspected thief, counterfeiter and arsonist.

"I bet some of the check-cashing centers even have your photo posted," a woman at the downtown branch confided. She was sweet, telling Colin things she wasn't supposed to. "Really, my manager said to call the police the moment I saw you."

"Wow. That's serious. I came here to escape trouble, and it followed me."

"Listen . . . meet me at the pizza shop across the street. We'll talk."

She was a short woman, her hair braided down the back of her head into a tail, and she was cheeky, as though she was forced at birth to be happy.

"This is my smoking break, so I can't be long," she explained once they were seated. "What I don't understand," she mentioned, hoping to quench her own curiosity, "is . . . if you're supposed to be all bad, then why aren't the authorities after you? This is a federally insured business, so it seems to me if you *did* steal money, they'd have gone after you. Heck, the counterfeiting alone would get the Secret Service on your tail in a heartbeat."

"I agree."

"But the notice we have up at work is something from, well . . . a *company*. I don't even know why we have it posted except it may be a corporate move—you know how many of these banks and other financial institutions work together and support each other . . ."

Colin had long considered that, assuming that the devils he once worked for probably *did* alert the authorities. But they'd only reported the arson. There was no way (Colin surmised) that the posse would report the money issues to the police because, of course, there would indeed be a federal investigation. Then the records would *really* be scrutinized, at which point it would come out who *really* was to blame. And in Colin's mind, that was Jerry Ade.

"They probably couldn't report me," Colin told the woman. "As the saying goes, don't throw stones if you live in a house of glass."

"I see. So your old job had some grimy activity going on, and what? They're using you?"

"As a scapegoat."

"Mmm . . . that's deep."

"Disgracing my name and hurting my ability to continue in the financial industry was their only option."

"So what're you gonna do? A good-looking guy like you oughta be able to make a living however and whenever he wants to. Or . . ." The evil showed in her squinted eyes. "I could reverse the game and put it out there about the grimy stuff goin' on in LA. I bet the Secret Service would jump on it. Plus, I know some people—"

"No, no . . . I'm done with all the thoughts of revenge," Colin told her. "Trust me."

"Shoot, Colin, I'd hire you quick, fast and in a hurry, but there's people *I* gotta answer to. If they knew about you being on the blacklist I'd get my head cut off."

"I understand, really. But more important, I'm glad you took the time to help me. The information you shared is *obviously* helpful. At least I know not to walk into another check-cashing joint."

So, with few options left, Colin stalled. The business he knew so well, one he had a wealth of experience in, was taboo. Bruce was impressed by Colin's story and how much he knew about the money business. And maybe he thought he'd earn points by introducing Colin to Reed, because that's exactly what he did.

The first words Colin heard from Reed's lips were the most memorable: "*I hear you know a lot about paper.*"

CHAPTER

6

Reed took Colin on as his business manager. The position was important: Colin had to keep a correct count of the phony money vs. the good money. Plus he was the best person to verify the quality of the "new" phony bills before they were distributed. Reed figured that if the bills could pass Colin's inspection, they could pass anyone's. Colin's know-how and experience helped to save money, make money and arrange safeguards that would shelter and protect Reed's earnings.

Three months into his position, Colin noticed a pattern that bothered him. "If you don't mind, Reed, I want to make a few suggestions to you . . ."

"Well, what do you think I hired you for, Colin? Suggest all you want."

"Uh . . . the suggestions I have aren't really about the money exactly . . ."

"I'm listening."

"Reed, we need to get out of the spotlight," he said. "There are too many eyes and ears around, especially in this busy club, and we're movin' too much money to jeopardize everything by doing transactions out in the open." Colin waited to hear Reed's reaction.

"Is that it? That's the suggestion?"

"Well . . . there's something else, Reed."

Reed took a glass of champagne from a waitress and nodded—a sort of toast to her beauty. "Go ahead," he said, sipping and panning the club like a proud mob boss.

"It's the flashy stuff. You and all our mid-level people are pushin' top-dollar whips, wearin' expensive watches and partying loud and often. All of this is an advertisement, Reed. They're red flags that can easily attract the attention of the feds. They might *already* be investigating the operation. You never know . . ."

Reed raised his glass again, this time to a woman winding her body and giving him sultry come-fuck-me eyes over on the dance floor.

Colin went on, "Nothing is ever guaranteed to be one hundred percent break-proof."

"Is that all?" asked Reed.

Colin was confused, unsure of what Reed meant by that. "Uh . . . yeah. Sure, that's it."

"Okay, then lemme share something with you." Reed hung his arm around Colin's neck and led him to the edge of the VIP area, an elevated area with a view of the entire club. "See that bartender there?" He pointed his glass toward a redheaded Italian girl.

"Yeah."

"Okay . . . now look over on the dance floor. You know who that chick is? The pink dress, black hair?"

"A girlfriend of yours?"

Reed laughed loud and hard. Then he swigged down the rest of his champagne. "Close. See, Colin . . . this is home. Ain't too many people I don't know in here. Matter fact, there ain't too many people in here that don't know me. Any funny business goes down, I'm the first to know about it. Anybody comes in here snoopin' like a fed or whoever, I'm the first to know about it. I got the keys to the front door, and there's three or four different ways to escape this joint. Not only that, the bouncers by the doors are hired guns. They work here, but they also work for me. The bartender? That's my Friday night piece of ass, but she also studies the customers. She peeped you a long time ago, son. You did some razzle-dazzle with that trick . . . said she was your sister when Bruce was tryin' to wash one of our bills. That was cute what you did, but nobody's mad. I heard you hit that. Good move. You won points in my book. Bruce is a moron anyway. You were the best thing he ever did for us—bringing you to me n' all . . . and the pink dress on the dance floor? Uh-huh . . . that's the daughter of the Jersey City chief of police. I'm not only getting every inside detail on Jersey City's finest, but she's also waxing my knob like a starved crackhead locked in a lollipop factory. And trust me, money—she can suck the hell out of a lollipop.

"So fuck all that talk about the spotlight. I *am* the spotlight. And don't you worry about flashy lifestyles. That's the benefits of all our hard work. If you can't show your bling and flash your cheese, then what are we in business for? Now let's get these Samsonites movin', and stick to the agenda."

The "agenda" Reed spoke of entailed movin' paper to the low-level functionaries, both quickly and efficiently. But naturally Colin went beyond what was expected of him. Just because he was now working on the grimy side of the money game didn't mean that he wouldn't do the best job he knew how, making suggestions where possible, making further progress until this organization was tight—at the top of its game.

Colin was also the idea man behind the safes that were welded into the floors of the Honda Civics. Reed sent out a dozen or so drivers each week, each of whom was paid $3,000 per trip to move the vehicles from point A to point B, nonstop. Each trip carried more than $500,000 in counterfeit $20 bills, earning Reed a profit of 20 percent each trip.

Reed's organization took in so much money every week that he hardly knew what to do with it. So he rented storage rooms at Put-Away, a self-serve warehouse where customers paid monthly fees and had their own keys. So far, Reed had 13 storage spaces, all of them stockpiled with profits from his counterfeit empire.

Colin collected an average of $10,000 per week for his role in the organization. He was wise with his money, opening a few brokerage accounts in a variety of company names, entities he felt sure could never be traced back to him. Any purchases of big-ticket items, such as a new Toyota Camry, were leased or paid for in piecemeal installments. In the meantime, Colin made sure to never spend more than $5,000 at one time.

He rented a penthouse in Fort Lee, close to where Reed had his million-dollar duplex. Despite these expenditures, Colin still managed to keep a few hundred thousand dollars stashed in his home. But Colin's lifestyle and the money he made wasn't everything. He had money enough to buy any luxury available to man. But he was simple. He didn't want a fancy boat, ten cars or a mansion on the Jersey shore. He didn't want a watch that was more expensive than a Learjet. What Colin wanted was someone to share his success with.

This missing link led to more one-night stands— encounters that were more or less rewards, due to Colin's status in Reed's organization—women who called Club Jaguar their home on the weekend, then returned to their children, their husbands or their daddies. It eventually became comfortable for Colin to see these women, to expect "the chicken head"—that local who accepted less, who had a low self-esteem—or the trick whose idea of independence was a smart attitude, a taste for the thuggest rap songs and a weakness for any attractive man with money, a car and the "hustle" to keep them cash-rich.

Colin became familiar with the stable of go-go dancers and the various other establishments where they danced around the city. And although he'd never taken one home, he was good for dropping $100 tips here and there—his weakness was seeing these women bust their asses for tips.

It was during one of his nights out when Colin spotted Toy, a bartender at Nuts & Screws. The courting began, then the love affair.

CHAPTER

7

Spirits were always high inside Club Jaguar. The dance floor was crowded, men and women out there winding their bodies, gettin' their grooves on as the DJ mixed old school, new school and everything in between. There always seemed to be that understanding in the atmosphere—that understanding that Vince Reed was ever-present, and that his money and influence was at the foot of the club's nirvana.

Tonight was no different than last Friday night—women shaking their asses, men pursuing them and Samsonite suitcases filled with money being passed in the VIP area.

The bass-heavy raps of Doug E. Fresh were fused with those of B.I.G., and B.I.G. was mixed with X-Clan, and Colin at some point considered the contradictions here—how Doug E. rapped about partying, how Biggie rapped about smokin' weed while getting head and how X-Clan professed about black consciousness. Still, the beats were infectious and the sweaty crowd loved it.

"Hey, Vince, how 'bout we do this toast," Colin suggested, looking at his watch as he did.

"Aw, man, what's the rush? Hang out a little . . ." Reed urged.

Colin merely tapped his DADO watch with his forefinger—the picture worth a thousand words.

"A party-pooper . . . I swear . . . A wright, y'all . . . gather round . . ." Reed called out to the others in the VIP area. "Let's get on with the toast!"

The group of ten or so associates pulled together, some

reaching for glasses from the waitress, while one or two hugged on their significant others. Reed was about to speak.

"This one's for m'man Colin . . . transplanted from the *west siiide*, and now a major, major player here in Jay Cee . . . so . . . I'll take this time to congratulate you on five years of hard work. Also, I wanna give you credit for holding together a family when I wouldn't stand a chance in hell of doin' that. I envy you, bro . . ."

Reed raised his glass, as did the others. After the sips and gulps, everyone went back to partying, while Colin informed Reed of his departure. It was always the same story with Colin. "I'm a married man now, Vince, I can't stay out late like I used to . . ."

And Reed would usually agree. But tonight was different.

"One thing, Colin, before you go."

"What's that?"

"We're about to do this last transaction of the night. Spanky is comin' through with his boys any minute now . . ."

"Vince, you done too many deals with Spanky to need me—even before I got to Jersey City. I'm tryin' to—"

"Ahh-ahh . . . no arguments. Just ten minutes. We do the damn thing, and then you can get back to that pretty woman and that doll of a daughter. Now, take another sip and relax. He shouldn't be long," said Reed.

There was simply no disagreeing with Vince Reed. This was his world, where things were done his way—do what he said and everyone was the better for it.

The sudden impact of doors busting open around one A.M. sounded like grenades had exploded near the front end of the club. A raid was in motion. And it wasn't merely the gangly locals who crashed the party—not D.T.s with shiny badges hanging like medallions over muscled chests. No. This was something much bigger and entirely unexpected. Something more complex and well thought out. The exits had been sealed off by armed men, while about 20 others in black vests, shielded helmets and other protective gear stormed forward with assault rifles directed at any and everything.

Reed was busy at the time of the invasion, making arrangements for later, expecting to get laid by the bartender and her cousin. Colin, however, immediately thought about the Samsonite suitcases sitting in the VIP area. He made the dash for a rear exit, but a gunshot sounded and sent him diving to the floor. And then the music died.

"Nobody move!" shouted one of the men, holding a 12-gauge pointed at the ceiling. He appeared to be in charge. He scanned the room. "Everyone within the sound of my voice"—he climbed onto a table for all to see—"my name is Special Agent Woods, and this establishment is now under siege by the United States Secret Service . . ."

During the agent's speech, one of the club's patrons made a move. An agent was after him at once, tripping him up with the butt of his assault rifle, and pressing the nose of the weapon to the man's neck.

Another shot rang out. Colin saw the 12-guage smoking, before Special Agent Woods spoke again. "Lay down! Everybody!" he barked.

Regardless what they wore, whether sequined dresses or two-piece suits, close to 200 patrons all obeyed, all of them stretched out on Club Jaguar's dirty dance floor.

Minutes passed as if they were hours, while Secret Service agents scoured the nightclub. Some agents questioned the staff, while others searched the inner workings of Club Jaguar.

Twenty minutes passed before the most obvious question was asked: "Whose are these?" called out Special Agent Woods, holding up one of the abandoned suitcases.

When nobody responded, he took both suitcases to a couch in the VIP lounge for further investigation.

Squawks from a number of clip-on two-way radios could be heard throughout the club as agents stepped over and between frightened and disgruntled clubgoers. Assault weapons swung beside some agents' black multipocket cargo pants, while other agents perched weapons on their hips, threatening the slightest hostility.

Colin was now worried more than ever, since it was inevitable that agents would discover the Samsonites were packed with phony money. At the same time he scanned the club, trying to read Vince Reed's expressions.

Would people share what they knew about Reed's organizations, perhaps the whos and hows? Did this mean that the game had come to a sudden close, and that everyone in it had to face the music? Who, if anyone, saw what? And why were agents now escorting clubgoers one by one to the V.I.P. lounge?

"Shit!" Colin chewed the curse so that nobody heard. He also turned his head and eyes away the instant a stranger pointed one of the agents in his direction.

Fingered as a principal in the counterfeit scheme, Colin was rushed out by three agents, as was Reed. The two were taken to separate areas and questioned. Colin was close to the coat check; he could see the VIP lounge, and wondered why Reed was doing so much talking. The words that Reed directed Colin to use *just in case* sounded in his mind: *"If a raid ever goes down, deny everything. You don't know anything about any money, and no, you never saw any suitcases."*

Colin had warned Reed that such an event was almost inevitable, what with how Reed was running things so loosely and with too much flash. Like he always said, nothing was ever guaranteed to be 100 percent break-proof.

Reed's dark, bald head glistened under the house lights, bobbing up and down in concert with his nonstop lip movement. Colin couldn't make out Reed's words from so far away, but he could see that he wasn't following his own advice.

How involved could a denial be?

In time, a white woman, pretty with long bronze hair, was escorted from her place on the floor (patrons were permitted to sit upright now) and led over to where Reed was being interrogated. Colin didn't know who the woman was—even though he had been working with Reed for the better part of five years—but he was certain he'd seen her face in the club now and again. *What does she have to do with this? Is Reed fucking her too?* Colin cursed again, less chewing this time, when the woman pointed in his direction.

Minutes later, Special Agent Woods approached. "So, you don't know anything about the suitcases, huh?"

Colin could feel his own temperatures rise—the one for his blood, and the one for his rears—knowing that Woods wasn't merely *questioning* him, but more so placing blame. The stream of thoughts and assessments flowing through Colin's head started with dishonor and accumulated into a pool of betrayal. Instinctively, he wanted to defend himself . . . to punch back harder, and redirect the agent's focus. He had the strong urge to point toward Reed; he even had details that would expose Reed's entire criminal enterprise.

However, even in this case, he couldn't do it. This wasn't nursery school, where children played "tattletale," telling the teacher, "So-and-so is to blame . . . so-and-so started it all."

No. Colin was bound by the code of the streets—an ethic that "true soldiers" practiced: *you lay in the bed you made*. You did a crime, and if you got caught you didn't go ratting out the next man so that you could get a break. Play by the rules, or don't play at all.

This was the life that Colin had committed to with rules and ways that he adopted. He knew long ago that if he went over the line, diving into the illegal end of the money game, he'd have to do it 100 percent. No half-steppin', no matter how grave the threat. It was a consciousness that kept him honorable, true to the game despite where he went or who he met up with. At least he'd never have to run and hide, or constantly look over his shoulder anticipating the next attempt on his life.

CHAPTER

8

Colin couldn't wait to see Vince Reed. It didn't matter how many "soldiers" stood by him, or how much of a mortal threat they posed. Whatever, if he had to die doing it, he'd face up to the challenge. But damned if Colin wouldn't find out why he, of all people, was chosen as the man to take the fall.

That was Colin's only conclusion . . . the only thoughts at the top of his agenda as he stood there in federal court before a U.S. magistrate considering bail.

Still in yesterday's clothes, with his hands cuffed behind his back, and with two U.S. marshals guarding him, Colin listened to the instructions of his court-appointed attorney.

The magistrate was expected to emerge any time now. Meanwhile, the U.S. Attorney—whom Colin immediately recognized as his enemy—and his team of legal eagles were all in a powwow adjacent to Colin and his spur-of-the-moment legal aid.

At times, one of the U.S. Attorneys peeped over at Colin, sizing him up as their next challenge. The court clerk was short and portly. He was also balding, with a pale white spot at the crown of his head.

"All rise!"

The courtroom had just nine people in attendance. Other than the clerk, Colin's defense attorney and Colin himself, so far as Colin could surmise, everyone but him worked for the same superpower, and he was simply the next item up for debate. Once everyone got up on their feet, the judge acknowledged the room with a quaint gesture of his hand. Something he seemed tired of doing.

"Please be seated," he said. The magistrate scurried toward his throne up there behind a massive oak front. With the United States and Department of Justice flags behind him, along with that official seal and eagle on the wall behind him, the older white man with slicked-back strands of graying hair looked to be a tremendous authority. Even with those beady eyes that kept shifting back and forth behind a pair of John Lennon spectacles, the magistrate appeared to be in command. Although, for an instant, Colin felt like part of an ongoing tennis match—smacked hard and often.

"I bid you all a good morning."

"Good morning, Your Honor."

This must be the start of the show, Colin thought—these tightwads with their distinguished manners and how they spoke.

"May I have the appearances, please?"

More formalities . . . as if the judge doesn't know these people already.

"Frederick Murray, Assistant U.S. Attorney, for the government."

"Brendan Lyles, appearing on behalf of Mr. Williams." Lyles nudged Colin.

"Good morning. Colin Williams, defendant."

"Let the record reflect that we are here concerning the matter of indictment number zero zero dash four twenty-two, the people of the United States versus Colin Williams . . . uh . . . Marshal, you may remove the cuffs. Thank you."

The magistrate nodded once the handcuffs were removed. Colin massaged his wrists as the formalities proceeded. "Before I can appoint you counsel I must put you under oath and ascertain whether you qualify under the Criminal Justice Act for this attorney's services. Would you mind stepping over to the clerk, sir."

Colin went through with the procedure. *So help me*

God . . . so help me God, if I find out I've been set up, he told himself.

The judge went on, "For the record, how old are you, sir?"

"Sir" again. This dude is sugar-coating an already twisted situation.

"Twenty-six," answered Colin.

"Now, I know you're presently in custody, but where did you reside prior to your arrest?"

"The Shangrila, in Fort Lee, New Jersey."

"The Shangrila, sir?"

"Yes, it's a condominium complex."

"Oh, I see. And you live with whom?"

"My wife and child."

"And how much is your monthly rent?"

"Twenty-two hundred."

"I see. And is your wife employed?"

"No. Not right now," said Colin, noticing how the U.S. Attorney took notes after each answer.

"And your family still resides at . . . the Shangrila?"

"Yes."

"Now, before you were arrested, did you have a job?"

"I was self-employed."

"And, for the record, what was the nature of the business?"

"Er . . . financial consultant."

There was a snicker from the group of Colin's enemies that caused the judge to pause. He cut a gaze in the prosecutor's direction. "And can you tell me at the present time what you have in the way of assets? Let's start with bank accounts. You and your wife . . . what do you have in the way of savings, checking and the like?"

Colin calculated the question, knowing there was no way he could be truthful. Doing so would be nothing less than an admission of guilt. "I have no bank accounts, no checking and no money," he said, deciding to play it down. He figured a man with no money might not add up to a big money hustler—the stereotype that might make him an excellent target. "My wife has her own bank account, I think. But if that's still there, there's less than five hundred dollars in it."

"No cash on hand at home?" asked the judge.

Colin thought about the cash stashed in his home, the brokerage accounts he had in various company names, as well as a few other secret investments. In his mind he pictured all the cash he'd amassed over five years—close to $800,000 if he wasn't underestimating the numbers. "No, sir. No cash on hand."

"Nothing in a safe-deposit box?"

Colin wagged his head, his expression a sincere one. "Nothing."

"Do you or your wife own any real estate?"

Colin wagged his head again.

"I'm sorry, Mr. Williams. You'll need to answer so the stenographer can record—"

"Oh. Sorry. No . . . no real estate."

"Any securities? Any stocks or bonds?"

"No, sir, none of the above."

There was a long pause, during which the judge scanned the courtroom, apparently confused; after all, this was being presented as a multimillion-dollar counterfeit scheme.

"Is it fair," the judge continued, "for me to conclude that you have no assets whatsoever other than your wife's small bank account?"

"Yes. That is correct."

The judge peered over at the prosecutor, then at the defense counsel before he addressed Colin again. "Mr. Williams, if you don't mind me asking, how do you make a—"

The magistrate's inquiry was cut short when a man zipped through the courtroom doors, breaking the near-silence. The marshals immediately cut their eyes at him, sizing him up as friend or foe.

"Your Honor, if you'll excuse me—I'm here to represent Mr. Williams."

Colin did a double take, taking a closer look at the white man—*another one*—with a stocky build, his jet-black hair swooped up in a pompadour, and a pigeon-toed walk. The attorney appeared to be an aggressor, looking dapper in a double-breasted pinstriped navy suit, coupled with an ocean-blue shirt with a white rounded collar and a printed burgundy necktie. Colin thought of him as a walking *GQ* advertisement, but was drawn by the man's instant magnetism.

"And your name, sir?"

"Messenger, Your Honor. Jeffrey Z. Messenger the Third."

"And you've been retained to represent the defendant in these matters?"

"Yes, Your Honor. A few of his friends have retained my services," Messenger replied. As he spoke, Messenger approached the public defender and shook his hand—more or less a dismissal. Messenger then placed a reassuring hand on Colin's shoulder as the magistrate spoke.

"Very well." And at that moment the switch was acknowledged—out with the old; in with the new.

Messenger whispered to Colin, "Vince Reed sent me. Don't worry . . . you're in good hands now."

Colin couldn't help taking a long-awaited deep breath. Maybe Reed wasn't a traitor after all.

"Your Honor, at this time I'd like to make a motion seeking release pending trial. By all accounts, it is certainly clear that Mr. Williams is neither a flight risk nor a danger to the community. I'm sure he can meet the burden of court appearances on his own. I understand that he has no resources with which to flee—he cannot run to another country because he essentially has no money to do so."

"Does he have a passport?"

The attorney listened for Colin's response before he answered the judge. "No. He does not."

"All right . . ."

A landslide of thoughts tossed around in Colin's head. First, he was thrown by how easily Messenger assumed the controls. Second, the way he responded to the judge was as if he knew Colin's life story inside out . . .

Messenger went on. "My client has longstanding ties to the Fort Green community. He's spent—I'm sorry. Would you excuse me while I consult with Mr. Williams?"

The judge nodded. Colin whispered to Messenger.

"I'm sorry, Your Honor. My client has longstanding ties to the *Fort Lee* community. Forgive my mix-up."

"Go on, Counselor."

"Yes, my client has spent all his life in Fort Lee. He went to high school there. His wife and daughter are there. More important, Judge, every time Mr. Williams is scheduled to appear, I will see to it *personally* that he does so in a timely fashion."

Colin kept his comments to himself, but he realized now that Messenger was selling a bag of shit to the judge. *High school in Fort Lee?*

"Your Honor," interrupted Fredrick Murray. "The defendant has admitted under oath that he is poor, that he has no job and no assets. It is obvious to us all that he is likely to commit more crimes to support himself and his family."

Messenger intervened. "Your Honor, I find that argument to be extraordinary. I also find it to be offensive, the suggestion that the only way for a poor man to support himself is to engage in criminal activities. If that is the notion behind that comment, and I hope it is not, then what I implore this court to do is to look upon Mr. Williams as the man that he is: a flawed man . . . a man who has made mistakes, to be sure, as we all have in some way or another. But I think this is a man who is entitled to be judged on the basis of reasonableness and fairness and, hopefully, not have his error measure him continuously for the rest of his life."

Messenger gestured to accommodate his argument; his hands seemed to dig into the issues, molding the relevant points and banishing those he disputed.

"What I want to say is this, Judge—Mr. Williams has not been convicted of a crime of violence. He has not robbed anyone with a gun. He has not sold narcotics. He has not bludgeoned anyone to death on the Turnpike with a flashlight. I cite these recent examples because in each of those cases the courts have permitted the defendants to be released pending trial."

"Thank you, Mr. Messenger. Mr. Murray?"

"Thank you, Your Honor. I will be as brief as I possibly can. I can neither confirm nor deny a lot of the statements made regarding the defendant being grounded in his community. But I will say that the nature of these charges suggests the deceitful character of Mr. Williams—"

"Your Honor," Messenger intervened, "isn't *every* alleged crime based on deceit? And since I suspect it is, then my client should be treated no differently than every other defendant who comes before you."

"Your Honor, I will recite freely from the indictment, which says that Mr. Williams is responsible part and parcel for distributing more than ten million dollars in counterfeit bills per month. That's a network that stretches into more than four states, with almost thirty associates; plus there is a four- to five-year record of this activity. Mr. Williams played a role—"

"Your Honor, I object. My client is innocent until proven guilty."

"You're quite right, Counselor. You will temper your accusations, Mr. Murray."

"Thank you, Your Honor."

"It is—*ahem*—alleged that Mr. Williams played a principal role in these activities, and we believe that to be indicative of how he will behave if bail were to be granted at this point in time. In the Marks case, the courts specifically found mail and wire fraud charges to be two key reasons to revoke or not to grant the defendant bail pending trial."

"Your Honor, with all due respect, Mr. Murray is blowing hot air. The Marks case is in no way relevant in this matter. Wire fraud and mail fraud? *Please*, Counselor!"

"Well . . . uh . . . by Mr. Williams' own admission, he has never submitted a federal tax return, again showing his manipulative and deceitful character. And finally—"

"You're pulling straws, Murray," snapped Messenger.

"Finally, there is this issue of the possible sentence, if the defendant is found guilty . . ."

"Big if."

"Counselor."

"Excuse me, Your Honor. But I just can't stand by and allow this smoke-and-mirrors campaign to continue."

"Counselor, let me remind you that this is merely a bail hearing—not a trial. Allow the U.S. Attorney to make his point and I promise to give your concerns fair consideration. After all, I am the judge in this matter. Continue, Mr. Murray, and please . . . finish your point."

"Thank you, Your Honor. As I was saying, the characteristics that the defendant has exhibited provides us ample proof of flight risk."

"All right, all right. Enough. I'm ready to resolve the issues before me."

"Your Honor, if I may—there's one more thing," Murray said.

"Please keep it short."

"I made the point that Mr. Williams is likely to commit additional crimes—not because he's a poor man, as Mr. Messenger raised, and which I find to be an irresponsible interpretation of what I've said—but because Mr. Williams is a con artist. He is a criminal . . . a counterfeiter . . . and a fraud. Finally—"

"Enough."

"But, Your Honor—"

"I will not repeat myself. Now, Mr. Messenger, do you need to respond?"

"Yes, I do, Your Honor. And I will be short. There is a reason that my client, Mr. Williams, sits in this courtroom. It is alleged that he committed a crime, and so he is eligible, like every defendant, to a fair trial, the foundation of which must consider him innocent until proven guilty. The statements of my adversary are simply the government's version of Mr. Williams' life. Most of what Mr. Murray claims will be challenged at trial. Particularly the counterfeiting charges. My client was not in possession of the counterfeit bills found at the club where he was arrested. Moreover, we intend to challenge both the charges and the veracity of what has been set forth here today. I don't believe the government will be able to prove its case."

"All right, Counselor, you've made your point. I've heard both sides. The defendant, Colin Williams, was arraigned yesterday in this court and now submits his motion for release pending trial. He has pleaded not guilty to counts one through seven regarding conspiracy to distribute and distributing counterfeit currency, as well as the substantive offenses of counterfeiting and financial fraud . . .

"Mr. Messenger has moved this court to decide on a motion for release pending trial, pursuant to Title Eighteen of the U.S. Code, section three one four two six. Under that section a presumption of detention exists unless the defendant establishes by clear and convincing evidence that he is not likely to flee or pose a danger to the safety of any other person or the community if released. I have considered all of the factors, and I have considered them closely.

"Therefore, it is my decision that Mr. Williams is not a flight risk and poses no danger to the community, and since the defense counsel has committed to having the defendant here on time, I see no reason why I shouldn't give Mr. Williams the benefit of the doubt."

Colin was sizzling with nervous energy, engrossed in the words that came from the judge's lips—grabbing at them with his ears before they were spoken, and with his eyes, as though they were objects. And then, once the words did gain exposure, joy entered the equation, the butterflies swirling about in his body, in his mind.

Damn! Messenger is a pro!

Colin could see the light again, not merely the dreary overcast that ruled the courtroom. He found himself calculating again, assuming that since the lawyer could manipulate the judge so easily, so skillfully, then the trial by jury should be a walk in the park.

As the judge delivered his decision, Colin noticed a slight disturbance among the prosecution, how one was showing his two-way pager to the others. Murray seemed to show a special interest and eventually asked the judge for an emergency recess. The judge allowed him five minutes, but for Colin those minutes felt like hours.

"Your Honor, it's been ten minutes," Messenger complained during the quiet wait.

The judge motioned to the clerk and the proceedings continued, despite the prosecutor's absence. A handful of words hadn't been spoken before Murray shot back into the courtroom. He whispered to his associates, then motioned for the judge's attention.

"What is it now, Mr. Murray?"

"Your Honor, please, if you'd excuse me . . . something just came up, something critical to this case. If you would, before you make your final decision—"

"But I have *already* made my decision."

"I implore you, Your Honor. This is beyond critical and regards the lives of others."

"Oh?" The judge looked down at the defense table, directly into Colin's eyes. "Very well, then, should we expect some form of documented evidence regarding this . . . critical information?"

"I should have something within the half hour."

"I'll give you fifteen minutes," said the judge. "And this had better be good."

The mallet was slammed down onto its wooden block. Court was recessed.

"Oh shit," Colin muttered under his breath.

CHAPTER

9

Colin imagined that one of the prosecutors had found out about his true financial position—maybe they'd searched the condo and found all the cash between the mattresses . . . maybe one of the brokers from the various money market funds had identified Colin and his assets were uncovered.

Now, all he could do was weigh the situation—why he had lied about his finances, his intentions to win the court's sympathy. Colin wasn't aware that this was an often-used tactic, how defendants hoped the powers that be would somehow conclude: *he couldn't possibly have done all that's been alleged . . . he's so damned poor!* But now, on second thought, Colin wondered if that was a bad idea—an idea that had now backfired on him.

And then, just when he thought he'd figured it all out—the reason for the holdup—something altogether unexpected dropkicked any chances he had for bail.

"What in God's name was *that* about?" Jeffery Z. Messenger III demanded.

The court had just reversed itself and rejected Colin's appeal for bail. The trial date was set for three months down the road, and Colin was cuffed, taken through the maze of secret passages, hallways and corridors to the basement where cubicles were set up for lawyers to meet with their clients. There was a mesh screen between the two, so thick not so much as a sewing needle could be passed. However, the lawyer and his client could still see and hear one another.

"They're all lies," Colin replied. "I had nothing to do with any arson. Yes, I worked at SCE, but the story they told out in the courtroom is a lie. Every bit of it."

"So then you've made *me* out to be a liar. I stood there and told the judge that you were a Fort Lee resident with strong ties. I said that you attended school here, for God's sake!" Messenger paused. "Not *all*, huh? How can you have strong ties if you lived in LA just four years ago?"

"It's actually closer to five."

"Okay. Then why am I out there telling the judge you've lived in Fort Lee all your life? About school, and family ties and yadda-yadda-yadda . . . and to add the elephant to your lifeboat, they're claiming you're a pyromaniac! You lied—I lied—everybody's friggin' lyin'!" Messenger fumed. He ran his hands through his hair.

"Okay, listen . . . we have to organize a defense for you. If we're going to trial, then we have to get past this—just forget all about what just happened. We need to concentrate on what the jury will see and hear. And don't worry—this magistrate only presides over the bail hearings. You'll be assigned a trial judge and then we'll have a fresh start . . ." Messenger took out a yellow legal pad and jotted the date in the upper left-hand corner. It was the beginning of a long uphill climb.

Vince Reed was proud of himself. He felt himself to be one step beyond the ultimate puppet master. Getting the heat off of himself by diverting the attention of the Secret Service was just the start. Making Colin the fall guy and still looking like a hero was bigger than a con; it was the art of a craftsman. Hiring Messenger to handle Colin's legal woes was a positioning that was akin to protecting a pawn with a knight, therefore controlling the chess game.

But Reed never counted on Colin's past to throw a monkey wrench into the process. He also didn't expect such overwhelming obedience by so many witnesses, and how they followed his lead during Colin's trial. Reed's original intention was to get Colin out on bail and have enough witnesses to speak favorably in his defense.

They'd say: "I never saw him with any suitcases . . . in fact, I've only seen him at the club one time, the day of the raid . . ." "I've been a bouncer at Club Jaguar for seven years, and this new guy—yes, I'm talking about the defendant—well, I'd never seen him before, so I gave him closer attention; you never know with strangers, and we can't afford to have someone come and terrorize the place. Anyway, I watched him since he came in . . . no, he didn't have a suitcase. No, I didn't see him handling any money other than buying a drink or two . . ."

This had been the plan—to organize a series of eyewitnesses who would vindicate Colin. However, Reed learned some interesting details that forced him to change his course.

Jeffrey Messenger had a box of evidence—photos, phone records, taped conversations, and other material—detailing a six-month investigation entitled: Operation Funny Money.

"Reed, there's over a thousand photos here with shots of every customer to come into Club Jaguar within six months. Notice I've separated them as best I could . . ."

"Okay, but anybody could—"

"Reed, you were their original target. That's why you have more photos than the others. They thought you were the kingpin behind the counterfeit scheme."

"Then they're still hunting for my hide."

"I doubt it. Right now, because of the events in court, the prosecutor feels they already have the big fish. And they're staking everything on it. Colin could end up with thirty years in the pen."

"So he's in the hot seat," Reed realized.

"Exactly. And the bigger picture is, if I get him off, the investigation is back on. They'll be hunting for you again."

"So what's the deal? What are his chances?"

"Depends on our witnesses," said Messenger.

Reed smirked. "I guess that answers my question, esquire. I think this is where we say good night. Keep handling his case, let me handle things on my end. Oh . . . and let him give you his outgoing mail."

"How's that?"

"Do I need to repeat myself?"

"No, I understand *what* you said. I just don't know why—"

"Leave the big decisions up to me, esquire. Just follow instructions, got it?"

"Of course."

"I'm especially looking for letters to his wife, Toy, or any other friends. We'll see that"—another smirk—"the letters reach their destinations."

"What should I tell him? I mean, what reason is there to give *me* his mail?"

"I don't care *what* you tell 'im, esquire, just see to it that *I . . . get . . . his . . . mail.*" Reed poked Messenger's arm to emphasize his demands. "Good night, Counselor," he said.

Messenger exited from Reed's car to load into his own.

"Think we'll have problems out of him?" asked Bruce, who had been sitting in the backseat all the while.

"Not in the least," Reed said as he watched Messenger's vehicle disappear from the Meadowlands Arena parking lot. "Because he doesn't want his little daughter catchin' a stray bullet . . . if you get my meaning."

"I do."

"Now . . . before we stop in to watch a bunch of horses run circles, there's something I want you to take care of—or, at least, I want you to start setting it up when you get back to Club Jaguar."

Reed's wishes were Bruce's demands. And within a day and a half there was a cast of witnesses ready to appear in court—only they were doing so on behalf of the prosecution, not Colin Williams.

At trial, one woman said she'd seen Colin taking two Samsonite suitcases out of his Camry in the parking lot outside of the club. "I knew they were Samsonites because I used to sell luggage at Macy's department store," she said.

Another woman confirmed the parking lot story, saying that it looked peculiar for a man to be carrying two suitcases into a dance club. *"He stuck out like a sore thumb."*

One of Club Jaguar's bouncers testified, "Two guys were

fighting just feet from the front entrance of the club. I ran up behind the other bouncer, ignoring the man standing at the entrance with two suitcases in his hands . . ."

The bouncer couldn't account for everything, but he helped to paint a piece of the bigger picture, how the crew of Club Jaguar staff ran from their posts to stop a potential brawl. "When I got back inside—we threw the two guys out of the club—the man with the suitcases was gone."

When U.S. Attorney Murray asked the witness how he knew that the potential brawl was a diversion, he answered, "I put two and two together. Those guys were homeless dudes I've seen in downtown Jersey City. They hardly have money, always feedin' their drug habits." But later, the bouncer explained, when he was done for the night, a few hours after the raid, "I saw those same two fags eating—"

"Sir," the judge intervened. "You'll need to refrain from derogatory terms regarding sexual preferences in your testimony."

"Judge, when I say fags, I don't call all gay folks faggots . . . it's just the fool-assed ones, the bitches who can't keep their heads on straight."

Laughter erupted in the courtroom.

"Please! Order in my court!" demanded the trial judge. He was already frustrated at how so much street lingo and slang had earned a place in his courtroom. After a powerful *bang!—bang!—bang!* of his gavel, the courtroom went silent. "Sir, you'll need to tame your language in my courtroom and how you refer to people, or I will personally make an example of you and find you in contempt of court."

"Sorry, Your Honor. I'm just keepin' it real."

"Well, save that for the bathroom walls. Meanwhile, in my courtroom, just concentrate on keepin' it *right*."

"Yessir."

By the time the prosecutor backtracked and had the bouncer pick up where he left off, it was clear that the two "fags" had gone to a local diner later that night, where, amongst a table of friends and a mountain of food, a toast was made: "Here's to the suitcase man!"

"After I overheard that, I put two and two together. The suitcase man—"

"Would you mean the defendant, Colin Williams, who sits at that table?" The prosecutor pointed to Colin and his attorney.

"Yes, I realized that he set up the disturbance . . . paid the f—the troublemakers so he could slip his suitcases in."

"And tell me something . . . Sir, have you ever seen suitcases brought into Club Jaguar in the past?"

"Why . . . no. Not a chance. They'd never be allowed inside. This ain't a hotel."

Jeffrey Messenger cross-examined the witness. "Sir, there's just one question I have . . . I'm confused here. Why in the world would anyone in their right mind bring a suitcase, two of them, to a nightclub? And if they *did* manage to get them in, wouldn't it be obvious? Wouldn't you guess there's trouble? Maybe weapons? Or worse, a bomb?"

The bouncer immediately took the defensive, both by his facial expression and by the tone of his voice. "You said you had *one* question, which *one* did you want me to answer?" He turned to the judge for help.

"Mr. Messenger, please keep your questions simple, if possible, so that the witness may respond in kind."

"Of course, Your Honor. Let me ask you this"—Messenger directed the question toward the bouncer—"Can a person bring a chair into Club Jaguar?"

"No," he answered with a sigh—the indication that this was nonsense.

"How about a frying pan?"

"No."

"How about . . . a toolbox?"

"Maybe a repairman, during the day?"

"How about a clubgoer, during business hours."

"Nope."

The judge interjected. "Yes or no, please," he told the witness. Then he said to Messenger, "Please . . . could you make your point?"

"I was just wondering . . . you've been bouncing at Club

Jaguar for years—you control what comes through the entrance, and as you say, there are no chairs, no frying pans, no televisions and no toolboxes allowed during business hours. Is that correct?"

"Yes, sir, it is."

"So, then, answer me this: why—if the usual procedure is for you to screen clubgoers at the front entrance—would anyone in their right mind even make an *attempt* at bringing a *suitcase, a large, obvious, burdensome Samsonite*, to the front door of the dance club?"

"Well . . . uh . . . I guess that was the reason for the distraction. To get the security to lose focus."

"Lose focus?" Messenger repeated in a tone of disbelief.

"Yes."

"I just wonder if you've been hired for the right reasons."

"What's that mean?"

"Well . . . If I was a club owner, I can't imagine hiring you to—ahem—*lose focus*."

Messenger said that he had no further questions. But, as far as he was concerned, he'd put on a good enough performance to persuade even the witness that his was an effective interrogation.

The bouncer's story, the story from the woman who had been in the parking lot, and the stories of more than a dozen other witnesses were in fact all fabricated accounts of what had happened on the night of the raid. They were all cock-and-bull tales that Reed had them rehearse over and over again with none other than Jeffrey Z. Messenger III pretending to be the prosecutor.

They had all been coached so that the full weight of the problem fell on the shoulders of Colin Williams. Now, with Colin's downfall, the Secret Service's investigation was complete. They'd nabbed their man. Case closed.

Making Colin the patsy, the scapegoat, the fall guy, lifted an incredible burden from Reed's organization. It was a sacrifice, as far as Reed was concerned, that was worth millions of dollars. With such tremendous odds against him, Colin never had a shot at a fair trial. Everyone—the prosecutor, the judge, the witness, *his* lawyer and inevitably the jury—was out to bury him. He might as well have been a great big grapefruit, with his skin peeled back.

It didn't matter that Colin's fingerprints weren't found on the suitcases. What *did* matter was the many witnesses who said he did have possession of them.

"And how could more than a dozen witnesses be wrong?" the prosecutor asked the jury in his closing arguments. Each Samsonite contained $500,000 in counterfeit $20 and $50 bills, and despite the paper being worthless (having been confiscated and inevitably burned by Secret Service agents) Colin was convicted on the "intend loss" as opposed to the zero value of the phony currency.

His culpability, coupled with all of the so-called "relevant conduct" that the prosecutor stacked against him during the sentencing, left Colin in water so deep that his drowning was assured.

The judge was lenient, for what it was worth, not giving Colin the top of the guidelines (the 20 to 25 years that the offense called for), since Colin was considered a first-time offender. He hadn't been arrested or convicted of a crime— even in Los Angeles—so his slate was figuratively clean. Furthermore, the judge said during sentencing, "I want to see Mr. Williams leave prison early enough so he might still have some importance in his daughter's life, provided prison does him any good."

When all was said and done, Colin was sentenced to prison for 14 years. The best-case scenario for his release was an "85 percent date," or 11 years.

CHAPTER

10

For one year, the time it took for Colin to weather his court proceedings, Vince Reed carried the payments for the penthouse where Toy and Lady, Colin's wife and daughter, were living. Reed also paid utility and food bills, as well as pre-K classes at a private school for Lady, who was now four years old.

"I don't understand Colin. Why doesn't he write more often or call? Why won't he let me come to court to support him?"

Toy's questions were easy for Reed to respond to, so long as he kept track of his string of lies. "This is a difficult time he's going through, Toy. He doesn't wanna drag you through his problems, and I agree with him one hundred percent."

"But he *is* dragging me through this! Do you have any idea how it feels when Lady comes crying to me at night, *'Where's Daddy? Where's Daddy?'* I'm confused, Reed. Sometimes I just wanna die!"

"Don't say that, Toy. He wants what's best for you. He's still looking out for your finances . . . through me, of course."

"But money isn't *everything,* Reed. Sometimes a woman just wants to be held. Some affection. It's been almost a year without my husband . . . can you imagine what it's like? To have a husband, someone you're committed to, and he's missing in action? A man I've changed my whole life for, but who's no longer around to love me?"

Reed dealt with all of these cries and pleas. He had an answer for everything, but more important, he had the money to help smooth things over. There were roses he said were from Colin. There were gifts he said were from Colin. And there were the letters. All the time that Colin was going to trial, in and out of the courtroom in handcuffs and that awfully loud pumpkin-orange jumpsuit, Toy was kept away. Reed's word was all it took, since he was her only lifeline to money and, so she thought, to Colin. And just in case, Reed had enough of his goons around to enforce his words. There'd be no surprise appearances at Colin's trial.

At the same time, Colin's attorney served as the perfect messenger, often manipulating things so that Colin's messages were given to Reed. On the other hand, Reed had someone writing letters to both Colin and Toy, letters which were designed to bring their marriage to certain collapse with every passing month.

Vince Reed, the puppet master.

Both husband and wife grew more and more miserable without each other, thanks to the miscommunications. Toy had long since changed the home phone number and kept it unlisted, making it impossible for Colin to reach her directly. It was Reed's suggestion so that Toy wouldn't be "harassed" by the reporters covering the case. Reed also had the doorman at the Shangrila censor Toy's mail, just in case Colin disobeyed his lawyer, perhaps in an attempt to get a letter to Toy. None were sent. But that was no wonder, since Colin had a new friend.

Kitty Turner wondered if Colin would recognize her from Club Jaguar when she first went to visit him at the Bergen County Jail. But there were considerations that Kitty hadn't thought of. First, she wore clothes and makeup that transformed her into a stunning work of beauty. Second, Kitty was a "gift" from Vince Reed. She made sure there was money in Colin's commissary account, and she accepted his collect phone calls, often serving as a sounding board for his woes. Kitty was also the one to "craft" the letters for Reed, those that were supposedly written by Toy. So, she was as much aware of his troubled marriage as she was with the scheme that kept him behind bars in the first place. Finally,

Colin was more and more desperate for consolation. He was willing to listen to and perhaps believe most anything. His trial proceedings always ended with painful results. He didn't have any friends in Fort Lee, only acquaintances and associates, most of whom were on Vince Reed's payroll.

All told, Colin was too blind to see the bottom line: Kitty was just another pawn under Reed's power, doing what he wanted when he wanted it. She was also Vince Reed's "Sunday fuck." They'd spend the night out, go to dinner, talk about business and he'd coach her on things to say or do regarding Colin.

"He's our sacrifice, Kitty-Kitty. He may not know it now, but in the long run he'll know why we did what we did. You just keep him happy. Make 'im fall in love with you—I know you can do it, 'cuz you're a triflin' ho underneath those looks I bought."

"Why do you have to talk to me all mean, Reed? You know I'll do anything for you."

"I know. But you also like it when I talk greasy to you— *don't you, bitch?*" Reed squinted as he spoke.

Kitty rolled her eyes at Reed's hard rock ways, just as she usually did.

"I didn't hear you," said Reed, reading her mind.

"Hear me *what*?"

"I didn't hear you say you like it. You like it when I talk greasy to you, don't you?"

She took a deep breath and closed her eyes.

"Oh, you wanna play? 'Cuz, bitch, I'll make you take your shirt off right here in the restaurant. Now, say I won't."

"Take it easy, Reed. You win. I *love it* when you treat me greasy. Okay? Are you happy?"

"And tell me what white trash is gonna have my dick in her asshole tonight."

"Vince," Kitty whined. "People are gonna—"

"You know I don't give a fuck about who hears or sees. Plus, they're all about to see those pretty titties I spent eight Gs on, if you don't answer my question."

"All right already, Vince. It's *me.* I'm white trash, and as *usual,* I want your dick in my ass tonight." Kitty twisted her face, as if to say, *Satisfied?*

"I thought so."

Kitty was just another trick, as far as Reed was concerned. A missionary, with no boundaries on what she'd give. Now that Colin was stored away for what seemed like an eternity, Reed intended to line Toy up as another of his tricks. It was perfect timing for him to make his move, maybe have her replace Cheryl as his convenient Wednesday fuck. In Reed's eyes, considering how he was taking care of all her bills, things would work in his favor. It was only right, for one hand to wash the other. Reed knew as much about Toy as Colin had shared. Except, during the past year, knowing her better couldn't be helped. Toy was in pain, she was lonely and she needed attention. She wasn't a woman with a trade, with career goals or great expectations in life. She simply wanted to be happy and healthy and loved.

However, Reed already knew that, having grown up in the inner city. These were the wants of many, if not most, girls in the hood. Perhaps it was a social disease or a practice in conformity; still, it was a reality he knew well. *All women are the same*, Reed had realized long ago. The only thing that separated them was the spirit; otherwise the pussies and the pretty faces were a dime a dozen. The thing that made a man appealing in the eyes of a chicken head was cold cash, and Vince Reed had more of that than he knew what to do with.

Now, just hours after Colin's sentencing, was the time that Reed decided to show his *other* side. This was the thought in his mind as he steered his Lexus into the driveway of the Shangrila. He could see the Camry, Colin's car, parked in its assigned space, and he smiled. *She's home.*

He parked in the visitors' area and looked up 30 floors to the penthouse windows and terrace. It was as if he could see the outcome of this visit. He knew that Toy's was a broken home—a miserable one. And Toy was so much woman, bottled up, shacked up, locked in—waiting for some miracle to come her way. She needed everything to get back to normal, or she'd have to get on with her life and find someone else—some sense of fulfillment.

Those thoughts empowered Reed to harden his game face, even as he looked down at his crotch. *Humph . . . fulfillment.* In the elevator Reed recalled things Colin had told him about his wife; intimate details. He'd sometimes brag after a big score, how he was going home to "his Toy," as if she were his personal plaything: "She's probably home right now, waiting for me in one of my Brooks Brothers shirts and no panties." Colin, the proud husband. Reed also recalled seeing a photo of Toy at home, hair down, in a see-through negligee; another photo showed her in a cut-off T-shirt and booty-hugging shorts, gazing outward with those come-fuck-me eyes.

"I see you got y'self a cold freak," Reed had said to Colin, since he'd had balls enough to show the pix.

"Why you say that?" asked Colin.

"Because Toy's a Jersey City girl. And I know Jersey City girls well. I can see right through them."

"What's so different about Jersey City girls that you can see through 'em?" asked Colin, as serious as he was unimpressed.

"Fo' real, it don't matter if she's from here or not. That's just how I do. I study women like cats study Animal Planet . . . within a matter of minutes after I meet a chick, I can tell what she's about. I can see if she's weak or strong-minded by her gestures, her hygiene, her breathing patterns, her tone of voice . . . and if I get close enough to touch her, I can get a good idea of her soul power."

Colin was quiet for a spell before he broke out in a laugh. "Get the fuck outta here," he said, punching Reed lightly in the arm.

"You laugh, but I'm dead serious. I'm like a mind reader when it comes to women . . . a psychic . . ."

That was Reed's game, knowing people . . . and women *were* his toys; not because of marriage or because of being soul mates (as in Colin's case), but because that was how he saw the opposite sex. He seduced them with his casual frankness, he imposed himself whenever he had the chance; and in the end he was pleasured, thrilled and satisfied. Reed was abrasive when he had to be, but he did so just enough to remain a feared man—just enough to always have his way. In many ways, Vince Reed was a devil.

When Toy looked into the peephole, she experienced a spasm of fright. It was Reed, and she *really* needed to see him. She was down to her last ten dollars, and she was impatient to find out the results of Colin's legal affairs.

At the time the buzzer rang, Toy had just finished showering. She'd wrapped her still-wet body with a plush, pink towel and ran for the door.

There he was, his image distorted—like he was in a fishbowl—there on the other side of the door. Vince Reed, the six-foot-tall, dark coffee brown hunk who was once, or maybe still was, her husband's boss.

She'd anticipated his arrival sometime this week since this was about the time he came to drop money off—the tenth of the month—plus, as he'd mentioned, Colin's trial would end "any day now."

"One minute," Toy said in a sort of singsong tone. She ran back to her bedroom for a robe. Before she opened the door, she paused to check herself in the wall mirror that sparkled and reflected nearly the entire foyer.

I hope you have good news, Reed. I sure could use some right about now . . . Colin . . . I miss you so much! Toy's thoughts were spinning. So many questions . . . so many assumptions.

Woven in with her concerns about Colin were the nuances about Reed. His presence was so powerful—her lifeline for the time being. The thin mustache, and the shaved head that always reminded her of Michael Jordan, made Reed out to be an appealing bachelor. There was that awesome diamond bracelet dangling on his left wrist, and that expensive-looking Rolex on his right. And, of course, the diamond solitaire pinkie ring.

Toy had once asked about the ring and what it stood for, but instead of explaining what it *meant* to him, he'd talked it up as being worth more than $100,000. Toy was in awe of Reed from that day on. And now that she thought about it, she realized that Reed had once again exercised his "power" to always manage to appear unannounced, bypassing the building's strict rules—the doorman was required to use the intercom for every visitor. However, Toy never minded the intrusion since this man brought nothing but relief in such miserable times.

Still, there was something so mysterious about Reed, and it at least piqued her interest. His image was bigger than life in her eyes, and yet she always stayed on her side of the line, minding her manners. The Toy of yesteryear might have fallen for this man without a second look. But she was a different woman, a married woman, who would never do anything to dishonor the love and devotion she had for Colin. And besides, this was the man whom Colin had to deal with. Surely, the two had an "understanding" when it came to each other's women.

"Hey, Reed," said Toy, giving him a peck on the cheek—no more and no less than a married woman should.

"Oh—*damn* . . . did I catch you at a bad—"

"No . . ." Toy replied. "Come on in. We're all adults here. I just got out of the shower . . ."

"I . . . *see* . . . "

Toy was stalled by the way Reed spoke and looked at her. But in a snap, she shook the notion of any sexual hints, smirking back at him with her own expression: *you so crazy.*

"How in the world did you get past Simpson downstairs?"

"Oh, him," Reed said, as if the doorman were of little concern.

"You always do that," Toy said with a feigned anger, already headed back to the bathroom.

Meanwhile, Reed shut the door.

"It'll only take me a minute to get it together," Toy shouted. "Make yourself at home!"

The devil was there in Reed's eyes, as though he'd just conquered his foe. He was Tyson after knocking Spinks out in less than two minutes of the first round.

He moistened his lips, preparing for something that even *he*, Mr. All-Women-Are-the-Same, realized was a tough job. He was about to devastate this woman. But at the same time, he looked forward to licking her wounds.

He'd been here before, in these swanky surroundings that Colin called home—the sunken living room just off the entry hall, the white marble floor leading up to thick champagne carpet. Reed grimaced, knowing that: one, he was paying for all of this luxury, and two, one day soon it would be *his* naked toes curling in this carpet, warming up to that fireplace on the side of the room, with Colin's woman performing God-knows-what service for him. There were a number of houseplants to add that flavor of earth and nature to the man-made conveniences of the residence. A few paintings graced the walls along with enlarged photographs of Toy and Colin posing together; another showed them with their daughter, Lady.

Those will be the first to go.

When Toy emerged from the bathroom she was wearing a white button-down dress shirt with hair-thin red stripes. The shirt—belonging to Colin, Reed guessed—stuck to the still-moist areas about Toy's breasts, her nipples making their dark impressions. At the same time, Toy was busy with a plush pink towel, drying damp tendrils of her golden-brown hair. "Good news?" she asked, more or less cutting to the chase.

She plopped herself on the couch, carefully so. And Reed took her caution to mean that she had no panties on under the dress shirt. His guess was confirmed when he noticed Toy making the effort to keep the shirttails low over her naked thighs. She sat there with an overwhelming honesty about her. No presumption whatsoever.

"I've taken real good care of you two, haven't I?" Reed began, as if he were responsible for the oxygen she breathed. "I mean, from the looks of this little nest you're living in, life ain't too bad, is it?" He stood and paced before Toy, pontificating as he did—the ultimate authority in her life.

"Sure. Um . . . I mean, we're doing pretty good, considering. I can't say I agree with all the, you know, *crooked* stuff, especially since that's what got us into this whole mess in the first place . . . all this court stuff, and not seeing Colin for a year now. But, like Colin used to say . . . you don't take risks, you don't grow rich." A pained smile graced her lips, and Reed saw right through it; right through to the false sense of confidence.

"I know that quote well . . . it's like I thought it up myself," he said. He was closer to her now. "Toy, you should also know that with the risks come the possible consequences." He reached down to put his hand to her head, which she had wrapped with the towel her hair all swept up into a makeshift turban.

"Okay," said Toy, clearly unaware of where Reed was going with the discussion.

Now he stroked Toy's temple and cheek, following a drop of water with the back of his forefinger. He caught himself and backed off, not wanting to progress too fast toward his goal. He needed to temper every gesture, every word. Contemplating what to say next, Reed drew in a chestful of air and turned back toward Toy with a fresh resolve, his arms folded.

"What's wrong?" Toy eventually asked, a slight tremble with her words.

"You want it raw? Or sugar-coated?" Reed had long anticipated this moment, these words, surprising himself at how things were working just as he'd planned.

And now he could see what he couldn't plan—Toy's reaction.

She was visibly shaken. Her eyes were turning bloodshot.

Somehow, her God-given beauty was fading to plain-Jane looks.

"Just . . . *tell me*!" Toy muttered, a slight growl seeping through her tightened lips.

"They took Colin away from us, Toy." It was a flat comment that made "they" seem like aliens, and Colin, their captured earthling.

"What do you *mean*, 'took him away from us'?" Toy stood up, no concern this time to the shirttails spreading, showing that brief view. "I thought you said he'd be getting out soon! His letters even said he would get probation! Look . . . I'll show you." As if this would make all the difference in the world, Toy bounced off to a table and grabbed some letters from the drawer.

Reed could tell Toy was in a red zone at the moment and maybe she could only see, hear and imagine what she *wanted* to as opposed to what was reality.

Reaching out to stop the madness, Reed grasped Toy's arm. This was the only way. "Lose the fantasy, girl. The dream is over. They gave our boy fourteen years in the pen. They're sending him to Marion, Illinois."

Toy could hardly speak, her mind repeating the things Reed had said: *Fourteen years . . . Marion, Illinois.* Not a sound escaped her lips until one gasp. The words seemed to be stuck in her throat as she back-stepped, separating herself from the messenger with the bad news. Eventually, she let out a single word: "*How?*"

"Here . . . I knew you'd have a hard time believing me, so maybe you'll believe your husband's words." Reed took out and unfolded a sealed envelope. It was marked for Toy. "He had it passed to me in the courtroom today . . . I guess he already knew his fate."

Toy took the envelope as though it were a fragile artifact. She sat with it, afraid to open it.

"Toy, I know this is hard to swallow . . . I know. I had a hard time dealing with the truth myself. On the way over here I almost crashed my car, I got so upset . . ."

Gradually, Toy began opening the envelope. She got the letter out. It shook in her hands.

Dearest Toy,

I need to make this short and sweet. Today I will learn my fate, and it is only right that I say what's on my mind. I must clear the air so that you and I can both go on with our lives.

For the past year I've been living a fantasy in my letters to you. I hope you've been getting them all. But the truth is I was just being optimistic under grim circumstances.

I'm going away for a long, long time. You might as well call it a lifetime. I'll be almost 50 years old when I leave prison. Too old for a lot of things. You will have outgrown me by then. Our daughter will be going to college. And, to keep it real, you'll probably be with a number of other men during that time.

But that's okay with me. I accept this fate. This is the way it is. So I've asked Reed to help you as best he can. He's my friend, baby. I trust him with my life. What happened to me is nobody's fault but mine. I made a dumb mistake, and now I must pay the price . . .

Toy was sniffling, and tears ran endlessly as she read on. Reed ran his hand along her neck and upper back to comfort her.

I also asked Reed to look out for you and make sure you're happy. If anyone can do it, he can. You just have to trust. I won't drag this out, so good luck to you. It was nice while it lasted, but remember I told you life is about risks . . . I took it. Enjoy your life.

"No, no, no, no, no! There has to be more! He hardly mentioned Lady. What about our family!"

Toy sobbed loudly, like a dying siren. Gusts of emotion

that had been trapped inside of her came out as if a dam had burst. She was raspy, crying into a throw pillow that she held to her chest and face, hugging for dear life. She wailed bloody murder into that pillow, muffling most of the rage and horror, soaking it with her tears. Reed said nothing. He merely caressed her—showing not compassion, but affection.

Toy moaned and toiled about there on the couch, unaware that everything below her navel was now exposed to the hungry eyes above her. The lusting man inside of Reed chuckled deceitfully while he focused between her legs. It was a moment of suspended lechery that made his dick hard. Now that he'd reached this point, Reed considered what he'd do next; where to touch and what to say.

He sat by her side and gave her his shoulder, pulling her to it to cry on. But he didn't need to try hard, since Toy poured herself onto him, draping her arms around his neck and molding to him as she wept.

Reed took every bit of Toy into his arms, pretending to be concerned. He wasn't possessive like he wanted to be, but managed the compassionate embrace nonetheless. His erection was still his secret while he inhaled Toy's scent—it may as well have been the aroma of a toxic spring taking over his senses, making him sick with the want for her flesh. He closed his eyes, imagining Toy as that next woman he'd conquered: his Wednesday fuck. Soon enough.

By nightfall Reed had called the sitter, explaining that she should keep the baby overnight. The two pills he'd brought with him had Toy out cold and she was in no condition to care for a child.

CHAPTER

11

While Toy was asleep, Reed enjoyed himself. He stripped the dress shirt from her body and the towel from her head before he laid her on her bed.

Following a few minutes of quiet review, he became familiar with her soft skin and ample curves, smoothing his hand on, in and around her body. He used a little lotion, as an excuse in the event Toy woke from the drugs. He fingered her cold folds and played those same fingers in and out of her mouth. He then rolled her over and pulled her ass cheeks apart for more evaluation.

"Damn, I can't wait to make you mine . . . and I do mean one hundred percent mine," he said softly.

He gave her ass a light smack, the impression of thrills to come, as Toy continued her peaceful sleep. He turned her over once again and fixed her so that her head was close to the edge of the bed. Then he loosened his belt and lowered his pants. Within seconds his hairy scrotum was dragging along her nose and lips. When Reed was done, there was no part of her face he hadn't defiled. "I would whack off on you, but I'll save it for later," he said. He got himself dressed, threw a sheet over Toy, and let her rest.

It was close to 11 P.M. when Reed returned to the bedroom with a tray of fruit salad, tea for Toy and coffee for himself. He woke her by wiping her face with a cool, damp washcloth.

"Oh . . . *God*. I—I fell asleep? What . . . *time* is it?" Her voice was raspy.

"It's late," said Reed. "Here . . . sip some of this tea."

"Oh, my . . ." Toy suddenly realized that she was nude under the sheet, and she pulled it up to conceal her exposed breasts. "What happened?"

"I took care of you. I took *good* care of you. Don't worry, I know my stuff. When my grandmother was bedridden, I was the only one who would help. I bathed you, massaged you and gave you some juice."

"You did? I did? I don't remem . . . ohh . . ." Toy sighed helplessly, addressing how life suddenly got out of hand. She let her head drop back to the pillows for more sleep. A place where she'd feel safe for the time being.

In the morning Reed woke Toy with breakfast in bed: an egg and cheese omelet, orange juice and toast. He even dressed the plate with strawberries and orange slices.

"Mmm . . . that smells real good," Toy said as best she could with her groggy voice. She moaned as she lifted herself up to get at the food. "I feel like I've been sleeping since last year."

Reed could see how life had been virtually vacuumed from her, more or less overnight. "We've gotta get some pep back in your step, woman."

"Omigod!" Toy said frantically. "The *baby*!"

"Don't worry yourself, Toy. I called the sitter. She picked up Lady from preschool yesterday and kept her for the night. They'll be here later."

"Oh," she uttered breathlessly. "Thank you, Reed."

"You cried a river of tears last night—no condition to care for a child. No sense in upsetting her too. Know what I'm sayin'?"

Toy nodded in agreement, still a bit unsure about things. And yet, she thanked him again.

"It's no problem, baby. That's what I'm here for. Remember what he said—" Already, Reed was omitting Colin's name from the picture. "You can trust me."

Reed hid his joy at how it was so easy to hijack the Williams' household; to take control of the steering wheel— to drive this baby. "Whatever you need, just ask. Life is gonna change for you and Lady. From now on it's gonna be a different world altogether . . ."

Toy said nothing, but her wet eyes focused.

"Your man and I had a pact, Toy. We made a commitment to each other that if either of us met with tragedy or fate—that's prison or death—the other would pick up the pieces, take care of the family . . ." Reed smoothed his palm about Toy's cheek, cuddling it. She didn't reject his TLC. "So, I hope you don't mind, but . . . you're *my* responsibility now."

Toy was already feeling like Reed's responsibility, considering how Reed had been paying her bills all this time, not looking for anything in return. Quiet as she kept it, she was already feeling guilty, wanting to return the favor somehow. A tear eased down her cheek where Reed's hand had caressed.

"What's gonna happen to Colin?" she asked.

"All right. I want you to listen to me. I'm gonna say this once to you—once and for all. Dude is goin' away. *Far* away, Toy. And for a long, long time. He'll be about forty-eight years old when he gets out of prison. That's if he gets out of prison. You'll be thirty-nine, Toy. Beyond your prime. I . . . I wanna tell you something that he and I spoke about, but only if you promise to keep it between us."

Reed knew there was no way for Toy to reach Colin now, not with his controls in place. So his want for secrecy was but a ploy, much like a lot of his hocus-pocus talk. If Colin was doing anything right now, he was playing right into Reed's scheme, having jailhouse phone sex with Kitty.

Toy nodded as a sign of her vow, obviously anxious to know any- and everything that Colin might've said.

"Dude doesn't want you to wait for him, Toy. He doesn't. In fact, he doesn't . . . this is crazy. I can't tell you this."

"Please, Reed. Tell me, *please*," she pleaded.

"Toy, he doesn't think he'll live to be a free man."

"I don't believe you! How could you say that? Oh God! We have a *daughter*! We have *dreams*! You're *lying,* Reed! You're *lying*! You are LY-ING!"

Toy pounded Reed's chest with her fists, again and again,

until she lost energy, until her palms lay on his pecs. It was as if she was having a bad dream—a nightmare. Only, it was so real. She could feel that physical side of the illusion.

Reed had snatched up the tray so that it wouldn't get all over the bed. At the same time, he endured Toy's ranting, knowing that this phase was part of the withdrawal from that drug Colin and Toy had together. They called it "love," but it left a sour taste in Reed's mouth.

Toy didn't want to give up or lose faith, but her body and mind were going separate ways. She was both confused and exhausted. Reed held Toy with a careful embrace, finally calming her. She sank into his arms, muttering sounds that were no longer words.

"Shhh . . ." Reed whispered the hush into Toy's ear while placing his finger softly over her lips. "Remember . . . I got you, girl. I won't let you fall, you hear me? We're gonna follow his last wishes, so start thinkin' different world. Say that for me. Go on, say it: different world."

Toy stalled, the way one would before making a confused decision. Reed urged her with a tighter grip on her arm and sincerity in his eyes. Vince Reed, the actor. Eventually, Toy came around, seeing things his way. "It's gonna be . . . a . . . different world," Toy said with some trepidation.

Reed helped her along. "And . . ."

"And," Toy repeated.

"I am your responsibility, Reed."

Toy responded accordingly.

"That's it. Good. See? That wasn't so hard, was it? Now, you get comfortable with seeing my face more often. Bills, food, clothing . . . *whatever*. You ask for it, you got it. Starting with these."

"What's that for?"

"Take 'em, baby. They're the keys to a brand-new Ford Expedition. I even knew your favorite color—blue—and I got you the leather interior. Gucci-ed up. Is that a word? Well . . . it is now."

Toy stuttered, unable to get a word out.

"You gotta take your beautiful daughter here and there,

and I wanted you all to be safe. You're a prize, baby. And you should be treated like one. A truck is only gonna make you more secure in a world of so much unpredictability."

What Toy couldn't say with her lips was expressed across her face: *wow*.

Reed tucked his curled finger under Toy's chin. "I'm gonna show you what happiness is, doll. Trust me."

CHAPTER

12

When Reed leaned in to kiss me, I froze. I didn't expect it, and I sure enough didn't know how to respond. I could feel my face twist up with disbelief. I felt awkward and . . . well . . . not dirty, but definitely naughty. My bones chilled.

But the way he kissed me was exactly what I needed at the time; I just never quite knew how to ask for it. There's been nobody to turn to; Colin is, really, the only love I've known. I could never imagine another man's lips against mine. The old me—ho that I was—would've jumped right out there. But I'm a mommy now . . . my daughter means the world to me, and so does her future. I know it sounds crazy, but everything I do—even kissing her father's boss—will affect her life in some way. I don't know exactly how, I just feel that in my heart.

So, I guess giving in to Reed's advance was a bit selfish . . . more for me than anything else. Also, the affection helped ease my tension. My pains. I was starting to feel like I was a whipping tree, where slaves were hung and beaten. Only I wasn't the slave, the whip wasn't directed at me. But I was still feelin' the agony. My periods were irregular; I was experiencin' constant headaches, and in bed I was so lonely I'd cry. Lady would come in my bed.

"Mommy, don't cry," she'd say. And the way she crawled in my bed and wiped my tears was so adorable that I'd hug her for dear life. I'm all about love—giving and receiving. I guess I wanted—I *needed*—to have that back in my life.

CHAPTER

13

TOY felt a bit numb. A bit subdued. Her eyes watered, but not in total sadness. More like in acknowledgment of this new revelation; the feeling of change.

Is this really what Colin wants? He wants me to be with another man? Happiness without my husband? Does this mean divorce?

It was a heavy burden to think these things without the convenience of simple answers; without Colin's input. But ever since Colin's arrest, Toy had had these "up in the air" feelings, but refused to address them. And now there was this latest letter. It was there in Colin's own handwriting, how he was saying to go on without him. Toy began to see the light. She couldn't stay dumb about things that much longer. Colin had somehow become a trickster, having held back on such important details that would affect her and her child.

> For the past year I've been living a fantasy in my letters to you . . . It was nice while it lasted . . . Enjoy your life.

As far as Toy could see, Colin was just another man, and she had been blind. Just as Stan had used and discarded her in high school, so too had Colin.

At least Reed was compassionate enough to step in and be the man Colin wasn't—telling her the truth. Toy suddenly become angry at her husband. Her soon-to-be *ex*-husband. The answer was right there in front of her. She needed Reed's affection.

And from then on, things began to happen in a blur. Like an on-and-off dream. At one instance, Toy was conscious of Reed's lips, his aroma, and then she wasn't. There was the music—had he selected one of Colin's Barry White CDs? There was also Reed's hands touching and fondling her . . . possessing her. And then they weren't. The stops and starts of her senses were driving her crazy, making it difficult to determine what was and wasn't real. And yet she wanted more.

Toy swore she felt Reed's body on top of hers, moving in sync with hers, as if they were swimming together, drowning, in some pool of pleasure. She couldn't resist—she sank deeper and deeper as more and more of her cavities were filled. And somewhere inside of these lost moments Toy felt surges—her body jolting, and her insides filled with a powerful, undefined force that left her exhausted.

Toy woke up to daylight, feeling well rested, but also fatigued at the same time. "Did I fall asleep again?" she asked, her words slurred.

Reed was there at the edge of the bed standing over her, pulling on a shirt over his thin-but-muscled body. Toy knew that shirt to be one of Colin's, but that was the least of her concerns at the time. Reed didn't voice a response, but instead gave a smart aleck's pout, and Toy wondered what that meant.

Her hand on her head, Toy blinked hard, trying to squeeze out what was on her mind. "This might sound crazy, but I can't tell if I was dreaming, or if certain things really happened."

"Certain things, like what?" asked Reed.

Toy bit her bottom lip before saying, "Did you give me the keys to a truck? An Expedition?"

Reed smiled, then he meandered toward the nightstand and picked up a set of keys and jingled them before her.

"Oh boy. I guess that answers my second question," said Toy, covering her face—her guilt. She said nothing about the sex, since she was more than certain now that—

"What's wrong, boo? Are you okay?"

Toy sighed, not knowing what to say . . . whether or not she should acknowledge the events of the previous night. "Oh . . . yeah. I just wondered . . . when did you have time to buy me an Expedition?"

Reed chuckled. "Now, I didn't mean to give you the impression that I was God—"

But of course he did.

"It was nothing, really. I already have a number of cars on my account, and since those sales nuts always try to sell me the next best whip, I just made a phone call. I asked them what they had on the lot, and since I knew you liked blue, the rest was a piece a cake. They delivered the truck an hour ago. It's downstairs if you wanna try it out."

"Wow. I guess"—she smiled for the first time in days— "this *is* a different world."

"Told ya. And I'm just gettin' started. Wait'll we start travelin'."

"Oh?" Toy shifted to a seated position. It felt like she was just her head. "I think I need to pee," she said. Reed came to help her get a silk robe on. "Thanks. I think I can manage."

Just then the intercom buzzed.

"That should be the sitter. Go 'head . . . handle your business," said Reed. "And freshen up some—you look *atrocious*," he added in a parental tone.

In the bathroom, Toy stopped in front of the mirror. *He's right. Who is this woman?* She touched her fingertips to different areas of her face, assessing the damage. There were slight bags under her reddened eyes; her hair was all over the place; and— "Jesus," she drawled after cupping her hands to her mouth to smell her breath. "You got the devil in your mouth, girl."

Toy untied her robe and squatted on the toilet. There had to be a well full of liquid in her bladder, and it felt good to empty it. She didn't notice as she was cleaning herself, but Reed was standing right there in the doorway. Toy gasped when she finally saw him.

"Didn't mean to scare you. Like you said, we're adults, right?"

Toy pulled her robe together, still seated. *"Reed!"*

"I know, I know. But really . . . you don't have nothin' to be ashamed of. And . . . that, uh, wasn't the sitter. It was a delivery." Reed took his arm from around his back, presenting Toy with a bouquet of roses. It was an awkward moment with how she was on the toilet and all, but she couldn't *not* accept them. She couldn't *not* express her appreciation.

"They're very sweet, Reed. *You're* very sweet. But now, can you give a woman some privacy?"

Toy, with the pretend disgust. Reed snickered mischievously. "Of course, boo. Can I put those away for you?"

"Thank you. They are beautiful."

"Mmm-hmm. What I was gonna say was—" He bent down, took the flowers and held his face inches from hers. "I hope to be seeing a lot more of you in the near future."

Toy's eyes searched his, looking for his purpose. But Reed turned away to tend to the roses. Forearms settled on her knees and head lowered, Toy thought about everything that had happened to her in the past 24 hours. By noontime, Toy had brushed her teeth, showered and pulled a comb through her hair for a wet n' wild look. Taking one last look in the mirror, she wondered about Lady. It was Saturday; no preschool, a day when mother and daughter normally did errands together, cleaned house and did laundry. She'd never been separated from Lady for more than half a day, and now she missed her horribly.

"Mommy! *Mommy! Mommy!"*

Toy lit up at the sound of her daughter's voice. She let the dish she was washing slide back down into the kitchen sink, grabbed a towel and turned to see Lady running toward her.

"Well, hel-lo, my little fushniken."

"Mommy, I stayed the whole night at Kimberly's! We had marshmallows, and we played checkers and we watched Cartoon Network!"

Lady was just over four years old, bright and full of excitement. It was only now, watching her daughter glow with happiness, that Toy appreciated Reed's arrangements.

"You're in no condition to take care of a child," he had said. And Reed was right. There was no sense in involving Lady with the adult woes in the Williams household. No sense in curbing that selflessness, that untainted joy that she exuded so whimsically.

"You *did*?!" Toy managed her own big, bright smile as she helped Lady free from her jacket and backpack.

"Yes. And . . . and . . ." Only now did Lady notice her mother's visitor. "Oh. Hi, Mr. Reed."

"*Ahhh* . . . you *do* remember me."

"Yes, silly! You gave me the doll!"

"I sure did, sweetheart," said Reed, trading sidelong gazes with Toy and the sitter. "Toy, I'll pay the sitter," he offered. Escorting Kimberly to the front door, Reed pulled out a wad of money and began peeling off bills for her overnight services.

"Make sure you stay available for us, Kim. These are gonna be some tough days ahead." He gave her an additional $1,200, and she turned frantic, her eyes about to fall out of her face. Toy smiled in the distance.

"Don't spend it too fast, baby." And there was the wink to accompany Reed's warning.

"Mrs. Williams, you know I'd take care of your daughter for nothing if I had to."

Toy and Lady waved good-bye. Reed closed the door behind Kimberly, vowing to do something about this whole "Mrs. Williams" mess.

The wall hangings, the name Colin Williams were all things Reed needed to address. Reed turned to face this new reality. Toy and Lady: his new *family*?

Toy stood behind Lady, her hands cuddling the child's head and face from behind—the protective mother.

"Looks like we should get to know one another," said Reed with that practiced smile, already prepared to contribute to Lady's candy allowance, training-bra fund and college tuition. Anything to keep her happy and out of the way.

CHAPTER

14

Within weeks of the Club Jaguar raid, Reed's counter-feiting operation was back to normal. However, now they were less flagrant about their activities. It had been Colin's suggestion earlier on, to play down their exposure, their ex-traordinary lifestyles and spending habits. But it was only after he was swept up by the feds that things had changed. Colin had hit the nail right on the head—an on-point warning—but nobody had listened.

Today, those same perceptions were the new reality. And with the feds falling back from their investigation, Reed was able to make the necessary adjustments. Colin's arrest was of little consequence—Reed filled his position within days. All he did was move two mid-level functionaries up the lad-der, and in doing so he also saved himself a chunk of money.

There was another thing; Reed had a new contact, some-one who had full access to the scrap paper that was disposed of at the U.S. Treasury in Philadelphia. Further research showed that the same scrap paper could be recycled and made into a similar version of Grade-A money green, the stock on which real money was printed. In laymen's terms, this meant cutting out the middleman so that Reed could print the bills in-house. A few desktop computers, a few commercial printers, and he'd have all that he needed to do the job himself. So, as it turned out, the loss of Colin Williams added up to Reed's gain. His new focus would re-sult in more money for everyone now that the printing could be done when and where he called for it.

Not that Reed wasn't already amassing a million dollars a

month—he was. But with the new procedures in place, in a couple of months he was netting ten times that amount.

Reed's social life wasn't doing bad either. Although he now kept a limit on his stable of women. Since more money meant more business meetings, more discipline of associates and, overall, more running around among Delaware, New York and Philly, there was less of his time to spread around. But if there were three "dime pieces" to have to call on for his convenience, then Rachelle, Danielle and Toy were the winners for the job.

Rachelle, daughter of Jersey City's police chief, and Danielle, who was the spitting image of Toni Braxton, each lived in apartments on the north side of town, while Toy, more or less his trophy, was still at the Shangrila with her daughter.

Over the years Reed's "hot list" of convenient women went through changes, depending on who did what for him. Since Rachelle's resources were "in the family," it was essential for business purposes to keep her. A few freak sessions each month and the lease payments on her apartment and car were his depth in the relationship. Danielle's mother was the senior V.P. at First Union Bank. He didn't know all the details, but frequent sex with this pretty girl gave Reed access to five bank accounts that were assigned to "phantom" beings. Through her, he wired, deposited and withdrew funds with no questions asked; no taxes to file, no papers to sign and no authorities to address about any transaction.

Whether those women did or didn't satisfy Reed's "thrill factor" was of great importance, otherwise he'd need to fill that void. That was partly why Reed was still attached to Toy after all these months. No, she wasn't the daughter of a key law enforcement figure; nor was she related to a banker, able to wash and rinse his money. But what Toy *did* have, in Reed's eyes, aside from the supermodel looks, was the willingness of a trained mutt.

He broke her in, however deviously, pursuing her to be in his world—that *different world* he harped about. Sure, Toy took the longest, and maybe the most effort, to persuade. But in the end, Reed could expect to have her whenever and however he wanted. At the time he put the move on her, she was desperate, lonely and in search of support for her and her daughter. So long as he provided that, he knew he had her continued obedience. And one more thing: Reed had a lot of money invested in Toy. And even though money was something he had an overabundance of (especially since now he was having a hard time making use of it), he didn't take risks in order to piss money away. Toy was still a substantial investment in time and money. And come hell or high water, Reed intended to get his money's worth; he'd continue to milk that cow until he was satisfied.

In that first month since Colin's sentencing, Kimberly, the babysitter, made more than $6,500. Toy began to see less and less of her daughter so that she could show her gratitude. Besides, Reed said he just wanted to get to know her better; said he wanted to introduce Toy to that "different world" he'd promised.

Reed persuaded Toy to indulge in her first try at marijuana. He took her everywhere he went, flaunting her for all to see—like a shiny new Rolex. He was even bold enough to introduce Toy to his "friends" Rachelle and Danielle.

Toy didn't know how to drive so the Expedition Reed got for her just sat there until he could teach her to drive it. And when he was comfortable enough with her driving, he had her drive his Lexus, chauffeuring him to and fro, always staying put in the car if he had to conduct business.

As time went on, Toy became just as content with Reed as she had been with Colin, wearing little to nothing when he stopped by the Shangrila, and going topless when she stayed over at his duplex, not far from the condo, since that was his "rule." And, naturally, she wore nothing at all when they slept together.

Sex graduated from casual to extremely deviant. Toy accepted Reed in ways that surpassed any of her previous experiences with Colin, perhaps twice-over. She learned to enjoy his spanking her. She'd forgive the lack of condoms, and she learned, however painfully, to enjoy anal sex.

The taste of his uncircumcised dick became as familiar as a morning coffee, as did his ass and his semen. At Reed's whim, Toy satisfied him without reciprocation.

"I'm coming over," he'd tell her on his cell phone.

"To stay?" she'd ask, somewhat hungry for him.

"No. In and out. I got moves I gotta make . . . matter of fact, be waitin' at the front door for me. I don't wanna hear about bills, your daughter or what you wanna do this weekend. I don't even want you to say a word—understand?"

"Sure, baby. Everything all right?"

"Of course it is. I'll be there in ten minutes . . . and you betta be butt-naked," Reed would tell her.

When Reed got inside the penthouse, Toy would be right there in the foyer, per his directions. Naked.

"Shhh," he would say, his forefinger to his lips. He'd point to the floor as if poking at a touch-tone telephone. And Toy always understood the gesture, lowering to her knees as he assumed a cocky stance before the wall mirror. So accustomed to his ways was Toy that she'd have a pillow in hand to prevent her knees from getting bruised. Then, as expected, she'd unzip or unbutton his pants and suck him off— sometimes for a few minutes, other times for a half hour or longer—until he ejaculated down her throat. Only after the act would Reed toss a few $100 bills on the foyer table before he turned and left the penthouse without so much as a good-bye.

If that wasn't extreme enough of a thrill, Reed would occasionally violate Toy in one orifice or another, taking what he wanted by force and against her wishes. And on every occasion, Toy merely endured the humiliation, the pain and/or discomfort, just because it pleased her man.

These were the ways of Vince Reed. Twisted. Insensitive. A victimizer. He was always the one in total control of everything and everybody in respect to his world. He lived out his thrills and fantasies no matter the cost or embarrassment to the next person. He was proud about having that certain angle on people, where they did as he wished, and were usually left unable to peg him or figure him out. For his way, he made no excuses.

After three years of twisting Toy every which way, Reed had an itch to stretch the limits of his thrill rides. After all, that was what Toy had become for Reed. It was a thrill to have this fox, someone else's wife, at his beck and call. It was exciting to explore just how far she'd go.

Other than that, he had no more use for her.

On a summer's night, when the sky was clear enough to see the twinkling stars and the shadow of the moon, Reed's Lexus rolled into the gated community of condominiums where he had lived for close to eight years. Reed's duplex was farther back on the winding road that snaked from the entrance gate, past a string of residences.

This was Brendanville; a community within Fort Lee where middle- and upper-class executives all owned similar duplexes, each with abundant plots of land, pools and immaculate gardens.

Toy was driving, while Reed lay back in the passenger's seat. Kenny Lattimore's latest song was playing, setting a sensual mood in the vehicle.

"What're you thinkin'?" asked Toy.

"Nice night."

"Mmm-hmm . . . I was thinking the same thing. Too bad you have a busy day tomorrow . . . I would've loved to stay on the boat for the rest of the weekend."

"Yeah. I guess. But like they say: too much of a good thing can kill ya."

"Hmm. I could *never* get enough of this life, Reed. I really am the happiest woman in the world right now—"

"Hey! Watch the road!" Reed raised his voice, but it wasn't a shout.

"I'm good. I was just saying . . . well . . . you're wonderful."

"Yeah? I thought you said I hurt you."

Toy was wide-eyed at Reed's comment. "Sometimes you do, Reed." She put a hand over on Reed's knee.

"Both hands on the wheel, Toy."

"Okay, Daddy," she said as a shy young girl would.

"Shit." Reed sat up.

"What happened, boo?"

"I forgot. I need something from the 7-Eleven."

"Want me to make a U-turn?"

"Nah," said Reed, a decisive tone in his voice. "Pull up in front of the house." When she did, he hopped out, circled to the driver's side and opened the door. "I'm gonna take the car and get what I need. You go on inside. Shower up and have it waitin' for me, baby . . ." Reed kissed Toy on the cheek when she rose from the driver's seat. "When I get back I wanna find a porno star in my house."

"Oooh . . . sounds like *somebody's* horny." Toy reached her arms around Reed's neck, wanting to feed him a more intimate kiss.

"Now get in there and get ready for Daddy," he said.

Toy strutted up the walkway, her stiletto heels clicking, her black skirt swaying.

CHAPTER

15

I looked over my shoulder to blow a kiss, but he had already taken off. I hadn't even opened the door yet—*rude ass*. But this *was* a gated community. It wasn't like a girl had to worry about being out alone in the dark. Besides, there was a guard posted at the entrance in that small hut 24-7. Crime was serious these days, but never in Brendanville. The Brady Bunch could've lived here. I couldn't wait to get inside, wash up and put on a see-through teddy—I was thinking the pink one since Reed says it reminds him of my pussy.

Nasty-ass slut, that Reed.

But I can't lie. I was hungry for it. I was ready to be his porno star for the night—and maybe the next morning too. I took out my spare key and opened the door. The place was dark, and I wondered what had happened to the lamp. It usually came on automatically by a timer device.

I shrugged it off and went feeling for the light switch. But before I touched the switch—before I even got to shut the front door all the way—someone's strong arm hooked around my neck. At the same time, a hand covered my mouth real hard.

I was so scared, and I couldn't think. From then on, all I can remember is shaking, and darkness and . . . *oh my God*.

CHAPTER

16

Toy shivered in fear as the intruder dragged her across the entry hall. Being manhandled like she was, from her perspective, she couldn't see who her attacker was. It was too dark anyhow. There was a man's grunt.

"In here," a woman commanded. The voice was muffled, as if she had a muzzle over her mouth.

But Toy couldn't make further assessments, too afraid to draw any kind of sensible conclusion. Before she knew what was happening, a cloth of some kind was tied around her head, covering her eyes. The woman's voice said, "Bad timing, bitch. You done fucked up our little break-in . . ."

The voice was farther away than the person restraining her—of that she was sure.

Two of them? Three?

". . . and now we're gonna break you!"

Toy screamed the instant the hand moved from her mouth. At once, the scream was answered with a slap across her face. Then another to the opposite cheek.

"Shut the *fuck* up!" a man's voice ordered.

Unable to prevent what was happening to her, Toy was wrestled to the living room floor. Her wrists were tied to the legs of some furniture. And then her ankles. Within moments, she was stretched out on the floor. The ropes about her were pulled and her limbs were manipulated, provoking gasps and whimpers. She could only see those words in her mind: *and now we're gonna break you!* She twisted and tugged, a futile attempt to free herself.

The attacker smacked her again, turning Toy into a limp, obedient captive.

"Stay put, bitch. And if you scream again, I'll kill you!"

Toy whimpered, praying that Reed would hurry home. Then, with every bit of will she could muster, she wailed, "REEEEEEED!!!"

The next smack was harder.

"Bitch! Wha'd I tell ya? Din' I tell ya to shut up? Huh?" The man sounded like an angry hillbilly.

"Tape her mouth shut," the woman said.

Toy wriggled, still challenging the reins that bound her. Now, the ripping sound of tape. Toy could feel the man—a husky one, she guessed—straddling her waist as he pulled the tape down onto her mouth.

Her clothes were ripped off, the black skirt and the matching top. She had on no bra, since that was how Reed wanted it for the cruise. And now, every bit of her was exposed but for the foot with the stiletto still hanging on. Her worst fears were coming true as she lay there.

"Hurry up." The man's voice.

"Don't worry, babe. This won't hurt." The woman spoke into Toy's ear, no longer muffled.

Toy suddenly felt a cold tool pressed to her temple. A gun? She whimpered and struggled like never before, pleading for her life under the tape.

Reed made a U-turn just as he came to the front gate. He flashed a thumbs-up sign at the guard and proceeded back home. *Fuck the 7-Eleven*, he decided. He parked the Lex in his driveway and sat for a moment, meditating. He reached under his seat to his stash—that bottle of Tiger Bone Juice. He look three long swigs, capped it and put the bottle back.

Smiling anxiously, Reed hopped out of the car and took the cobblestone path to the porch. The front door was open some. He turned to his left, then his right, to see that all was okay in the vicinity. Peace and quiet was met by his deep inhale and exhale. Finally, Reed slipped in and quietly closed the door. He crept toward the living room where, as he got closer, whimpers, pants and other carnal sounds filled the air. The sounds at once amused Reed. They could've come from a porno flick playing loud on the TV. Or better yet, they were probably coming from—

At the entrance to the living room Reed looked down on the activity playing out just 15 or so feet away. He didn't make a sound as a table lamp cast its modest glow on the three figures there on the floor.

Toy was lying on her back, her mouth and eyes covered, her wrists tied and stretched back behind her head, butt-naked except for a stiletto.

The male was kneeling on the floor facing Toy, video camera in hand. His thick legs were situated so that they helped to keep Toy's ankles pinned. He had dirty brown hair, an unkempt mustache, meaty fingers—his tattooed knuckles read LOVE across one hand and HATE across the other—and one or two missing teeth.

The other woman had her bronze hair tied back in a pony-tail, hastily affixed. And now that she realized there was a spectator, she looked his way, her face brightening in the gloomy light.

Reed smiled when he saw the empty soda bottle in Kitty's hand, pressed up against Toy's temple as if it were a gun. Both attackers were looking toward Reed, while he leaned against the wall like some desperado. Reed merely flipped his hand at their hesitancy, urging them to carry on. And as the performance continued, Reed was the quiet by-stander enjoying the show. A show he'd prearranged.

It was a $1,000 job. All the hillbilly, Knuckles, had to do was smack the girl around a little bit and videotape as Kitty sexed Toy both orally and with a strap-on. Knuckles was a friend of Kitty's and didn't know Reed personally. Although, in Reed's opinion, that was all the better.

Kitty was partially naked herself, wearing studded shorts that just covered her privates, but not enough to be a pedes-trian. The T-shirt she had on was tied off at the waist. She kept looking over her shoulder at Reed, as though he were directing, perhaps for some gesture of encouragement—something. But Reed only waved Kitty on, essentially telling *her* to run the show herself, to continue with what she was doing. He'd see it all later on video, anyhow.

Thus encouraged, Kitty peeled off her shorts, revealing a printed thong. She then shifted her body so that her squat was just above Toy's face. The camera closed in, focusing on Kitty's crotch and how she rubbed it against her victim's nose, cheeks and forehead.

It reminded Reed of three years earlier when he had Toy subdued by the pills, and how he'd also rubbed himself on and about Toy's face. Reed didn't reminisce for long since there was so much more to see. Kitty buried her face between Toy's legs, lapping her folds, munching loud enough to cause Reed to smile, and Toy to moan.

When he was satisfied with watching, Reed eventually joined the fracas, mounting Toy and banging her until he ejaculated inside and out. He was done. And besides, he had plenty of video to remember the event: raping Toy. Reed signaled Kitty and Knuckles with a "wrap it up" gesture. There was one last thing he needed them for.

Reed stood, used Toy's skirt to wipe himself off and went back toward the front door. He pulled the door open, then slammed it swift and loud. "Baby . . . I'm *back*!" Reed stalled his approach long enough for his co-conspirators to be ready. "Hey, Toy? *Toy! Oh shit!!* Who are you? What the . . . what are you doin' to—HEY!!! COME BACK HERE!!!"

He rustled about with the others, making a big melee, or, at least, *sounding* believable. Knuckles and Reed both kicked some furniture around, cursed each other, and did some stomping, pretending to fall against the wall and floor. To be convincing, Kitty joined in; well . . . at least she broke a vase and shrieked.

Reed saw that and really cursed.

Toy, in the meantime, writhed and thrashed about on the floor, likely concerned about Reed, hoping he'd overcome her attackers.

When all was said and done, there were the exaggerated footfalls through the house to the back door of the residence.

Reed moaned, trying to sound hurt and in pain.

Toy struggled even more in response to Reed's pretended anguish, ignoring her own battered, violated circumstances. Reed mattered more to her right now, although he was doing fine, lying there just out of Toy's reach, watching her, amusing himself with grunts and gasps.

She wriggled and contorted her body with a greater effort, her muffled voice blocked by the duct tape over her mouth.

Wagging his head, almost laughing at how foolish Toy looked, Reed wondered if he might one day tell her the truth about this.

Toy made more violent attempts to break free from the ties, and eventually they gave. She untaped her mouth and loosened the blindfold. *"Reed! Ohmigod!* What'd they *do* to you?"

Reed only uttered a deep, strained groan in response. He had curled up in a fetal position, facing away from Toy.

"Oh, baby," Toy cried, managing to lift herself from the floor, despite her injured loins. "I'll call nine-one-one." Before she could take one step, Reed had reached out and grabbed her arm.

"Help," he said, his voice desperate and afflicted.

Toy quickly crouched down. "Reed . . . you shouldn't move. Something could be broken."

"Help me get to the couch," he told her, his body leaning heavily on her as she did so. Once he was situated, Toy suggested again that she call 911.

"No," he told her. "I don't want the police involved."

"But . . . but baby . . . they . . . they . . ."

"They *w-what*?" Reed moaned.

But Toy hesitated. She didn't know what Reed had observed. She didn't know if he'd seen the actual rape. "Look at me, baby. Don't you think that somebody should be *arrested* for what happened to me?" Toy indicated her bruised face and naked body. "They *assaulted* me!" she cried.

As desperate as she was to tell her man what happened, she was just as afraid *not* to. She had so much to say, but she didn't know how he'd take it . . . how he'd see her from now on. She didn't have much more to offer Reed than her body, and if that didn't keep him—Toy couldn't take Reed abandoning her and her child. She'd already lost one man in her life.

"Trust me, baby. I'll find out who did this. I'll send my boys on a manhunt; whoever did this fucked with the *wrong* person. An arrest wouldn't satisfy me. I wanna see heads rollin'. Are *you* okay?" Reed pulled Toy to him and hugged her. "What did they do to you?"

Toy put her hands to her face, partly covering her tears and partly masking the smell of sex from him. She boo-hooed there in the cradle of Reed's shoulder and chest.

He rocked her and said, "It's all right, boo . . . it's all right. Everything's gonna be fine. I'm just glad you're alive and healthy."

Everything's not fine, thought Toy. And all she could do was cry harder.

Reed could smell the odors of sex. He could sense Toy's frustration, only guessing why she closed up like this. *Here we go with the crying spells again*, he thought. And it immediately reminded him of when her man got drop-kicked in federal court.

He took Toy's chin, raising her worn, bruised face to his. Only now did he wonder if he'd gone too far; if *they* had gone too far. *Damn. I told Kitty to smack her around a little . . . to make it as real as possible, but . . . man. These redbone bitches bruise easy.* Reed was about to say something, maybe to soothe her hurt. But there were no words he could think up. What was done, was done. He instead kissed Toy's face, immediately familiar with the smells—the sticky residue left from the duct tape, and Kitty's fishy scent. The flashback images of Kitty straddling Toy's face suddenly excited Reed, and he kissed Toy again just to savor the taste.

CHAPTER

17

All I could do was keep alive. Yeah. I know that sounds like an artificial idea, being Jesse Jackson's famous saying and all, but doing time leaves you very few choices. If you're lucky enough to get a sound sleep, hopes and dreams and reminiscing about good old times are all convenient remedies, however temporary.

But when you wake up it's back to life—back to reality. And honestly, there's no perfect answer when you've lost your liberty. Prison is filled with cluster and cults; pros and cons of one kind or another. And it's not an easy place to get along without some "people skills." Not an easy place to find or foster hope.

"Respect" is a word I'm always hearing, a metaphor for that line you just don't cross—in other words, don't infringe on the next man's rights and privileges.

"Keep your mouth shut and mind your own business" is another high-ranking phrase on the top ten things to know in prison list.

And then of course, there's the popular catchphrase, "If you can't do the time, then don't do the crime," which is sort of like pouring salt on an open wound, since you can't undo what's been done. That's more like a phrase they should teach in grade school, high school and college so that people like me could be exposed to that so-called "ounce of prevention."

Nonetheless, this is prison life. Someone's always whistling that damned *Godfather* theme, as they appreciate all of this—the tight security, the limitations of life's simple pleasures, communal living, being told what to do and what not to do . . . the smell of other men, their various odors and gases reflecting the day's meals, and listening to the stories, fables and "somebody done me wrong" tales . . . and somebody's always running their mouth to attract attention, sympathy or merely a human sounding board.

"A man could get burnt out from this shit," Lee told me one day, out of the blue.

Lee has a number of names, depending on who's addressing him. There's O.T.—for old-timer; there's O.G.—for original gangster; and, of course, he's officially an "old head" since his age has begun to challenge his hair follicles.

"What? Chess?" I asked, positioning my bishop in front of his rook, threatening it. Naturally, Lee saw the attack coming and immediately slid a pawn to intercept the threat.

"No. I'm talking about time, as in jail time. And by the way," he said, not stopping for a breath, "you done lost yo' rabbit-ass mind if you think I'm fallin' for that weak move."

Now it was my move. So I answered, "If you liked *that* one, then you should *love* this one. *Check!*" The bishop move threatened his rook, but it was merely a deception since it was blocking my own rook and it's straightaway a threat on his queen. Lee made a face of distress mixed with disgust.

"You lookin' good . . . fo' real, nigga. You lookin' real motha-fuckin' good." He unleashed his knight to serve two purposes: to intercept the check I put on him and unlock the rook that I set up to threaten his queen. "Now . . . since you wanna check somebody, lemme get your queen!"

I sucked my teeth, realizing my loss even before Lee executed his capture. "Whatever," I said, then I went hard and sacrificed my queen, chopping down on the rook and producing the sound of hard plastic colliding. A pawn in the neighboring square was knocked off of the table as a result of the somewhat violent exchange. I reached to the floor to pick it up.

"Damn!" said Lee.

"You *damn right*. I told you before, I don't *need* a bitch!"

"See . . . now you done gone crazy," said Lee, and he took my queen—all suave, as usual, smiling as he did.

I advanced with another pawn, freeing a channel for my other bishop to attack. "I told you . . . I don't need a bitch," I said with a certain confidence. And my face was dead serious, like this was a true-to-life bloody battle.

"See what I'm saying, son? You *are* burnt out."

"Whatever. It's not my move," I huffed.

"Oh yeah? Then we better get rid of this since you won't be needin' it." He took a free piece.

"Shit," I grunted, and I swept the pieces from the table and onto the floor.

Lee's eyes widened. "It's just a game, young'un. Relax."

I was already up from my seat, headed for my cell.

CHAPTER

18

The cell block that Colin and Lee lived on had three tiers. Each tier had a walkway outside of its row of 20 some-odd two-man cells. Each cell had bars as thick as a quarter's circumference and were electronically controlled by the officers inside the "pod"—a glass-enclosed octagon at the forefront of the cell block. The game tables were in the open area of the ground tier, where convicts played chess, cards or checkers, or wrote letters.

If games weren't his thing, a convict might otherwise have his eyes pinned to any one of a half dozen televisions affixed high, out of reach, with specific sets designated for sports, Spanish programming, black entertainment or news and general programming. Each TV was muted and had its own FM frequency whereby viewers tuned in on their Walkman radios. There was a fenced-in recreation yard, a law library and educational classes as well, but some convicts found the most peace in their cells, reading, talking shit or sleeping the time away.

Colin's way of doing the time was reading, playing chess and sleeping. He had his chores (just as all convicts did, contributing to the upkeep of the prison): mopping the second tier once a day—twice if the weekly inspections came around. But short of that Colin chose to be left alone.

Lee was Colin's closest friend, as far as being a "friend" meant in prison. They talked every day, sharing each other's life experiences—Colin spoke of the world of counterfeit money, while Lee detailed the how-tos of robbing banks—or they'd dissect the world's ills, taking sides on how the USA was playing "bully" with Iraq, or how R. Kelly was being unfairly treated in comparison to Woody Allen, both celebrities having been involved with underage girls. And when they weren't talking, they battled on the chessboard.

Keep the "bid"—the prison term—simple. Be consistent. Focus. And somehow, make each moment a productive one. This was the plan that Colin stuck to, one that kept him out of trouble.

Lee came to the second tier an hour later. Like Colin, he had on gray sweatpants, a sweatshirt and Nike sneakers. Only, Lee's "leisure wear" was purchased compliments of Colin, since Lee seemed to have no loved ones at home; or at least they weren't sending him money. Colin, on the other hand, was getting along fine since Kitty was sending him $200 money orders every month.

"What was *that* about, youngblood?"

"Ain't shit," Colin answered and sucked his teeth.

"You ain't caught up about Toy again, are you?"

Again with the teeth and gums, Colin said, "Now you *know* better than that, old head."

"Well?"

"I dunno, Lee . . . just . . . this whole shit is gettin' to me. The time. The fools I gotta deal with all day every day . . ."

"Somebody botherin' you?"

"Not like that. Just . . . I mean, we got one fool who walks up and down the tier brushin' his teeth all day, toothpaste foamin' from his mouth like he's havin' an epileptic fit. Why we gotta smell his hygiene all day? Always flossin' his teeth up and down the tier, and probably flingin' his crusty scum all over the place—"

Lee was stirring with laughter at how detailed Colin was; images that the elder was all too familiar with.

"And another fool . . . that Jew-boy from England. I don't know *how* the fuck *he* got to be a convict. They say he got millions, but he's livin' scraggly as a mangy mutt. He picks his nose all fuckin' *day* . . . I mean, pinkie just disappearin' up in his *nose*! And he does it like he's all alone—like a dozen people ain't watchin' his ass with twisted faces. Mustafa thinks he's Stevie Wonder, singin' all goddamned day, tryin' to impress or irritate somebody . . . and Carlos in the cell next to me talks in his sleep. Big Eddie snores like a fuckin' jackhammer—I can hear him from fifteen cells away. And *oh my God*! Goldfish thinks he's goin' home next week."

"So? What's wrong with that?"

"Nigga, Goldfish got twenty years! He thinks he's goin' home every week."

"That cat does his law work, so you never could know. Don't hate."

"O.T., did I ever tell you you as funny as a bag of rocks? That law work is for the birds; jailhouse lawyers be sellin' dreams that ain't shit but illusions. *Illusions!*" Colin said loudly.

"But, if I remember correct, you were appealin' your sentence, Colin."

"Yeah, yeah. I got my direct appeal done. I had the oral arguments—*all* that shit. But look at me, Lee. I'm still locked up with the freaks, the queers *and* Goldfish. It never fuckin' ends, this bullshit!"

"Damn, youngblood. You got a lot on your mind. Maybe you should hop in the shower—jack off a little to get your hormones balanced."

Colin displayed an expression of boredom in response to Lee's remedy.

"But, just to let you know that I'm paying attention, let me drop a jewel on you; something you should remember for the rest of your bid," Lee continued. "See, you're mistaken when you say it never ends, because it does; one way or another, you're leaving here, whether it's by box or bus. The thing is, what are you gonna accomplish *now*? What are you gonna get done *during* this time? Sure, the courts, witnesses and whoever else set you up and got you here. But now that you're here, what're you gonna do? Curl up and die? Some cats stretch their muscles. Others stretch their minds. Tuck does the pen pal bit; got women writin' him from all over the world, sendin' him money and whatnot. And, okay, so Gold-fish is workin' on his appeal and his head is in the clouds. But guess what? At least he *has* a possibility to look forward to. And so do you, as long as you keep your head up . . . as long as you can accept change as a part of life. As they say, youngblood, it's not where you're from, it's where you're at. That means accept what and who you are, right where you are.

"For a lot of these cats, hope is all but gone. They can't comprehend their toes from their knuckles. They'd rather sit and watch TV all day. They know more about the basketball players they watch than they do their *own* lives. When they're not stuck on TV they're talking shit about the cars they *used to drive*, the money they *used to have*, and the women—they don't even have significant soul-mate rela-tionships to speak of. Instead, they talkin' 'bout Halle Berry, or rap beefs. But I bet if you ask five of these jokers what they are or who they are, or where they expect to be in fifty years, not one of them will have a direct answer . . ."

"Lemme get back to you on that," Colin said—an exam-ple of Lee's point.

"*Exactly right*. And that's what I call a sailboat without a sail, a bird without wings or—"

"A vegetable."

"Right again. They're living some fantasy life in here; the government's paying for our bed, our heat, food, hot water. So you ain't *really* gotta lift your finger. You can just lay around, sit around and B.S.—but you'll be bullshittin' y'self. Which is exactly the problem on the street. We didn't care about our tomorrows, only what was happenin' on the TV, or what *other* folks are doin'."

Colin wagged his head, absorbing the old-timer's wis-dom. Colin was experiencing cognitive dissonance—that in-ner conflict between what and what not to believe. He almost realized the truth in Lee's explanation, but he also had a voice at the back of his mind, saying: *don't believe anything he tells you; he's a worthless, conniving convict*. But then, what did that make Colin?

"The truth, Colin, is that we will never be more than who we are at this very second." Colin twisted his face some.

"You heard me right: we are who we are right now, *where* we are right now; and *whatever* you're involved in—then that's who you are right now. If you're a reader and you're someone who stretches his mind, then that's your reality, your constitution. Something like the saying, 'You are what you eat.' If you eat pork, that very swine you eat becomes a part of you—its atoms, its thoughts that live within those atoms—it all goes into your mouth, then into your digestive system, your bloodstream, your heart and mind. Now, I can't say that eating pig is gonna make you think like a pig, or look like a pig—I ain't no mad scientist. But I do know that the pig's DNA, once digested, is now in your body."

"Hey, Lee, easy on that shit! You know I don't eat that shit—"

"Okay, but I'm speaking hypothetically. If our bodies are made of eighty-five percent water, it's common sense that constant refreshment of that supply is gonna keep us operating as we were meant to."

"True," said Colin, hoping Lee would get to the point.

"I say that to say, most important, don't give up hope. Even if you *practice* having hope you'll be stretching your I-have-hope muscles."

Colin snickered.

"I'm dead serious, youngblood. Don't start none, won't be none. And another thing: garbage in, garbage out. Feed your body and mind the best food—good stuff for the body is vegetables, fruits and whole grains. For the mind, that's your choice. If you read smut that's all you'll think about. If you read self-help books, then guess what? You're gonna be a better person. And be productive, youngblood. If you put enough matchsticks together you can build a house."

"Or a bomb," Colin slipped in.

"*Exactly* right. So then you really have that choice, *don't you*? You can do something good with your time . . . your life . . . or you can do something horrific. Something wicked. Just look at what those cats did with them airplanes.

On one hand, the planes were responsible for commerce, employees, food on the table, and clothes on people's backs. That's the good they did. But because *thinking* made it so, the men who flew those planes into buildings caused the opposite effect . . . billions in damage, deaths by the thousands and so on and so on. My point is anybody could've pulled that off. Any-body, you see. And it didn't take a genius to be wicked or evil . . . just the same, it don't take no more effort to be successful, or a world leader. I'll tell you what it does take . . ."

Colin was quiet, waiting for the hook here, the cure-all for his life.

"It takes consistency, Colin. And a goal."

Colin was at a loss for words, still battling that cognitive dissonance in his mind. "If you have all the answers then, tell *me* something . . . why you up in here?" he asked finally.

"Well, that's the other thing I didn't mention, never take advice from a burnt-out fool like me." The words were followed by a tight-lipped grin.

"See, Lee! You's a crackhead ma-fucka," Colin said within his own righteous laughter.

"But, seriously, youngblood . . . who knows why two people meet, or why two vehicles collide . . . why we take the left turn instead of the right." Lee noticed the bag of chips Colin had stored in his footlocker. "Now, how 'bout hittin' me off with some of those barbecue chips. All this counselin' got me hungry."

"Lemme find out that's why you came up to see me in the first place," Colin suggested.

"Of course," Lee said, unhanding the bag from Colin.

CHAPTER

19

Prison is like that—some days you get the blues and others you're on cloud nine. But I can't lie, there's a whole bunch of good times that I've had. Laughin' with Lee, meeting new people and hearing about their treasures and war stories, and I've felt saved on more than one occasion; saved, in the sense that so much tragedy goes on in the inner city—scratch that . . . *in the world*! Sometimes I feel that fishbowl effect, where I'm on the inside while all the craziness is taking place "out there." Folks gettin' shot up, planes fallin' out of the sky, whether planned or accidental, and this whole terrorism thing—is that some kind of *movement* nowadays?

I've also noticed how much prison encourages the worst in me. My vocabulary turned "horrendous" (my mother would've said). I use the word "nigga" in every other sentence. And the word "bitch" too. Sometimes I feel like I'm so damaged by my past experiences with women that they've *all* become bitches until they've proven otherwise. That is, every one when she's grown; and my mother, who I haven't seen or heard from since I left LA.

But this prison culture has undeniably changed me. My heart has grown callous and so has my mind. I can't believe, when I was young, how much of a choirboy I was. "If my friends could see me now," I always said to myself, since I know a sea of acquaintances that are as soft as cotton balls. They'd never survive a soft prison facility, much less the penitentiary.

I'm not upset at how I've changed, and I even (somewhat)

appreciate being exposed to so much, so fast. In a way, now I feel I'm better prepared for life's challenges, its schemes, and I believe I'll appreciate success so much more when it comes. And it *will* come.

Would I change anything, if I had it to do all over again? I'm still trying to figure that answer out.

CHAPTER

20

"No shit, Lee. I *was* a choirboy up until I left home to be on my own. It felt more like an escape from protective custody."

"That's what parents are *supposed* to be—protectors. I mean, some parents you *have* to get away from, by any means necessary. But, for the most part, they supposed to groom you so you'll do right. So you'll learn about how to contribute to life and not end up here. I do know one thing—your momma ain't no bitch."

Colin raised one eyebrow. "So what's *that* mean?"

"That means if she ain't one, then your *other* lady friends ain't. Your *wife* ain't." Lee poked Colin lightly in the chest, emphasizing his words. "So stop using that as a generalization for all women because of the actions of one. 'Cause, like I said, you are what you practice to be. That voice is gonna be you . . . the mind that uses that word is a pained mind . . . a scarred and bitter mind . . . even a ruthless mind."

"Easier said than done," muttered Colin. "What're you, Mr. Ethics all of a sudden? You use foul language just like me, Lee."

"Well, maybe for me it's too late. Can't teach an old dog new tricks. But you, you're still young. Your lady, or whatever lady you decide to get with when you get out of here, is gonna suffer from that attitude . . . that state of mind. And in the end, you're gonna suffer too."

"I thought you said never take advice from a—"

Lee completed Colin's sentence, "—an old, burnt-out fool like me. Yes, I know what I said. But don't keep tryin' to psychoanalyze me. Work on your own constitutions, young-blood. Fix y'self before it's too late."

"I know . . . I know, old school. But it's like you said: a man could get burnt out from this. And I feel like the world clobbered me. Word . . . my wife is gone, I ain't seen my baby girl for three years . . . the courts takin' forever to answer my appeal, plus these goddamn freaks in here. I guess I am suffering—I *am* bitter and scarred, and all that shit you said. And I'm 'bout ready to bust. I *swear*. One of these days a dude is gonna cross me the wrong way and I'ma blow my top. The government probably don't know it, but they got one fucked-up, locked-up, backed-up brother on their hands. And what, they expect me to be a model prisoner for *fourteen years of this*?"

"Easy, youngblood, easy."

"Shit, old-timer . . . sometimes I feel like they betta *never* let me up outta here. I might be the next ma-fucka looking for a plane to hijack and do some damage. This country might end up at war with *me!*"

Lee chuckled and wagged his head. "*Whoa.* You trippin', son." He patted Colin's shoulder, hoping to calm him. "It's gonna be all right, youngblood. Really." He got up. "Come on up to my tier. Lemme show you some stuff I think might help you."

Colin joined Lee. "I hope it's a quart of vodka. That's the only thing I see helpin' my ass."

The two strolled along the second tier, a runway of sorts, with convicts sentenced to 10, 20 even 50-year sentences—crimes that included everything from bank robbery and gun-running, to drug conspiracies and, of course, capital murder.

Colin avoided eye contact with "the fool" passing by, his dental floss working feverishly between his teeth as if he was a walking billboard for oral hygiene.

And if timing wasn't the devil's best friend, right behind Mr. Floss was the trio of Hasidic Jews. One of them with the hard-core defensive expression—as if he was ready to kick some ass; one with the frumpy walk and thick glasses; and lastly, the queen of England's favorite son, Mr. Nose-picker himself brought up the far right. Colin guessed that he'd only just finished digging for gold; he guessed what Lee said about "practicing" was true for everyone.

On the third tier where Lee was assigned to a cell halfway down, the scene was identical to Colin's atmosphere on "2" except for the different faces. Most of the cells had their books and magazines, their radios and photos or posters affixed to the walls with toothpaste—the prisoner's all purpose glue. Cells here and there had sheets tied up to block a passerby's view, meaning there was a privacy concern for one reason or another. A convict could be taking a dump—"feeding the warden," they called it. There could be a session of masturbation, or even some homosexual activity for the few who were willing and bold enough.

Just before Lee and Colin reached the halfway point, they passed Goldfish, overhearing his loud discussion about why the judge would *have* to rule in his favor, and how if he didn't Goldfish would sue this country "until it buckled to its knees."

Colin rolled his eyes and encouraged Lee, by eye contact alone, to pick up the pace.

As they approached Lee's cell, Big Earl, his cellmate, was lifting himself from his bunk. The two men acknowledged the other's presence as the huge convict left with a towel and soap in hand, and shower shoes on his feet.

"Okay. That means we have a few minutes alone," said Lee. He knelt to the floor and slid a box from under the bed. The cardboard stock scraped against the cement floor, sounding like one loud sweep of a heavy broom. Colin took a seat on the metal bench, which was secured to the wall under the desk. "This is where I keep all my short stories," said Lee.

Colin assumed that the box, which once held oranges, contained the elder's personal effects such as letters, legal documents and maybe photos. But upon closer review, he realized that the entire box was alphabetized from A to Z, filled with Lee's creative writing. "You mean *the whole box* is short stories?"

"Well, maybe that's not one hundred percent correct. Five percent of it is poems and essays. I got that whole Jack-of-all-trades thing goin' on."

"*Damn*, Pops! When do you have the time to write?"

"You kiddin'? I been doin' this bid for fifteen years, youngblood. I go through spells, see. I grind and slow up, I grind and slow up—whatever feels right. I slowed up some since you came to the block, but usually I'm good for an average of one or two short stories a day. I was once on a run for two months, when I wrote three short stories a day."

"That's . . . *damn!* You did a hundred and eighty short stories in sixty days?"

"I think it came out to one ninety, but it was a time of my life I won't forget. I was on a roll. Adrenaline pumpin'. And it's all here."

Colin looked down at the box, suddenly mesmerized by the mass of creativity.

"I used to be a fiend. Dedicated . . . writing day and night, like my life depended on it. Fifteen years of it . . . right here in the box. A lot of pain, pleasures, changes—this is my life, youngblood. A dream that is living and breathing like a bear in hibernation. Sometimes I feel like I am a bear—one with the world—only, I don't know, it's hard to explain."

Colin was busy reading one of the three-page stories, not really absorbing what Lee said. "What're you gonna do with all this stuff, Lee?"

"I guess I'll try to get some of it published when I get out. Maybe one of them big-time rappers like Jay-Z or Master P, or them Cash Money folks will recognize my craft and finance my growth."

"Shit, Lee, there must be over a thousand short stories here!"

"It's like I told you, youngblood, consistent work toward the goal. Check this one out," said Lee as he handed Colin a three-page piece entitled "A Black Woman's Blues."

Colin began reading, then stopped short at the first sentence. "Man, how you gonna write from a *woman's* point of view? This shit is bugged!"

"I can't explain it, youngblood . . . I just get *possessed*." Lee seemed to be looking for someone or something on the tier. "Listen . . . why don't you take the box to your cell and read 'em." Lee picked up the box and put it in Colin's lap. "Come on . . . let's get this down to your cell."

"You sure, Lee? What's up?" asked Colin, feeling rushed.

"Ain't shit. I just need to give my celly his space. He should be getting back from the showers any minute now, and I ain't trying to catch a new case."

"Y'all got beef?"

"Shit, I ain't got beef with nobody, youngblood. I'm too old for that mess. My beefs get squashed right where they start. I don't never let shit hang over till the next day. Not even an hour." Lee had that hard-faced maliciousness about him—that killer gaze. "But Big Earl got his own issues and I ain't tryin' to help him solve 'em. I'm too short for bullshit, ya dig?"

Colin and Lee left the cell just as Big Earl returned. There was a sign of hidden relief in his eyes, perhaps glad he didn't even have to ask for privacy.

"Damn," Colin muttered under his breath. "Y'all live too close together to have disharmony."

"Disharmony. Hmmm . . . mind if I use that title for a story?"

"What's this one gonna be about? Two cellies who can't get along?"

"I didn't know you were a mind reader," said Lee. "But don't worry 'bout me," he continued. "I keep my distance. I just sleep in that cell, ya dig? After all the time I done ain't nothin' left to say or do. Either I'm gonna go home like I'm supposed to, or I'm not. Remember what I told you—nothing dies, it only changes form. And I accept change one hundred percent."

Colin took a deep breath, trying to release the sudden tension that tightened his nervous system. He didn't take the idea of "friendship" lightly like the older convicts did. They were hardened, while he was admittedly still smelling the roses that came along in life. A threat to Lee was hard to ignore.

When they got back to Colin's cell the idea of beefs lost their power as he read more of *A Black Woman's Blues*.

Colin subsequently raved about the story's mastery, how it was so seductive on its various levels. There wasn't a wasted thought or an irrelevant word. ("There's no room for that," Lee explained.) And the characters were so real that Colin felt as though he knew them personally.

"Wow. This shit is . . . I mean, I can't even say it's shit. This *work* . . . this is incredible! Are all of them like this?"

"Well," Lee started humbly, "I'm my own worst critic, so I couldn't say. But you're welcome to hold the box . . . to look through them."

"Oh man . . . you think you wouldn't *mind*?"

"Good. I'm happy that you're happy," said Lee, knowing how Colin had been feeling horrible just minutes earlier.

The two spent the rest of their free time talking about writing, the discipline needed to create and how to devote quality time to the craft while keeping the necessary mood to pour life and soul into the work.

Then they went their separate ways. Colin returned to his routine—dinner, a shower, that end-of-the-day brushing and flossing—and after the evening's institutional count, he went back to reading Lee's work until the words carried him off to dreamland. *I can't wait to see Lee tomorrow*, Colin thought before his eyes shut down for the night.

CHAPTER

21

The next morning was something to look forward to since Friday's breakfast menu normally included French toast. Colin and Lee generally paired up to eat together, and many times joked about how incredible the meals were.

They knew damned well that their freedom was way more important than a prison meal. But interactions like these were what helped carry a convict through the shadow of misery from moment to moment. They helped to keep a smile going, the minute hand moving, the calendar pages flipping.

Breakfast was at 6 A.M. sharp. The cell doors were usually opened at 5, giving inmates time to shower and get ready for the day ahead. However, this particular Friday morning was nothing near usual. In fact, it would become a day that Colin wouldn't soon forget.

The instant he stepped out of his cell an air raid siren began sounding off. That was the signal for convicts to return to their cells at once. And whenever it sounded, whether it was a false alarm or a drill, or there was a fight going on, there was always a confusion of inmates and guards scurrying to and fro, as well as that loud roar of a voice barking over the cell block's PA system and bouncing off of every iota of the facility's steel and cement construction.

Colin shook his head, acknowledging that this was bound to be another one of those mornings—late breakfast, cold food and all-around aggravation. Just before he strolled back toward his cell, where his celly was still sound asleep, Colin noticed that a crowd had formed by the guardrail farther down the tier. Curious, Colin moved in that direction, deciding to be nosy before the guards began to holler at anyone still on the tier.

"Yo, what happened?" Colin asked of everyone and no one in particular, as he wedged himself in through the herd of bodies.

"He jumped," someone said.

"Nah, they said he was pushed," another convict argued.

"He only had a couple of months left," said a third man. "How he gonna jump and he at the end of a fifteen-year sentence?"

The more Colin heard, the harder it was to look over the rail. But eventually he did look and saw the attraction. Lee was down there, his body a twisted mass of contorted limbs and lifeless flesh lying in a growing pool of blood.

It just happened when they opened the gate? Colin tried to reason with himself. At the same time, he swore that he could smell the gore from where he was, some 20 feet up. From the third tier, Colin guessed, the drop had to be a good 50-plus feet. And Colin swore there was *no way* the old-timer had jumped.

"ALL CONVICTS TO YOUR ASSIGNED QUARTERS! NOW!"

The sirens were excruciating on the senses, penetrating the minds of every being in the cell block. Colin finally shot back to his cell, just in time before the electronic gates closed.

"Keep your mouth shut . . . mind your own business," were Lee's words, and they haunted Colin now, echoing in his head as loud and violent as the sirens.

There was a suicide just six months earlier, and Lee had preached that same important advice then. But now it was Lee, his friend, who was the victim. And the things Colin knew were driving him crazy . . . the beef between Lee and Big Earl, the unfriendly atmosphere between them . . . the "issues" that Lee talked about, ones he said he wouldn't allow to interfere with his going home.

So much information and conclusions pounded Colin. He wondered who saw what, if anything at all. Someone had to have seen something, he concluded. But the images were already developing in his mind—the younger, more powerful Big Earl grabbing Lee, the older, more helpless convict, and hurling him over the rail in one swift move . . . Lee falling three levels down and crashing to the cold, hard cement—instant death. It was all so easy to imagine; it didn't take a rocket scientist to figure it all out. And then, of course, there was always that final aerial perspective that Colin had, looking down at Lee's lifeless corpse.

But Colin had no choice but to keep his mouth shut; this was the penitentiary, where life could be (and was) swept away in one fell swoop. Friends or no friends, he had to follow sage advice: he had to mind his own business, no matter how uncomfortable. Except, however hard he tried not to think about it, Colin steadily sold himself on the possibilities of threats to his own welfare with every passing moment. Prison was just that unpredictable, where a hunch or a presumption could change or alter a man's destiny.

Colin began to feel the burden of his relationship with Lee. Other convicts who knew them as buddies would now watch him closely, as if under a microscope, maybe wondering about what he knew or what he'd been told. And with so much attention directed at him, Colin could never be sure who was friend or foe. He figured the best opinion to have was none; he'd ask no questions and show no hints of concern. If he failed at this, his life might be in jeopardy. Success, on the other hand, meant he'd be seen as coldhearted. And in a place like this, that was the safest way to be.

As an actor would, Colin programmed himself for the gloomy moods he'd maintain, the disinterest he'd project and how he'd use one of the "talkative" convicts—something akin to the prison's minister of information—as a witness, shrugging off Lee's death so that word would spread virally.

Before long others would be saying, *"That Williams cat is one cold motha-fucka."*

This, as Lee would agree, is how you make the best of a bad experience.

In the weeks and months following Lee's death, time seemed to fly by, thanks to Colin becoming a busybody. If you peeked in his cell you'd see him lying on his bunk, reading-reading-reading. As far as other convicts knew, Colin was an introvert, not necessarily building his mind, or being productive while expanding his knowledge in various areas. No, that would be *too* productive for this environment—a place where misery loves company.

But that was so far from the truth. In fact, Colin was so deep into Lee's literature that he frequently lost track of time. It almost didn't matter what day it was. He didn't even look forward to Friday's French toast any longer. All Colin cared about, all he devoted himself to, was reading that next short story. It was while reading Lee's work that Colin came up with the idea of taking the best short stories and transforming them into full-length novels. He began his crusade by sketching outlines for a number of the stories. He added characters that were his real-life neighbors—at least for *now* they were—with all their idiosyncrasies, habits and personalities. And why not? Since he had to cohabitate with them, tolerate them, and study them . . . why not use them as models, and absorb that wealth of criminal experience?

In time Colin found himself researching everyone he met or associated with. There were those who were born to victimize others, there were gang and mafia members, just as there were bank robbers, drug kingpins and killers. Colin grew crafty at borrowing from these men, their ways of thinking and their everyday routines. He didn't need to ask them who they were, since a person's actions always told exactly who they were—all a person generally had to do was listen. Colin became an expert listener, and turned what he learned into captivating prose.

At times he'd be elated by the reflection that looked back at him from his writing; other times he'd be moved to tears, somehow channeling the emotions, pains and pleasures of

his unique characters. The process became therapeutic, often helping to mold Colin's own choices and desires. And on
top of that, Colin read whatever books he could get his
hands on to further study the technique of creative writing.
If nothing else, the books he read educated him on the
ways of established authors. He also dissected their work
with a fine-tooth comb, focusing on how they seduced their
readers—how they maintained their readerships.

At least, Colin imagined, by zeroing in on the most successful authors, he could do no wrong; they were already
making money, they had their devoted readers, they'd established a niche. All he had to do was develop his own style
and ride the wave. Success leaves its clues.

Colin thought, *If I can't be the quarterback, then at least
I'll be a player on the field.*

Above and beyond the amateur strategy Colin thought up,
his big advantage was having that box in his possession. The
late Lee's ideas were a treasure chest of future novels. And if
Lee had any family out in the world, then as God was his
witness, Colin would see to it that they benefited.

Among Lee's short stories, Colin found some personal
papers and a few photos. And when the time came, he intended to follow up the leads. However, there was also a letter that immediately spooked him. It was addressed to him.

Dear Colin,
*By now you'll have gone through my work (and
this letter) and you'll probably hate me when you find
out the truth. Yes, youngblood . . . I took myself off
the count. Call me a coward, Colin, but I've been living in fear lately. I've been dreaming of the street, the
things I once did and the life I once had. But the hard
truth is I've been living a dream here in the pen that I
never wanted to end. Going back to the streets would
be my wake-up, and that's my greatest fear—that I'll
arrive there and I won't achieve.*

*I never knew success, youngblood. I never tasted it
except for the dreams and the writing. If that were to*

end—my penitentiary lifestyle—I'd be shit out of hope. 'Cuz let's face it: I'll never be able to compete with all the other writers in the world. I'm 62 and I'm supposed to leave prison to start from scratch? Oh, hell no! I'm afraid of the unknown, youngblood. And that's what the street looks like from behind the wall. It's the great unknown. Unpredictable. It's that same uncertain future that lurks with a woman you meet, when you go for a job, or when you have an idea.

And youngblood, I'm too old for any more unknowns. I'm not curious anymore.

That's my point in giving you my work. You're not too old, burnt-out or hopeless.

I already know my future—I know where I'll be come tomorrow morning, after the jump. But you? Colin, you have the world in your hands. You are Cassius Clay before he became Muhammad Ali. You are Red—aka Malcolm Little—before he became Malcolm X. You are Tupac Shakur, who might've become a world leader.

You still have possibilities, Colin. Follow thru. Be disciplined, go forth and never waver. Never cower.

Your friend,

Lee

CHAPTER

22

It was already eerie for me to have all of Lee's writing in my possession—the last remnants of his life—and to receive it all the day before he jumped was a *trip*. That whole day the powers that be kept us locked down in our cells and fed us premade brown bag meals while the feds came in to investigate. And I'd wondered if Lee was really pushed or thrown over; it just happened too quick. The minute they popped the gates—then, *bam!* Airborne. *Damn!* He couldn't be *too* afraid to take the big jump. That's heart right there if you ask me.

And then I found the letter and I freaked out. He actually planned that shit . . . giving me the box, makin' up that B.S. story about beef with his celly . . .

I'd heard the stories of how a lot of convicts are afraid to go home, afraid to face society again after serving so much time. *Fear of failure*, they call it. But what Lee did takes the cake. I'm not really mad at him, but I *am* spooked.

This was my fourth year locked up, and certain realities were setting in, to the point that, like Lee suggested, I was accepting the change. This would be home for the next seven and a half years—85 percent of the 14-year sentence.

I was stripped of my liberty; my wife and child had left me, and now my friend killed himself weeks before he was supposed to go home.

The suicide just about broke my spirit; the letter he'd written had me shaken, with watery red eyes. But I wouldn't cry. I wouldn't allow my emotions to get the best of me.

I think Lee was just mixed up about life and (just like he

said) he shouldn't have listened to himself—*never take advice from a burnt-out old fool like me,* he'd said. That message will probably always be with me. But I still don't believe Lee was a coward. I think he was more courageous than he knew himself to be. Certain death is something many men could never face if given the choice. And Lee had that choice.

In my sleep I went through convulsions as thoughts of Lee and certain violence in his stories possessed me. It was something like that dream I have once in a while, how I'm driving, about to fly off of a cliff. After months of this, I forced myself to deal with it; I used Lee's death to empower myself. I suddenly had a larger purpose than to merely survive and make it back to the streets.

I figured if I could just follow through with turning Lee's short stories into full-length novels, I'd fulfill his wishes. With his help I could be a writer whose stories might possibly impact generations of people like me.

Of course, I'd have to write stories of sex, violence and money; otherwise who would read my stuff? At least I'd have the vehicle where I could channel Lee's wisdom and my opinions, and maybe I could prevent others from getting caught up in the mess I did.

But more importantly, my efforts were keeping me alive when all other hope seemed to be lost. Writing and creating kept me moving forward, even if time seemed to have stopped. It kept me hopeful in an environment that wasn't made to facilitate progress.

So, like a juggernaut, I was steadfast, disciplined and consistent. I wrote page after page, chapter after chapter, book after book. Somehow, I imagined, I'd hit pay dirt.

CHAPTER

23

Toy was picking the best apples she could find from the fruit and vegetable section of the Pathmark supermarket, at the same time ignoring the eyes that one of the stock boys was making at her.

A woman's voice sounded just over Toy's shoulder, surprising her since Toy hadn't seen her approach.

"Wow," the stranger said. "You'd think these guys would have a little more restraint. *Jeez.*"

"Huh?" Toy was a bit taken aback by how the woman imposed on her space, and she also had a hard time (at least in the beginning of the . . . *discussion?*) acknowledging her. "Uh . . . are you talkin' to me? I'm sorry; I didn't catch everything you said."

"The college hunk, babe. He's, like, lookin' you up and down like you're a sweet summer sausage or somethin'."

Now that the woman clarified her position, Toy was at ease. Plus, the *sweet summer sausage* comment had her cracking up deep down in her gut.

"But, come to think of it, I can't really blame him with this outfit you're wearing. It's *fabulous!* Can you tip me off? Let me know where you bought it?"

Relief washed over Toy; at first she'd thought the woman was trying to pick her up. She seemed genuine. Knee-deep in her own issues. Toy opened up some, becoming polite toward the woman while still selecting fruits for her basket.

"I can't remember," said Toy. "It might've been a gift from my man."

And that was another thing. Her "man," Reed, was

somewhere in the supermarket, lurking. They were supposed to drive to New York City for an Alvin Ailey dance performance at Lincoln Center, an appropriate occasion for the silk crepe gown that Toy wore and that the woman raved about.

Only now did Toy understand why she was attracting so much attention from the ogling hunk, this stranger and maybe a handful of others who seemed spellbound as she passed them. *It was the dress*, and how parts of her body were revealed by the cut-outs in the oriental print. She also had a fox stole around her shoulders, and strappy high-heeled shoes. How could she have been be so naive?

So that's why he wanted me to wear this, Toy determined on the spot. And now it all made sense—the night out on the town, Alvin Ailey, this particular dress. *He's testing me. This night is nothing but a hoax.*

"You okay?" asked the white woman.

"Huh? Oh . . . yeah. Just . . . just daydreamin', that's all." Toy's quick answer was nothing like the thoughts weaving about her consciousness, how her mind was replaying the scene in the Lexus, just before she came into Pathmark a few minutes earlier . . .

"Didn't expect me to stop here, did you?" Reed said, his voice raspy and harsh.

"What?" Toy asked nonchalantly. She pulled down the overhead visor to check her makeup. She didn't necessarily need to fix up anything, but pretended to in an effort to work past the sudden knot in her belly. After five years with Reed, she knew his temperatures—their lows and highs.

"That's how you speak to me? Just like that?"

Reed didn't pose a threat, not just yet. And Toy took the opportunity to explain—no sense in sparking off a fire. However, Reed didn't let up. He reached over and grabbed Toy's neck.

"Ow!" Toy cried.

He turned her head so that her eyes were directed toward the market's all-glass exterior with its fluorescent SALE!

signs posted for this week's specials on turkey, pumpkin pie, and canned candied yams, all reminders that Thanksgiving was around the corner. "Your little boyfriend in the super-market—*that's* what." He let go of Toy's neck and she rubbed it, as her fox stole slipped off of her bare shoulders.

"This is silly, Reed. Do you always have to *hurt* me when you think I'm *fucking* somebody?"

Reed pulled back his hand, winding up in that same way before he'd swing at Toy. She cringed in an abrupt jerk, anticipating his assault. He never struck. Not this time. But he did point his finger like a sword just millimeters from her eye.

"Watch the way you talk to me," he commanded. "I told you about that shit." He turned to look in the store as if considering his next move. "Okay . . . so if I'm wrong, and if you're not fucking him, this college punk who stocks groceries for a living, then you shouldn't have a problem with doin' a little shopping. Right?"

Toy averted her eyes so Reed wouldn't see her rolling them. "Reed, we went over this two weeks ago, and I told you the truth then. I've never seen that boy, besides here at the market. Why can't you believe me?" She wanted to ask, *Why are you so insecure?* But she wouldn't dare.

"Whatever," Reed replied, not necessarily giving a direct response. "What you do is take your ass in that store and spend five minutes picking out fruit. If that boy steps to you, if he so much as tries to hold a conversation with you, I'm gonna whip *his* ass, then I'm taking you back home—"

He's jealous?

"Reed? What about Alvin Ailey?"

"If this goes down like I *think* it's gonna go down, the only dancin' *you'll* see is my two left feet up your ass!"

"Reed!"

Reed reached past Toy, opened the door and shoved her enough for her to know he was dead serious. "Get the fuck out. Here's a twenty."

Toy was apprehensive taking the money, wondering if this was one of *his* creations. Reed's eyes, however, ordered her to do as she was told. Toy lifted her ass from the car seat and at once felt the November chill stiffening her nipples. The $20 bill in hand, she shut the door and strutted around the Lexus toward the front entrance of the Pathmark.

Reed lowered his window. "Don't spend the whole twenty, 'cuz that might be the last piece of money you ever get from me." And he raised his window.

At precisely that moment, Toy didn't mind one bit if this was the last piece of money . . . she didn't mind if she never saw him again, she was tired of his bullshit.

Only her common sense drove her on—thoughts of Lady in private school, clothing, rent and so on. It was just too damned hard to break free of this fool-ass nigga.

And now Toy was inside the market, trying to give Steven subtle signals that Reed wouldn't see . . . signals that he should leave her alone—that she was being watched.

But this woman came from out of nowhere, standing right in the thick of it. Toy considered telling her to go fuck herself, that she was interfering—but then she had an idea. The woman turned out to be the perfect prop; surely Steven would be intimidated if Toy was shopping with a friend.

Suddenly Toy was on a mission, and she gave the stranger added attention, as though they'd been friends for years. "What'd you say your name was?"

"Oh . . . I . . . I didn't. But my friends call me Kat—with a K—as in kitty cat." The woman appeared to be caught off guard by Toy's question, but that didn't sway or stall the objective. Toy nestled Kat's elbow in the palm of her hand, urging her to join her in a pow-wow.

From the corner of her eye, Toy saw Steven's frustration and how he expected her to stroll toward the back of the store as usual. Toy simply exaggerated her disinterest and slipped her arm inside of Kat's.

"So, Kat, do you really like the dress?" asked Toy, with the best small talk she could muster.

"Love it. Think you can find out where your man got it?"

"You know, come to think of it, he could've got it on Columbus Avenue in Manhattan . . ." Toy evaluated the pears and then the oranges as the two conversed. "One of those boutiques with all the designers. I think this one . . . *oh yeah*. This is a Jean-Paul Gaultier—four thousand, ya' know." Toy did a little spin for Kat to see, knowing that she was also teasing her admirer.

"No kiddin'," said Kat. "Is that *with* the stole?"

"Mmm-hmm," said Toy, wagging her head with a heart-felt smirk. "I'm afraid this beauty is twenty-five hundred. Gotta make 'em pay, know what I mean? As much shit as we get put through, why shouldn't they pay?"

The two women shared a moment of solidarity; then they progressed toward the vegetable bins.

Steven moved as well, now across the way and toying with bottles of salad dressing.

"Speaking of men, when I come in here he really gets on my nerves with the whole stalker bit."

"You think?" Kat turned and looked, giving Steven a once-over. "He doesn't *look* dangerous."

"Maybe not. But he damn near chases me to the checkout counter, bags my groceries; I'd bet a dollar to a doughnut that he's followed me home a time or two."

"No shit. And you never came on to him?"

Toy blew out a lungful of hot air in response, as if Kat had just unleashed the taboo curse. "Chile, are you kiddin'? *Please!* My man would have my *ass!* Hell no, I ain't kickin' it with no college stock boy. He ain't gonna pay my bills or feed my kid."

Kat's eyes were ecstatic by Toy's comment. "So, why don't you just tell stock boy to get lost? And this whole sheer-dress/sex-kitten look isn't helping things."

"I know, I know, but a girl appreciates a little attention sometimes. Especially when the man of the house is out, into extracurricular activities, if you know what I mean . . ." Kat wore a doubtful expression. Toy went on, "But still, this wasn't my choice—the dress n' all. My man is out in the car or in *here* somewhere."

"Girrrl . . ." Kat's wary eyes danced left and right, looking for the spy.

"Exactly. We're suppose to be in the city watchin' the Alvin Ailey dancers. But—you won't believe this—Reed, that's my man, he pulls up to Pathmark all of a sudden, and I think he *wants* me to attract Steven's attention."

"He's settin' you up?"

"Ex-*actly.*"

"But you said Steven."

"That's the stock boy's name. Your hunk."

"Mmm-hmm . . ." Kat's face was a deceitful mess; her lips twisted, her eyes squinted and her brows furrowed. "You sure he's not *your* hunk?"

Sucking her teeth, Toy gazed into Kat eyes, and Kat read her loud and clear.

"Well . . . I don't really know you. How can I totally believe you when you totally know this guy on a first-name basis?"

"Because I'm *asking* you to believe me. At least give me the benefit of the doubt," Toy stressed. "Reed is right, this guy likes me, but I'm not fucking him."

"Relax, girlfriend. You haven't given me any reason not to believe you. No sense in getting all worked up . . . tell you what . . . why don't . . ." Kat did some quick thinking. "You finish your shopping while *I* take care of loverboy here."

Toy's distress faded. *"Who are you??? You are an angel."*

"I've been called worse. But just call me Kat."

"Hey," said Toy before they split. "Why don't you give me a call sometime? I'll see if I can get you info about the dress." She hunted for a pen in her purse. A matchbook served as the medium whereon she jotted her phone number. Kat agreed with a shrug and a smile and took the matches before the two went their separate ways.

As Toy laid six apples and just as many pears and oranges on the conveyor belt, Reed slithered up behind her no differently than a snake would.

"Boo."

"Oooh!" Toy's body jerked some. *"Baby!"* The young cashier smiled a conspirator's smile as she totaled the purchases. "That'll be seven twenty," she announced.

Toy let out a shivering exhale, less in response to the "boo" than to what Reed's restless hand was doing, hidden from the teenager. On the way toward the exit, with Toy's attention elsewhere, Reed looked over his shoulder to see Kat making small talk with the stock boy. His eyes connected with hers, however briefly, and he was satisfied. If Toy wouldn't tell him, Kat would later.

CHAPTER

24

For five years, Vince Reed lived his dream. He had even more money, luxury and power than he bargained for. He was pushing $20 bills nowadays—they were less risky and easier to move than the fifties. He had a large fleet of customized Honda Civics, complete with removable floor plates to hide stacks of counterfeit money. "Mules" were then hired to drive the vehicles, nonstop, from Jersey to Philly, from Jersey to Delaware, or from Jersey to New York.

Now that the facilities were set up and the recycling process was in place, including the new contact with the Treasury Department's money-green paper shavings, Reed was ready to service the entire East Coast. His operation was gradually mushrooming from $50 million (in counterfeit bills) to $250 million per month, most of which was packed in self-storage rooms.

Where there were local police on the payroll, providing both inside information as protection, now there were federal agents as well, to give Reed a more surgical perspective on law enforcement's efforts and objectives.

Despite all of the criminal success he was experiencing, Reed was content to call Fort Lee his home. If he were to make any significant departure from Jersey, it would be for good.

Meanwhile, Toy was used in every way imaginable. Without exaggeration, she evolved into his all-purpose, all-access, all-star blowup doll in the bedroom, and his marionette in every other way he desired. Her daughter, thanks to the convenience of money, became so much less an obstruction, sleeping over at this and that babysitter's home, and remaining evermore the rare reminder of Toy's past—her jailed husband.

Sex with Toy had become passé—less of an "event" and more of a well-regulated "exercise."

And that was what Reed recognized as a successful man's right: pussy, how and when he wanted it. One way or another, whether it was given freely or purchased, pussy was always attracted, lured and sucked in to the magnetism of money and power.

A month and a half after the rape Toy found out she was pregnant. The news pushed her dead smack in the middle of yet another dilemma. She didn't want Reed to know that there was full penetration (or any at all) during the assault. Toy never thought that she'd be subjected to a second abortion, reliving her long-ago post-prom encounter, and surrendering to such a physically taxing experience . . . another scar on her life, only because of the deception and domination of another heartless, evil dick.

Fortunately, Toy had a new friend, Kat, who was by her side every step of the way. She helped Toy through the devastating ordeal as she faced the abortion clinic once again, terminating her second unwanted pregnancy.

Since Kat, aka Kitty, was in place as Toy's close friend, a relationship that had blossomed ever since their meeting at the Pathmark, Reed was well informed as to Toy's personal business. He hadn't intended on making Toy pregnant during the staged rape, but the tiger bone milk was at work that night—an energy Reed couldn't control if he tried.

Thanks to Kitty, Reed was in the know about Toy's complaints of stomach complications, crying spells and her wishes to take her own life.

Kitty was there to keep her alive.

All the while, Reed kept his dirty secrets to himself, and he didn't push Toy for any more details than she chose to share. There was no telling how she'd act if she found out the truth—the extremes that this man had gone through just to "get off."

Instead of encouraging her to talk about it, Reed showed his sympathy in another way.

"There's a couple of things I wanna talk to you about," he told her one night as they cuddled before a blazing fireplace. "Remember the . . . situation that night at my place?" By his eyes alone, Reed indicated the seriousness of his comment, expecting Toy to know just what he meant. For weeks she had been bugging him about going to the police, and about the pain she felt in her heart. But Reed expressed his determination: "I'm taking care of it," he told her.

"How can I forget?" said Toy. "A month in therapy, and I'm still not sleeping normal."

"Well, maybe you will now. Here . . . take a look at these," said Reed as he handed Toy two Polaroid photos. "There were other pictures, but I figured these two would satisfy you."

"Oh God," Toy gasped, her face wrinkled up at the sight of blood and guts. "Do I have to? It turns my stomach to see blood. What is that?" She took another, more investigative look at the photos. "*God* . . . who *are* they? How do they know—"

"That's not important, boo. It's over. That's all that matters, and that's the last I wanna hear about it."

Reed tossed the Polaroids in the fire and they shriveled to ash.

Toy stared at what was left of the pics.

"One more thing . . . I'm goin' on a little trip . . ."

Toy was steadily gazing into the fireplace, squeezing herself further into Reed's embrace.

"Just some time to get away."

"How long?" asked Toy, as if he was a supply more critical than oxygen or water.

"Two weeks. Maybe three."

"Could you . . . could you at least call?"

Reed noticed a tear falling along Toy's cheek but didn't acknowledge it. "Of course," he said, knowing that the woman he'd be with had a phone at home.

It was that easy. Toy was no longer a challenge for Reed. No longer a mountain that he needed to climb. He had been there and he had done that. She was merely convenient these days.

Yes, he still flaunted her whenever he wanted to show off—after all, she was still one of the most attractive women on the set, and still had all of her plumbing in place. He used her when he wanted to impress a new associate.

It wasn't unusual for Toy to be on Reed's arm at clubs in Philly, in Jersey, or even at one of the gentlemen's clubs in New York City. Men would strain to see more of her, the dark areas of her breasts, and how their silhouettes played up against some sheer blouse.

If there wasn't the flaunting at the clubs, there were still the "experiments" he'd try behind closed doors. Once, Reed attached a used dog collar to Toy's neck and walked her around his duplex on all fours, half naked and begging him to stop. Another time he had Toy fix up some seafood— salmon, shrimp, lobster tails and crab legs. The abundance of food was set out on the dinner table.

"Take your clothes off," Reed ordered in a semiseductive, semicommanding tone.

Toy was never bashful to undress before Reed, but for some reason, this sounded different. Maybe he'd have her eat in the nude?

Not. Reed sat at the head of the table and had Toy climb up on a chair, then on the table, until she lay there amidst the feast. With so much of Toy's naked body staring him in the face, Reed ate, directing her to execute various lewd poses with the food; then he'd fed her, all while they held casual conversation.

When Reed was erect with desire, the two finished the occasion with after-dinner sex games in the Jacuzzi.

Aside from Reed's shenanigans at home, there were his other "whims" that Toy answered:

The blow job on the observation deck of the Empire State Building.

The fast food restaurant, where Reed stood behind Toy (as a stranger would) as she propositioned an impressionable cashier for a threesome.

There were also numerous occasions in the Lexus, or the Expedition, mostly while the vehicles were in motion, when Reed ordered Toy to "take it off," encouraging near-collisions by nosy drivers and passersby.

When the thrills seemed over and done with, Reed decided that it was okay for Toy to make money for him. Why not? Didn't he have dozens of other mules, men and women alike, who took "trips" in the Hondas, delivering good and bad cash to and fro? And wasn't Toy the most obedient mule he'd ever met?

Toy had asked Reed if she could drive for him on more than one occasion. But he always declined. "Just be here when and where I need you . . . you're my ride-or-die chick," Reed said now and again.

That was music to Toy's ears. It made her feel wanted and useful. She belonged and she was secure. The sex was off-the-hook, and usually raunchy, but she didn't mind. Reed was her man, he took care of her like no other and she'd go to any extreme for him. Sometimes, you had to take the good with the bad, she reckoned. And besides, she was in too deep to pull out.

And then, one day, he changed his mind: "I need you today," he said simply and matter-of-factly. "One of my drivers got herself . . . well . . . let's just say she's unavailable."

Naturally, Toy agreed. "Why can't I drive the Expedition?" she complained. She didn't necessarily appreciate having to drive a compact car. "*A Honda Civic?* For Christ's sake!"

"Don't question me," snapped Reed. "You're to take the car straight to Harlem. Don't stop for anything." When Reed was sure that Toy knew the directions and the destination, he cuddled her chin in his firm grip.

"I don't expect you to do anything more or *anything* less than what I told you. Is that clear?"

"Yes, baby." Toy, the pawn.

For all she knew, there could've been TNT in the car, since she had no idea why these Hondas were sent out and driven from state to state, only to return to Fort Lee where Reed owned a parking lot near Club Jaguar.

Reed had plenty of "drivers" on the payroll, and she didn't mind filling in. She didn't question Reed's directions: "Park right outside of the address I gave you . . . honk the horn three times and wait for a Jamaican girl to come out . . ."

At that point, Toy was expected to get out of the car and wait in a van while the Jamaican girl drove off with the Honda—"She should be back in less than ten minutes. Just wait for her."—and when she returned, Toy was expected to get back in the Civic and return to Jersey.

Whatever, Toy thought again as she reworked the details in her mind. If this was what Reed wanted, then so be it.

She set out at 7:30 in the morning, hoping to beat any major traffic crossing the George Washington Bridge. But it turned out that Toy wasn't the only person with that idea—not on a Wednesday morning, heading into one of the nation's biggest cities. The traffic that bottlenecked from the Jersey side took almost a half hour to work through. By the time Toy crossed over the Hudson River and weaved around the bends that branched off of the bridge, merging onto the West Side Highway, it was too late to take an exit. Toy was stuck in a traffic backup that seemed to stretch as far as the eye could see.

To add to her misery, the cell phone that Reed provided wouldn't operate; it required a code and that was something he hadn't told her about earlier.

As Toy snaked along the single lane of traffic that was allowed, she soon realized that an 18-wheeler was the cause of this mess. It had attempted to drive along the highway (where no such rigs were permitted) and had struck an overpass. Drivers vegetated for hours, turning the West Side Highway into a virtual parking lot until ten in the morning. *Who knew*?

When Toy finally reached the 125th Street exit, the Honda stalled on the down ramp. Instinctively, she checked the gas gauge and realized it was on E. *I've been here before.* She sighed, hoping that there was just enough gas left to restart the car and get to a gas station. *I knew I should've took the truck*, she thought, turning the key again. And again.

The car choked back into operation; Toy thanked God, and was carried for one more block to a BP station. She directed the vehicle to the left side of the pumps, the side that promoted "Full Service," and awaited the attendant.

"Fill it," she said.

The attendant smiled so that his pitiful gold tooth glistened. As he went about his duty, Toy suddenly realized what she had been in denial of for the past two hours. She stuck her head out of the window. "Excuse me . . . do you have a bathroom?"

"Yes," he replied with a heavy Spanish accent. "But it's no working." He then pointed across the street to the McDonald's restaurant, its golden arches towering over 125th Street.

Toy huffed and debated with her bladder, her thighs already tightly pressed together to hold it in. It had been a long wait back on the bridge, then the highway. The gas pump read $15 and counting.

Damn, this pump is slow, she thought as she studied her surroundings. The subway line was a monstrous sight, at least 100 or so feet overhead, with its graffiti-ridden metal links rumbling through. Cars, trucks and vans zipped back and forth along 125th. The intersection at Broadway had a doughnut shop, a five-and-dime store and a CD shop on the adjacent corner. The meter was at $18 now.

Jesus, one side of her brain panted. *He'll never know*, assured the other. Her body couldn't take it anymore, and she was forced up and out of the Honda. She had already turned off the ignition, and now she snatched the keys.

"I'll be two minutes." Toy told the attendant, her eyes telling him to finish pumping gas and to keep an eye on the car while she tinkled. She then strutted off, trying to keep the pressure on her nether regions as she crossed the street. A lemon sweater, lime skirt and white Reebok sneakers marked Toy as a sight to see, encouraging a horn's honk and a shout— *you go girl*—as she shuffled into Micky Dee's front entrance. Relief was already crying inside of Toy as she thrust her way into the ladies' room.

When her business was done, Toy hardly washed her hands before she rushed off, a little light-headed from the sensation of emptying her *own* tank.

Outside on the curb, hoping to catch a break in the traffic, Toy noticed the Honda had been moved from where she'd left it.

A blizzard of emotions attacked her as she craned her neck to see around passing vehicles. Even the gas pumps seemed to block her view. When she eventually crossed the street, the air felt sucked from her being. The car was gone. Not moved . . . *gone*.

Bewildered, Toy stormed toward the attendant's booth. The walk-up window was busy with two customers paying in advance for the self-service pumps.

"Excuse me," Toy said, not wanting to be rude, yet pushing her way past the payees nonetheless. "Did you see where your attendant took my car? The kid with the gold tooth? I think he's Spanish?"

"My attendant? I don't have an attendant, ma'am."

"What do you *mean*, you don't have—I . . . I . . ."

"Ma'am, I *am* the attendant. And you haven't paid me anything. I've never seen you before in my life, and what's more . . . you're cutting the line. Would you excuse them, please?"

"Shit!" Toy screamed, stomping her sneakered heel into the concrete. "Have you seen my car? A blue Honda?" she asked the patrons in a condescending, finger-pointing tone. They both held strange expressions until she was eventually ignored, their backs turned, returning to the business of paying for gas.

"Has anybody seen a blue Honda Civic?"

Toy's screaming was a waste of time—just another whisper in this cold, heartless metropolis.

She soon realized the scam: the chump who had approached her was not the attendant . . . he didn't work for the gas station at all. Toy was but a target; the naive girl from the burbs. *He probably saw the New Jersey plates on the car . . . fuck. Fuck. Fuck!!! What will I tell Reed?*

CHAPTER

25

Reed told me to take a taxi home. I tried to explain things; how and why and whatnot, but he said he didn't wanna hear it. "I'll be here," he said, with not the slightest compassion in his voice. Then he hung up.

I thought I had to pee *before*? *Jesus* . . . when Reed hung up the phone I thought an ocean was gonna flush from between my legs. Not only did I have to pee, but my bowels were lining up inside of me too. My nerves were sizzling like hot wings, and I had enough worry hammering in my head to compete with a demolition crew. I even bit off the fingernail of my right pinkie.

"Could you slow down some?" I asked the cab driver. I know he was probably just trying to make good time to get me to Fort Lee as quickly as possible. But I sure didn't wanna hurry home.

"Sorry, miss. You get carsick easy?"

"No. I just . . . just take your time, that's all." I had to think things over. Maybe I wouldn't go back home after all.

CHAPTER

26

Reed understood his power by now, how he influenced, impressed, inspired or intimidated people—especially women—specifically Toy. Therefore, he could see why Toy was stuttering on the phone. She feared him. She was scared to death of him. And maybe . . . just maybe, she'd take a detour and not show up at all. If that was all it took to get rid of her . . . if a hooptie and a million in funny money was the cost, the final bill for his using Toy to the extent that he had, then so be it.

I'm done with that bitch anyway, Reed thought, content to devote his attentions to a fresher, younger, wilder piece of ass. This might just be all the excuse he needed.

The taxi showed up at one o'clock in the afternoon. Reed took in that last deep breath, trying to tame his anger. He had already driven himself insane with *I told that bitch* this and *I told that ho* that. And now, she had the audacity to face him? He didn't want to have to kill Toy over something as unimportant to him as money and a dispensable car.

He could always print another million—especially since there was such an abundance of paper now—or buy another car. But there was the principle to consider, how she'd disobeyed him. That was more important.

Toy didn't use her key. She just rang the doorbell as if she were a stranger, a door-to-door saleswoman or a distant relative. Reed, once he opened the door, made a face as if to question her. And then he started to ask, "Why didn't you use—"

He never completed his question before Toy picked up on

his comforting expression. At once she fell forward into his arms like a lost child. He hugged her with one arm and reached to close the door with the other.

"I'm sorry, I'm sorry, I'm sorry, oh God," Toy bawled and sobbed and panted. "I'm *so* sorry, Reed. Oh please, please, please, forgive me. *Please!*" Her pleas were spraying from her mouth as fast and as immediately as the tears spilled down her already wet cheeks.

"Did you talk to the police?" Reed asked calmly, somehow focused and insensitive.

"No, Reed. I did like you told me, baby. I just left. I caught the first cab I saw. He's outside now. I didn't have enough to—"

"I'll take care of it," Reed said, reading between the lines. "Does *he* know what happened?"

"No, no, no. I haven't told a soul. I just did as you said," said Toy.

"Sure you did," he said flatly.

Toy looked up at Reed, wonder in her eyes. Maybe this was where he'd flip on her.

"All right. Go shower up. You're a mess. I'll pay this guy."

"I'm so sorry, Reed."

He said nothing, and his eyes crawled the length of her body—head to toe, then back. Then he left her standing there and went through the door, the money clip already sliding off of his cash.

Toy had nothing to give Reed to replace the loss. She was certain that there was more at stake than just the car. She didn't know what, since Reed kept his business from her. But the least she thought of doing was to give him her body.

As fast as she could, Toy pulled off her clothes and prepared the shower. Meanwhile, she got hold of the cordless phone, calling the sitter to see about Lady. Her daughter was the only person who could help Toy keep her sanity.

"I'll tell little Lady that Mummy's work—mummies work all d' time," explained the sitter. "Your baby misses you."

"I know, I know. Give her a hug and kiss for me, would

ya? Mommy'll see her later tonight. And thank you, sweetie.
You're a doll."

As Toy showered she thought about how far and how
deep things had gotten. This life of hers became so . . . so
unpredictable. There was excitement, a sense of mystery
and plenty of luxury to enjoy. She loved Reed. Couldn't
live without him—or, at least, she couldn't *imagine* living
without him. But she also knew that she was trapped.
Trapped by the money, by the circumstances that put her
here, and even trapped by her own willingness to do and be
and indulge.

It was a relationship that was both good and bad, like the
"Emotional Rollercoaster" that Vivian Green sang about—

"Loving you was never healthy.
Loving you was never good for me . . .
but I can't get off."

The money, the luxuries were intoxicating. It allowed Toy
the opportunity to live like the rapper chicks she'd once admired; that she somehow still admired. She could wear the
high fashions, the diamond necklaces and bracelets. She
could do things that even she knew she'd never do on her
own otherwise. Money unlocked all of that for her. The sex,
the spontaneity and feeling overcome with satisfaction was
also exciting. Even if she was used a bit now and then, at
least she could enjoy being Reed's freak. His Toy.

One of her "dirty little secrets" (quiet as it was kept) was
that she still went along. Always, Toy went along.

Toy came out of the shower fully intending to be Reed's
sex slave. She barely dried herself, wanting to appear as wet
and wild and sexy as she ever had. As she approached the
bedroom, Reed's voice grew less faint. He was sitting on the
bed talking on the phone, she realized, with his back to her.

"I don't *care*. We need to find that shit. See who runs
that scam over that motha-fucka. I ain't gonna be able to
sleep knowin' that a million in paper is just hangin' out,
doin' *nothin'*. I'll bet my blood n' bones that the lowlife who

took that shit don't know who or what he fuckin' with . . .
just get on it before that car show up in some scrap yard wit'
some old Fred Sanford motha-fucka findin' that shit . . ."
Reed swung his head around suddenly. The look in his eye
startled Toy.

She was standing in the doorway, dumbfounded by what
she'd just heard. Reed curled his forefinger at her and she
dragged her way over, a plush white towel wrapped around
her body, hair dripping on her shoulders, collarbone and
down her cleavage.

"Mmm-hmm," Reed murmured into the phone, listening
as he fingered the towel. His hand traveled up to the top,
where the towel was bound into a makeshift knot.

He loosened it so that the towel fell to the carpet.

"Mmm-hmm. Yeah . . . I know," Reed said, continuing
with his phone conversation. He looked at Toy's body in that
cocky, been-there-done-that way.

Toy still had the breasts of a fitness nut; just as perky as
when he'd first had her. Her skin was smooth—*impeccable*.
She was his flesh, to do with as he pleased. Toy turned
around so that her back was to him. She looked back over
her shoulder, wondering what he had in mind. The mystery
both frightened her and stimulated her.

Reed fixed the phone so that it was cradled steadily between his ear and shoulder. He had Toy spread her legs, his
hand cupping her genitals, fitting his middle finger up into
her opening as he would into the hole of a bowling ball. He
intensified his grip to more or less remind her whose pussy
this was. His.

Toy liked how it felt, and she wanted something to hold
on to so that she could enjoy it more. But she instead focused
additional effort on keeping her balance.

"Well, I want our people in Harlem and the Bronx on this
problem *immediately*. You could do one of two things . . ."
Reed placed his hand against Toy's lower back and pushed
easy so that she would bend over, hands on her knees. "Put a
price on dude's head or offer a reward. Simple as that . . ."

His other hand was still cupped on her genitals, the forefinger wiggling inside.

Toy let her hands glide down to her ankles, eventually touching her hands to the floor, achieving that balance she needed. Now she caught that upside-down view of Reed and worked herself into the enjoyment—the soft "oohs" and "aahs" that were familiar responses.

Gradually, Reed withdrew his finger and then gently slipped that same slimy digit into her asshole.

Toy's whimpers wavered back and forth between agony and pleasure, as Reed twisted and probed inside of her. Then he smacked her ass. "Shhh," Reed said. "Oh that? That wasn't shit. I'm just tryin' to fix somethin' over here," Reed said into the phone, sarcasm in his eyes. He motioned for her to straighten and she faced Reed with that awkward look about her.

His busiest finger gesturing, Reed directed Toy to get down and kneel before him.

She did.

He took the same grimy forefinger and skated it along her lips.

"Listen, I gotta go," said Reed. "Take care of that." He didn't wait for a response, he just put down the phone. Then he stared at Toy.

"Suck it."

Toy's face was awash with objection, dreadful confusion. "You . . . want me to suck the finger that . . . *you put in my ass?*"

"Don't make me tell you twice, bitch!"

The way Reed's voice sounded was so foreign to Toy; so low-pitched that it terrorized her deep down. She took hold of Reed's hand, her glow dwindling mightily as she briefly studied his finger, smelling the offensive odor it gave off. "I'll do anything for you, Reed. You know that . . ." She didn't take her eyes off of his as she eased his seasoned finger in her mouth.

"Good. Suck it like a lollipop," he said.

And she did. Her eyes were shut tight as she tried to

imagine that this wasn't as gross as it seemed, as it smelled, as it tasted. But the effects were all too unforgettable to get rid of. Maybe she had seen the worst of it . . . the furthest she'd have to go.

"See? Now that wasn't so bad, was it?"

Toy shook her head, unable to look Reed in the eyes.

"I bet you wanna suck Daddy's dick now, don't you?"

Toy didn't know how to respond; it sounded so much like a command—or was it a trick question since Reed already knew—

"I told you . . . I'll do whatever—"

She didn't get to complete her comment. Reed whipped his palm around, slapping her cheek hard enough for her to fall back to the floor.

"That's not what I asked you, Toy . . ." Reed's tone was casual, not at all fitting in with his violent outbreak. The voice of a psychologist. He got up from the bed and helped Toy back to her knees. "Come on, come on. I'm sorry, boo. I didn't hurt you, did I? Aww . . . Daddy's lil' girl is cryin'."

Reed was sitting on the bed again. Toy was as she was before, at his mercy, kneeling in front of him, except now her cheek was red and her hair mussed. Tears streamed down her face, dripping down the front of her naked body as she tried to subdue the boo-hoo sobs.

"Now . . . answer me. You wanna suck Daddy's dick . . . *don't you?*"

Toy got up the strength to hold her head up. She worked out a nod as best she could, trying to catch her breath. *Yes.*

"You do?" Reed chuckled. "Now what the fuck makes you think I want your nasty-ass mouth on my dick after you done ate some shit?"

He swung again, slapping Toy when she least expected it. She went down holding the opposite side of her face. She writhed and wept on the floor as though going through an epileptic seizure—like she was dying. She was in a rock-bottom state, and she wanted to die.

"I'm going for a drive. Have yourself cleaned up by the time I get back . . ." Reed had his smooth-as-silk tone again. "The best part of this is making up."

Even in this state of delirium, with all of her senses distressed and her vision somewhat foggy, Toy realized that Reed had finally done it—he'd pushed her past the point of no return. She couldn't be sure anymore about what was real and what wasn't. She couldn't feel comfortable or secure or pampered. She couldn't feel, see or think about the money, gifts or conveniences. Reed was a nut. Of that, she was sure. And he had the balls to bring up sex? "The best part of this"?

He had all-the-way lost his mind if he thought his dick would come anywhere near her ever again. Hopefully, he would be gone for long enough that she could gather her things and get away. Far away, if she could make it happen. Right now, all she could think about was her daughter, her lifeline. Her reason for living.

CHAPTER

27

Toy caught a taxi from Reed's duplex and mapped out her getaway for the five-minute trip to the Shangrila. There were certain things that had to stay, things she had enjoyed for so many years. There was all of her clothes; designer bags and accessories that probably added up to more than $100,000 in value. Her furs alone were worth $80,000. And there was her jewelry; she couldn't very well leave without that.

"*Oh God.*" Toy wept, realizing that this was much more involved . . . much more complex than she thought it would be. Before long, the surroundings got to her. This was home *way* before Reed came along.

Why am I running away from my own home?

And then the thoughts of Reed paying all of her bills weighed in on her conscience. There was no way Toy would be able to handle so many expenses all by herself, without a partner. Lady's tuition at private school was one of the biggest expenses—almost $2,000 a month—and then there were the payments on the penthouse. The rent was close to $3,800 a month, not to mention utilities. If Toy broke things off with Reed, she stood to lose all of that. But if she stayed . . .

"No. No. No! Don't think that way! You can't stay! You just can't!" Toy scolded herself in the bedroom mirror.

That instant made her more aware of the bruises—the cab driver hadn't been lying. Her cheeks were darker, and a slight swelling appeared under her right eye. If she had something in her hand, something big and bulky enough, she'd break that mirror . . . she'd destroy that image; that poor, desperate, helpless image.

The idea emerged about authorities, police, a courtroom somewhere. But the mere notion of challenging Reed under those circumstances crushed Toy and any confidence she mustered. Reed's business was already grimy, so how much further would he *really* need to go before he had one of his thugs attack Toy? And another thing—Reed had already shown the world that he could escape prosecution. So if the federal government couldn't touch him, how hard would it be to squash Toy's itsy-bitsy challenge?

While Toy dabbed a cold cloth against her face, the phone rang.

"Hey, girl. It's Kat. Haven't heard from you in a minute."

"Oh . . ." Toy sighed, not in as joyful a mood as her friend. "Busy, I guess."

"That's fine. I understand the married life . . . been there, done that."

"Kat, for the last time, I am *not* married. And, you know, now is not a good time at all for your basket of cheer. I've got serious problems."

"I . . . I'm sorry. Didn't know. Wanna talk about it? I'm all ears, hon. What else are friends for?"

Toy let a long silence pass before she agreed. Maybe Kat's call was for a reason. A godsend. And maybe she'd be able to help Toy make some sense of this . . . this pain and humiliation she'd been subjected to.

"It's crazy, Kat. Really crazy. I feel like a rag doll that's been tossed around, spit on and kicked . . ."

Toy was sitting in a booth across from Kat—aka Kitty—at the local Dunkin' Donuts. Toy had cried extensively, re-hashing her relationship with Reed from soup to nuts, minus the *extra* spicy details.

Her shoulder still damp from the tears, Kitty had an un-canny way of filling the role of big sister to Toy. Not that she was much older, but she was certainly more in the know . . . more on to the particulars of the Reed/Toy/Colin triangle than she'd dare let on. This whole act that she put on—the part of "Kat"—was working like a drug. And it was easier than she'd expected to be compassionate, to be that "friend in need."

Kitty wondered if her being white had anything to do with how easy this was—how she appeared to be so distant from those hard-knock realities that blacks experienced in society at large. If Toy thought that, she couldn't be further from the truth.

While Kitty had that all-American girl look—the Barbie doll face, the Bally's Fitness figure and the Julia Roberts smile—she knew she had to have what kids in school called a black woman's DNA. She grew up in Trenton, New Jersey, attended multiracial public schools and was even a star point guard on Ewing High's varsity girls' basketball team.

The other unusual attribute of Kitty's was her ass, the very thing that had attracted Vince Reed to her in the first place. Hers wasn't flat like a lot of white girls Reed knew. It was more of a well-rounded, heart-shaped sight to see. A sensation.

But there was more to Kitty than her appearance. She was a good con artist.

"I thought you liked sex," she said with a twisted grin across her upturned lips, the suggestion that Toy was the one who was trippin'. But even that comment was a coercive effort of drawing Toy away from the pain; a way of carving the experience with Reed into more of a rough-sex episode than abuse.

"Of course I like the sex, child. It's not that. Do you understand that he's been *beating* me? Do you not see my face? Look at my cheeks."

Kitty gave her a closer examination. "Now that you mention it, they do look a little dark. I thought that was just you in love, girl. A glow or somethin'."

"Oh, right. Some fucked-up glow *this* is," said Toy, holding up a compact with the mirror staring back at her.

"How does he hit you? With a fist?"

Toy wagged her head. "No. No not yet. It's just . . . he smacks me really hard, Kat. The fist might not be too far away."

"I have a friend or two that have been in your shoes, Toy.

And a lot of times the guy is drunk or stressed, or the woman crossed the line in one way or another. Did you—?"

"I can't believe you! You're actually saying it could be me who made him hit me? You're actually taking his side? You don't even know this guy. He's a monster when he's mad!"

"Toy, be easy. Calm yourself. I'm just sayin' that . . . well, sometimes even I could stand a slap here and there as much as I hate to admit it. I can be a total bitch at times, and I need that thug in my life who can keep me in check." Kitty realized that her statement was a reach.

"Okay, see, now *you* are a freak for pain, bitch. No— really. How you gonna say it's *okay* for a man to—" Toy cut her response short and took a hard look at her friend. "You know, I'm sorry I dragged you into this. Really." She gathered herself to leave the booth. "I better get goin'."

Kitty reached out and grabbed Toy's wrist. It was a strong hold—the first such aggression—that startled Toy. "Please. Sit," she said. "You need a friend right now, and whether you agree with me or not, the truth is gonna hurt. Now relax and stop running away from your fears."

Toy was stuck there, indecisive.

"I'm not the one who smacked you, Toy. It's me . . . Kat, your friend. Now sit and talk to me."

Toy sat and planted her face in the pocket of her palms. Then it finally came out. "It was my fault, Kat. You were right . . . I'm in denial. But I fucked up . . . didn't follow directions, and—well, he lost a lot of money because of me."

Kitty breathed an unnoticed sigh of relief. She already knew the process quite thoroughly since she'd started fucking Reed. Pretending not to know it all, she asked, "Like, what does *a lot* mean? Five thousand? Ten?"

Toy chuckled. "Girl, I think on a scale from one to ten, this was like an eighty-five."

"*Whoa.* Maybe you're lucky he didn't kill you," said Kitty.

"Well, thanks a lot!"

"Oh, stop it. You asked me for my opinion, didn't you? So I'm gonna be honest. I'm always gonna keep it real with—" Kitty's two-way pager vibrated. She looked down at her waist to check it.

CALL ME. NOW!

Kitty had ignored the previous two messages since Toy was wailing uncontrollably at the time. However, things had calmed tremendously. Maybe now was a good opportunity to call him back.

"Listen . . . I gotta make this call. Can you hold yourself together for a few minutes till I get back?"

"I'll try," Toy said, smiling slightly.

Kitty slid out from the booth, aware that Reed could turn downright ugly if his demands weren't met. From where the pay phone was, Kitty could keep an eye on Toy and still listen to Reed, the receiver having mostly disappeared under her waves of auburn hair.

"Me," she said once Reed picked up on his end of the line. "Yeah. I'm with her now. What did you do to her? She's a mess, Reed!

"Well, just so you know, we're at the Dunkin' Donuts shop. She did a bathtub full of cryin' and . . . well, now I got her calmed down. She's real easy to control . . . I gotta say, you broke her in good . . . no, not *like you did me*. Don't act like what was goin' on with you n' me, Reed. I was the freak of the week, and you were a mack on the come-up. But don't make it sound like any more than it was . . . yes . . . well . . . yeah . . . I know. You did. But so did—I'm not arguing with you. I just don't want you to look at me like you do her. I'm a lot more than her, baby. Her, Rachelle, Danielle or any other of those bimbos you fuck! I *am* calm . . ."

Kitty looked back across the shop and traded a confident smile with Toy. "Reed, I swear . . . you're gonna have to start givin' me a therapist's wages for all this *extra* shit I'm doin'." She sighed, listening to Reed's coarse tone and rolling her eyes. "Yes, boo. I can handle it. I think she's turning around now. She'll be normal again, or close to it . . . okay . . . yes. Look for us in, say, a half hour. Love you too. Otherwise, I wouldn't be doin' this."

She hung up and stood staring at nothing in particular, contemplating how she'd close the deal with Toy. Eventually, she took the stroll back to the booth, confident about her agenda.

"Stupid men. I'm tellin' you. If a guy wants to take you to bed, why can't he just *say so?* Why's it gotta be the whole beat-around-the-bush game? Just keep it real. *Jeez!*" Kitty, the actress.

Toy pretended to know what Kat was talking about, still caught up in her own dilemma.

"All right," said Kat. "Now back to you, girlfriend. You want my opinion?"

"Yeah. But go easy on me, would ya?" Toy saw the drive and confidence in Kat's eyes and gestures, and she secretly wished that she possessed the same.

"I think you're trippin'. In fact, I *know* you're trippin'. Okay, so the man smacked you around a little. But he doesn't do it every day . . . not even once a month. This was, what? The second time?"

"No. The first," Toy said.

"Okay. So, he hit you, and you're a little emotional right now. A little hurt and humiliated because this is a man you love . . . he kinda violated you . . . he shouldn't have gotten so physical."

"Exactly," said Toy, her thoughts flipping back to Reed's finger in her ass, then her mouth. *Yes. Violation is exactly what he did.*

"But you know, and I know, that men can be boys sometimes. They can get out of hand, rude and downright disrespectful too . . ."

Toy added a slow, "Mmm-hmm . . ."

"So do we toss 'em to the lions whenever they cross the line? Do we kick 'em to the curb? No—I don't think so. Lemme be honest with you, Toy. From what you say, you fucked up; you pushed your man overboard and he reacted

like the animal he is—the animal you *appreciate* him for—
and now, you're afraid and don't know *what* the hell you
want."

Toy's glassy eyes seemed stuck wide open—that revelation of truth.

"Hey. You asked me for my opinion; I'm giving it to you."
Toy said nothing.

"What's it worth to you if . . ." Kat appeared to reconsider her statement.

Toy jumped in. "No—go ahead. Say what you gotta say,
Kat. Don't hold back."

"What's it worth to you if I could, well . . . *fix* things between you and your man?"

"Fix things? How in the hell could you do that? You don't
even *know* him! You're no counselor."

"I know *you*. That's all that matters. I've known you for
almost a year now. All the stuff you've told me . . . plus I've
met him a few times. Trust me. I can handle this."

The offer hung in the air like a thick cloud.

"Wouldn't you like things to be wonderful again?"

Toy exhaled. Her eyes did most of the explaining: This was
unbelievable. "Yes, I do. But—"

"No buts, Toy. Tell me what it's worth to you for everything to be normal again."

Toy thought about it for a moment. "Everything, Kat. It's
worth *everything* to me."

"Okay, then . . . hand over Reed's digits." Kat extended
her palm, and at that precise instant Toy felt like a ball of
clay in this woman's hand. At Kat's urging she wrote down
Reed's number and passed it.

"Be right back. Don't move a muscle." Before Toy could
blink, her friend was back at the pay phone.

"He's not gonna show," Toy said, in her first show of
confidence since she met up with Kat. "You don't know him
like I do. There's, like, nothing I can offer him. Nothing he
needs from me, and nothing I can do for him that hasn't already *been* done. This whole mess has gotten way out of

control. You can't expect us both to just . . . turn back the
clock and pretend things didn't happen."

Toy and Kat had taken a taxi back to the penthouse, and
Toy was knee-deep into a tantrum, venting before her friend—
Ms. I-Can-Fix-Things—while pacing back and forth. "I
mean . . . what're you supposed to be, some witch or something? Like you're gonna go abracadabra, and poof, it's all
gonna be nicey-nicey again? If you wanted to help you
shoulda been there when he was smackin' the shit outta me!"

Toy was full of fire, a fire fueled by her fear and paranoia.
"This was a big fuckin' mistake. I shoulda never got you involved in this, Kat. Never. I can't imagine what you could've
told him on the phone that would get him to show up, like
everything is suddenly all right. Listen to me, I'm talkin' like
he's gonna show up—of course he's not comin' over here.
And we're waitin' here like two fools. Well, maybe *I'm* the
only fool . . . This is madness! Just a couple hours ago I was
packin' up and ready to leave, and now 'cuz a' you, everything is backward. This ain't how its s'pose to go. I *swear*!"
Just when Toy took a moment to catch her breath, keys could
be heard unlocking the front door.

Kitty wanted to laugh at Toy, how the poor girl went from
yelling and screaming, to—

"Oh God. It's him!" Toy's voice was low and desperate.

Kitty gestured at Toy with an abrupt pointer finger, in-
structing her to disappear while she had a few minutes alone
with Reed.

"I can't believe he's here!" Toy said in a hushed yet fran-
tic cry. She hurried off to the master bedroom.

When Kitty saw that Toy was out of sight, she scooted up
to the entrance to meet Reed. The door barely opened as she
muscled him back into the foyer, a virtual second lobby between the elevator and the penthouse threshold. She pulled
the door so that it was slightly ajar behind her.

"What's up?" asked Reed. "I thought you—"

"What's *up* is, she's scared shitless! This can go one of two
ways—either disaster, or . . . you can be the second coming

of Christ and get whatever you want from her. She's so soft, dude. Vulnerable . . ."

"That so?"

"Yeah. The way you like 'em."

"Easy with your mouth, woman. Don't let jealousy get between you and . . ." He pulled out a stack of $100 bills and peeled off ten. "Your bread and butter." He stuck the money into Kitty's cleavage.

Kitty twisted her lips, sure that there was some monkey in his remark. "Yes. I do know where my bread is buttered," she said. She took the money from where he'd stuffed it. "But what you need to know is you've been runnin' that chick up a wall, dude."

"Same shit all a you go through."

Kitty secured the cash in her jeans pocket, now confident enough to challenge him. "And you smacked *me* around?" Now she had her hands on her hips.

"You didn't give me any *reason* to. You didn't lose a car with a million dollars in it. And if you did . . ."

"If I did?" Kitty with one raised eyebrow.

There was a pause before Reed gathered the nerve he sought. Now, with his arms crossed, he replied, "If you did, I'd have smacked the shit out of you too, only harder, 'cuz you know better. *Now* what you got to say?" Reed pursed his lips and cut his eyes.

His words provoked Kitty's frozen expression. He didn't have to put a finger on her—she still felt as though she'd been hit. *Damn him!* Before Kitty could object, Reed spoke again.

"But you're the smartest cookie I got in the jar, Kitty . . . er, Kat . . . or whatever your name is." Reed's clever smirk.

Kitty took the mention of violence as a long-distant threat, and she stared at him until he turned into a fuzzy blur.

"And to be honest with you, Kitty, I don't care if she stays or goes. She's served her purpose."

"So"—Kitty put her hand against his chest—"why did you put me through all this? Why did I just do your dirty work, convincing her to—"

"Because that woman in there is Toy. *My* Toy. And I'm not done with her yet. Now, if you'll excuse me, I need to get my dick sucked."

Kitty rolled her eyes and again got in Reed's path. "There you go. It's always sex with you. Always a damned thrill! Why don't you go find a Jaguar chick for the night—that shouldn't cost you a dime. Play with *her* mind if you want."

"Oh, what're you, catchin' feelings for Toy, now?" Reed stepped back as though hit with a bright idea. "Wait a minute . . . you didn't . . . *you two?*" He eased up to her again, pointing in Kitty's face. "You haven't been eatin' that trick's pussy again, have you?"

Out of the blue, Kitty reached out and smacked Reed across the left cheek. His face barely moved, but a broad smile fixed his lips.

"Now, that's the white trash *I* know. Come on . . . slap me again. I *liked* that shit," he growled.

"Fuck you, Reed! You said you'd never mention that. You *swore!*" Kitty growled, all too aware that Toy wasn't far away.

"Yeah, so what. Sue me. I'm a crime boss, remember? My business is lies and deceit. And another thing . . ." Reed's hand clenched Kitty's throat, pinning her against the wall, toppling over a potted plant. "I made you, *bitch*. And I can *un*make you just the same. You got that?"

"I'm not afraid of you," Kitty uttered, trembling.

Reed drew her back an inch, and then thrust her back against the wall. "I *said . . . you . . . got . . . that?*"

A cross between a pant and a whimper, Kitty finally replied as he asked. When he released her she folded over, holding her neck.

No, this motherfucker didn't just . . .

"Come on, woman. You ain't hurt." Reed grabbed Kitty under her armpit, pulling her up straight. Kitty cursed Reed by her expression alone. "Aw, stop that. Stop it . . . not you too. Come on, girl . . ." He pulled Kitty into his embrace like he was doing her a favor; this was just the comfort she needed.

Unraveled and confused by Reed's brief (but violent) assault, Kitty's emotions overcame her good sense. She molded to his muscled frame, provoking memories of their on-again, off-again intimacies. For the moment, anyway, it was difficult to deny the affections of a lover.

"Don't get weak on me, boo. You're still my favorite cookie, ain't you? My vanilla fudge?"

Kitty nodded, her face rubbing out her tears against his chest, sucked further into Reed's wicked, unpredictable lure.

"Good. Good. That's more like it. That's my girl."

"Don't you ever think about the people you spit on? I really care about you, man. I want you to live forever. But . . . you've changed so much. The money . . . the power . . . it's made you so wild . . ." Kitty smoothed her hands along Reed's chest and then caressed his cheeks. Her watery eyes dug into his. Then she raised up on her toes to kiss him. It was intended to be short, but graduated into a firm, engrossing tongue-toss, speaking to the longing they both had.

When they stopped, he said, "Don't worry about me, girl. As long as you handle things like I say, we'll always be all right. Any smart person will follow the leader. I haven't steered us wrong yet, have I?"

Kitty wagged her head, easily pulled into Reed's magnetism.

"Okay, then. Run along and let me go handle my business."

"Could you be a little nicer to her? She's been through a lot."

"I'll do one better. When I finish dippin' my stick, we'll be over your place for dinner."

He sent Kitty on her way with a swift smack on the ass.

"Toy! You home?" Reed's voice was faint from where Toy stood on the terrace side of the patio doors with the aerial view of the nearby George Washington Bridge and the distant New York City skyline.

At the moment, however, nothing he had to say could influence her decision. She was standing ever-so-close to the railing, next to the patio chair she'd dragged over, intending to use it as a step—her *last* step. All she'd need to do was hoist herself up, swing a leg over—no waiting, balancing or deliberating, and just like that . . . one, two, three . . . her body would fall 30 floors.

Death. It didn't look so bad right about now. Just a second or two and her dilemmas, her issues and her life would come to an end. Eternity would begin. She'd welcome the transition with open eyes too. By her own choice.

On the terrace floor was the cordless phone; she'd tried to reach the babysitter, to speak to her daughter. But there had been no answer. And that felt like the right answer; like an omen. It was all the indication she needed.

Her life had turned upside down, all within a matter of years. She'd been through the worst of times, as far as she was concerned. And now, there was nothing left to say.

Reed's voice again.

She heard it. She didn't hear it. Didn't care. It didn't matter . . . not anymore.

So there. Stick this in your ass and suck it! With one foot on the chair, Toy hoisted her weight up, determined to get this over with.

CHAPTER

28

"Want me to take care of Lady after you're gone?"

"What—?"

Just the mention of her daughter's name made Toy turn her head, her attention shifting directly toward Reed. He leaned back, unconcerned, against the open patio door, hands in his pockets, ankles crossed. It was so casual a manner that he could've been some stranger idling by a street corner light post.

"I'm *sayin'* . . . I don't mind molding her. When she gets older I could break her in—you know how I do." Reed looked toward the sky, as if to picture the occasion.

Those same ideas, those instant images switched around in Toy's head, in a bizarre frame-by-frame spin. She had planted her foot firmly on the edge of the chair, already set to help spring herself up and over. But Reed's interruption snatched at her conscience. *Lady? Break her in? You?*

The plastic chair slid from underneath her so that she was left unbalanced. She fell to the terrace floor like a drunk Lucille Ball. Toy, as *I Love Lucy.*

"Better be careful," Reed quipped, with that utter boredom in his tone. "You could kill yourself."

Toy could hear Reed loud and clear now, her senses knocked back into some semblance of reality by the fall. His sarcasm was never more evident, and once again, Toy felt humiliated. Besides that, the sharp pain set in, shooting straight to her head by way of her bruised elbow and hip.

"Owwww!" she cried.

Reed's immediate reaction was a practiced one. He kept

his composure despite wanting to help Toy up from the floor. She was a hopeless wreck, distressed and whimpering. Pitiful. "So. I guess this means it's over between you and me . . . or, you and *anybody*, huh?"

Toy didn't answer, but she did wince within those hateful eyes, the way she cut them at Reed.

"I would help you up, but then I'd be assisting a suicide. I could get locked up for shit like that . . ."

A guttural howl escaped Toy's lips when she tried to move, and for a time Reed wondered if there was someone else nearby—on the terrace below—because never would he have imagined her this way, with the sounds and all. She tossed there, hugging herself, then pulling her body into a fetal position. The wailing progressed.

"Damn, girl. All a this because of a couple of smacks? Because of the freak shit I made you do? If I knew you were so fragile, I—"

"Y-you're sss-so cru-el," Toy cried. "All I ever did . . . everything you asked for . . . I . . . I've *always* been good to you."

With his arms folded and his tone condescending, Reed wagged his head. "The thing is, that don't impress me, Toy. If you're gonna be with me, shit like that is *expected*. I'm *supposed* to get everything I ask for. A woman is *supposed* to be good to me. What the fuck? I'm *Vince Reed*, baby. This is my world. I'm the leader, and everybody else follows—if you don't know, you need to ask somebody."

"You don't deserve me, Vince Reed!" Toy coughed up the words despite her sobbing. "You don't . . . *care* about me! All you care about is gettin' your dick sucked and hurtin' people!"

Toy's attitude went from submissive to snotty, however beaten by the fall. But Reed encouraged this; speaking out required strength, a strength that kept her responsive and alive.

"Yeah," Reed replied with an I-can't-help-myself sigh. "I do tend to use people, don't I? I guess I hurt 'em too." Along with the testimonial there was that guilty expression—a phony one—as though he was that kid caught with his hand in the cookie jar; a kid trapped in a grown man's body.

It was one hell of an act, if Reed said so himself.

Still in tears, Toy took advantage of Reed's apparent soft spot. "Yeah, you do," she quickly agreed, wiping her tears away.

"Okay. And . . . you're right, I guess. I kinda do like to get my dick sucked, but I wonder . . ." Reed let his words die off.

"You wonder what?"

"Well . . . I . . . I wonder if you love me that much where you would take you own life because of me . . . because of my fucked-up ways. Because of my twisted desires?"

There was a confusion that Toy showed, maybe receiving the mixed messages that Reed cast; maybe rejecting them.

Reed went on, "So what, I snapped. So what, I got a little wild—a million dollars ain't no chicken feed, woman. Just like a football coach has a team to run, I got a organization to run."

"A million?"

"Yeah, a million. Of course my profit would be a percentage of that, but any Joe off the street who finds money in that car? Believe me, they'll be spending that million one bill at a time."

"I didn't know," said Toy.

"You weren't supposed to know. You were only supposed to follow instructions. You were—listen. I don't wanna go back into this. You fucked up. Okay. I went off on you. Okay. You did your damage, I did mine. Here's the important question: do you wanna leave your daughter motherless for the rest of her life 'cuz a some bad decision?"

Toy was sitting cross-legged, raking her fingers through her hair.

Reed went to crouch by her side. "*Well?* What's it gonna be? Are you gonna stick around to see Lady graduate college? Or are you gonna make a mess down there next to my Lexus?"

Toy didn't answer. She simply shifted her weight so that

she was body-to-body with Reed, her face hidden. It was as if she was struggling between acceptance and her own sense of pride.

Whatever she was thinking about, Reed was sure that she didn't want to die. Reed, the negotiator.

"Cut the bullshit, Toy. Come inside, 'cuz you don't wanna kill yourself. You're just feelin' a little out of place right now. A little out of whack . . . what you need is peace of mind. You need a nice massage and a good meal—*am I close*?"

"I—*ooh!*" Toy grabbed her elbow. "All that and some TLC."

"I know just what you need. Now . . . how 'bout we start over. I'll hold back on the beat-downs, and you keep on bein' as sexy as you wanna be."

"Oooh . . . sounds good the way you say that. Can I get Jamaican rum too? So I can *really* be sexy? 'Cuz right now, I'm hurtin' somethin' vicious," said Toy.

Reed chuckled at how easy this was—the smooth talk, as if he really gave a shit. He guessed that it would take less than an hour before his dick was back at home—in her mouth.

Toy was submerged in a hot bath by five in the evening, with the menthol crystals penetrating, it seemed, every fiber of her being. It was that same effect that Ben-Gay had had on her sore muscles back in her high school cheerleading days, how the ingredients were absorbed into her pores, tingling and prickling and soothing her nerves. And right now, that certain soothing was hitting all the right spots, just when her body had given up and thrown in the towel.

Reed walked in the bathroom with an unnecessary knock on the door—a gentleman all of a sudden. His eyes roamed the bathwater with its suds bubbled up on Toy's legs and breasts.

"Comin' in?" she asked, trying to return to the spontaneity that her man was accustomed to. "There's room for two."

"No. I just brought you this. I figured you'd wanna relax your nerves." Reed bent down beside the tub and passed Toy her drink. She sipped, let out an "ahhhhh," and placed the tumbler on the ledge.

"Feelin' better?" he asked as he picked up a sponge and helped to bathe her.

"Much. Thanks."

"Your friend invited us to dinner at her place," said Reed. "I don't know how you pick 'em." He ran the sponge along her neck and down the middle of her cleavage. Toy instinctively reclined and raised one leg, hanging her foot over the edge of the tub. Reed glided the sponge along that leg, her ankle, and back down her thigh. Toy shivered and let out an appreciative moan.

"Tell me somethin'," she remembered to ask. "What exactly did she say to you, anyway? What kind of power does she have to just, well . . . turn this whole thing around like she did?"

Reed shrugged. "It's *your* friend. Maybe *you* should be tellin' *me* that."

"You sure she doesn't have you under some spell? Like, maybe she's a witch?"

Reed was amused, listening to Toy on one hand, but busy with the bathing as well; with the sponge submerged, it felt silky as he stroked her thighs, her midsection and her soft, intimate folds. "The only spell I'm under is yours, baby. It's because of you I act all crazy sometimes."

Toy smiled in a way to include both sweet and sour recollections. It had been a long, topsy-turvy day. But Reed somehow got Toy to feel good again. Sexy even. The way he looked at her naked in the tub, the soft sponge serving as his virtual hand, exploring her as if he had an all-access pass. Meanwhile, his smoky voice was a natural aphrodisiac.

"Remember earlier, at your place? When I came back from Harlem? I came out of the shower dripping wet?"

Reed's nod was hesitant, not in total agreement with revisiting the event.

"*Well* . . . I kinda got off on the stuff you did to me. How you made me . . . y'know, suck your finger. Not that I liked all of it—it was real nasty, and I had to brush, floss and wash my mouth out ten times. But except for the beating at the end? I think that was the kinkiest shit, y'know? And I was totally ready to be punished—I just didn't know how you'd do it."

"You're crazy!"

"No. I'm serious. You're a little rough with me, and I'm okay with it, as long as you don't go too far. Today, I was willing to be your love slave, Reed."

"You were, huh?"

"Mmm-hmm," she replied, wearing a girlish smile and flashing her fuck-me eyes. "You're a slut, Reed. But I love it."

Reed laughed out loud.

"What's so funny?"

"You! You? The nice girl from Jersey City? Miss All-American Girl, with the supermodel looks? You're an under-cover freak!"

"Only 'cuz you made me that way."

"Nobody makes anybody. You make your own choices in life. Okay, well, maybe I encouraged the choices. But at the end of the day, you're the one who decides to say yes or no."

Toy smoothed her wet hand along Reed's wrist, and it progressed until the buttons on his shirt were undone.

"Well . . . yes."

"Yes, what?"

"Yes, I want you to do that again." Toy's attention dropped from his face, down to his crotch. "But I want you to use *that*."

Reed smirked and raised up to his feet. "I have a better idea. Let's drop the whole slave bit, and just make love like animals."

A sensual leer in her eyes, Toy said, "Help me up, baby. My elbow is still a little sore."

Reed helped Toy; bathwater and the last of the soapsuds glistened on her skin. Then, with that pampering attitude, he took a towel from a rack and dried her.

"Remember this towel?" Toy asked with her arms up, flopped over her head to give him the most access.

"No. Should I?"

"Maybe not. I'm probably just being sentimental. This is

the towel I had on the day we first made love, almost five years ago."

"Yeah. That *was* special. Just like it always is," Reed said.

"Ohhh . . ." Toy cooed, and she molded to him. She showed her gratitude with sweet kisses that started at the earlobe. "You sure you don't want a love-slave tonight, boo? I wanna go there."

The words were escaping Toy's lips without thought. All she knew was that she was happy again. She was feeling loved once more and it felt *for real*. Her breathing was a lot deeper and her heart raced. She trembled like a virgin facing that first time, new to his touch. The next thing she realized, she was lowering herself to the floor, knees first. Reed offered his favorite pastime—a blow job. Toy went straight for his meat, unbuckling, unzipping and unleashing. His pants to his ankles, Toy used both hands to grasp and jerk him. Her mouth was sloppy-wet and wanton. As was his custom, Reed's hand brushed through her hair, massaging her scalp, pulling and releasing her head to orchestrate the pace. The passion progressed when Toy sighed and moaned, and his dick grew into a massive, throbbing weapon.

"You ready?" asked Reed.

Toy looked up at him, although her mouth and tongue remained busy. She had no idea what he meant.

He tugged her head back some so that her lips sounded something like a suction cup as they were pulled away. "So, you liked it, huh?"

It was an unexpected comment, especially since he'd just been so charming . . . so romantic.

"Turn that ass around!" he ordered.

Toy didn't have much choice since he controlled her, catching a handful of her hair, spinning her around so that, still kneeling, she was bent over the bathtub. She could feel Reed behind her, lowering himself so that he too was kneeling. He pushed Toy so that her thighs were flush up against the side of the tub, then he smacked her ass. Again. Again. Again.

"I'm glad . . . you kept . . . that ass . . . alive . . .'cuz a nigga's sho' nuff about to bust a nut!"

Toy's body went through a series of sensations, the fire where he smacked; the electricity in her nipples, in her head; and now . . . in her—

"Oh God!"

It was a choked-back exclamation; more of a forced plea that teetered on the cusp of pleasure and pain. As Toy grabbed hold of the tub, his dick pushed inside of her, filling her as far as—she *swore*—her belly button. The edges of her ass were sizzling, like a match was held to all her sensitive areas back there; but otherwise, the size of his dick thoroughly consumed her insides, touching places that had indeed been green with inactivity.

The confusion of aches and elations ended when Reed withdrew. Toy let out an exhausted gasp, nearly losing her grip, almost falling into the used bathwater.

"I'm not done, you dirty whore! Get around here and suck me off! Now!"

Smack! The unexpected sting shot through Toy's body, starting from her ass.

Within seconds, Reed was working himself in and out of her mouth, just another hole where he could spill his seed. The deeper into her throat, the better.

They arrived at Kitty's apartment in time for an eight o'clock dinner. Chicken wings—hot and spicy.

"Hot and spicy?" said Reed. "Sounds sexual."

Kitty pursed her lips to keep her mouth shut since she wanted to say, "Everything is sexual to you."

And according to the words Reed whispered to Kitty when they came in, Toy might not want to hear any references at all about sex for a couple of days. Kitty realized what Reed was talking about when she noticed Toy's discomfort, how she couldn't sit straight at the dining room table. This was the first time Reed had come to Kitty's place with Toy on his arm; the first time he'd felt comfortable with closing the gap, putting an end to those loose ends, instead of the secrecy and the phony name, Kat.

And why shouldn't he be able to bring her by? Kitty had

considered earlier. After all, he was paying her rent. As she came to think of it, he could bring the Pope, the Virgin Mary or any vagabond off the street if he wanted to, so long as he was giving up that cash.

"I was thinking," said Reed, apparently wanting to get it out of the way. "Do you mind if I use a nickname besides Kat?"

"What's wrong with Kat? That's the name my mommy gave me," she lied.

"Well, I was wondering if you'd mind me calling you Kitty. As in kitty cat?"

Kitty made a face—more marvelous acting. "If you were *my* man, with all the money I hear you got, you could call me *whatever you want*. But, since you're a friend of my friend, go ahead. Kitty will be my nickname," she said with a glance toward Toy for her endorsement. "Is there anything *else* about me you'd like to change or alter, Mr. Vince Reed?"

Sarcasm poured from Kitty. Amazingly, it was all way above Toy's head. At least she didn't give any indications that she was on to the con.

And now Toy was abuzz with laughter.

"You two are *hilarious*!"

Reed and Kitty shared a telepathic moment.

"Hey," Toy went on. "Since we're all riding the vibe up in here, maybe you could tell me what kind of spell you put on my man. We were tryin' to figure out if you're a witch or somethin'."

"God, Toy. It's nothin' like that. I just like to think I bring out the best in a man. Come on, help me with the dishes and I'll tell *all*." More sarcasm from the Kitty *Kat*.

"You two have your little girl-girl chat. Do you mind if I rest up on this couch over here?" Reed's inquiry was more of a declaration since he was already in motion, already flopping down like the beer-bellied man of the house. He made a quick cell phone call to confirm a late-night meeting, and then he dropped off into a deep nap.

"I wish I could have that talent," said Toy while she and Kitty were drying the dishes.

"What, cooking wings?"

"No. Your talent with men," said Toy as she took a dish from Kitty. "You seem to know them inside out."

"It's not all me, Toy. You must be doing something at home that made your man come back. All I did was play cupid."

"I think I'm doin' my job at home, Kat—"

"My new name is Kitty, *remember*?"

"You're serious about that, aren't you?"

"Of course, Toy. Your man is too powerful to disobey," Kitty warned. "So, Kitty it is. Now enough of that. Why don't you tell me *your* secret. What's so special at home, Toy? *I'd* like to know. Maybe then I'll be able to keep a man."

Toy bit the lower corner of her lip, sighed guiltily. "I . . . I guess I'm bending over backward for him. Isn't that what we're supposed to do? Y'know—how do they say it? A freak in the bedroom and a lady in public. I'd say I do my thing . . ."

Kitty pretended to doubt Toy.

"Okay, you beat it out of me. *I put it on his ass!*"

The two women laughed themselves to near tears.

"He really doesn't seem that bad of a guy . . . I mean, from what I can see. After all, what's a *real* relationship without a little spat here and there? Plus, he's still here, right? He's takin' care of you," Kitty pointed out.

"True."

"And don't forget about how your husband cut you off. Called it quits, didn't he?"

"Mmm-hmm. But I can't help thinking what it would've been like, y'know? To live out our fairy tale together."

"You've taken my advice before, haven't you?"

"Of course, Kitty. You're like my guardian angel, for God's sake."

Kitty contained her smile, and her face took on a serious expression. "Then get that man out of your head. I'm sorry I mentioned him. That's the past. You're in a new world now. Reed's world. You're Reed's responsibility now."

Those words echoed in Toy's head, resounding like a

thousand church bells ringing all at once but all out of sync. Hadn't she heard those exact words years ago? Wasn't it Reed—? Toy was dizzy for a moment and a glass slipped from her hand, shattering on the floor.

"Toy! You okay?" Kitty was startled, a strange look on her face. "Wait! Don't move . . . you're barefooted and I don't want you cut."

Kitty bent down to take up the larger pieces of glass. Toy braced herself, her hand gripping the edge of a counter, the other holding her forehead. Eventually, she shook herself out of the daze. *It's just a . . . a coincidence. Of course it is.* Warning bells and whistles touched Toy's conscience in one way or another, but she ignored them. *It's just a coincidence,* she told herself again.

"What's goin' on in here? A brother can't get a nap without shit crashin' in his head?"

"Nothin', babe. Just a slipup," said Toy as Reed entered the kitchen.

Kitty had grabbed a broom, was sweeping up the shards of glass. "Well, well . . . look who almost slept through the hurricane."

"Huh?"

"That meal," Kitty said. "I must've done a good job since you blacked out."

"Yeah. Plus it's been a busy day. I could stand a meal like that *every* night. I might have to discuss things with Toy . . . see if we can move you in. Havin' a cook like you might be *real convenient.* Besides, think of what a novelty you'd be: a white girl cooking *soul food* for a black couple." Reed chuckled his way out of the kitchen, leaving the two women to share a strange look.

"Excuse him, Kat. I mean, *Kitty.* He gets all stupid sometimes, especially when he drinks this tiger bone milk stuff he has."

"Tiger *what?*"

"Exactly what I said when I saw the bottle in the car. But then I notice he does stupid shit, he says stupid shit . . . anything goes with him. Then, later he's back to normal."

"Oh. Well, it's no problem. Really. It kinda sounded interesting anyway," said Kitty.

"Interesting? Tiger bone milk? It's probably just some carrot juice mixed with some kind of—"

"No, not that. The threesome. It sounds interesting."

"Right." Toy froze up. Then she huffed. "Now *you've* even gone and lost your marbles." She wagged her head and avoided eye contact as she wondered, *What is the world coming to?*

Some time later, Reed was reclined in the passenger seat of the Lexus. Toy was driving. The bulge grew in his pants. He'd gulped some of his notorious milk and seemed to stare off into the night. It was that night when Reed came to some decision in his own mind . . . when he psyched himself into a fit and ordered Toy to pull the car over . . . It was that night that once again in his very unpredictable way, Reed flipped again. Toy simply did as she was told, becoming the butt-end recipient of this man's pent-up rage. Again.

When that River Road episode ended, Toy found herself back in that miserable crisis, lost in her yesterdays, overwhelmed with worry about her tomorrows and so removed from the present that she could've disappeared.

CHAPTER

29

In the early months of his prison sentence, Colin had a strange feeling of being both guilty *and* innocent. Guilty, because *yes*, he was indeed involved in the counterfeit money scheme. But he also felt innocent, since he had no choice but to bear the weight of accountability for the entire Vince Reed operation. Not that he was a soldier or missionary anymore to Vince Reed, but he'd long ago realized that you had to take this kind of hit like a man. You couldn't cry now, not *after* shit got hot and messy, telling on every last soul just to get another chance at freedom. It was people like that who were labeled as weasels and rats, the same people who would sell their mommas to the burning flames of hell to save their own necks.

For Colin, this was no way to live. He'd have to deal with it. That was his resolve. Everything was pinned to him; the huge amounts of money, the intricate network of associates, and the smoking-gun evidence that was conflicted that night at Club Jaguar. All he could do now, all he had left, was to have faith in the appeals process. He could only hope that there would be a reversal somewhere along the way; that his sentence would be vacated or, at least, cut down. But Colin also knew, as it was with most appeals, that the turnover rate on convictions was less than ten percent.

Disappointment after disappointment darkened his hopes with every passing month. There seemed to be a convict with bad news to bear whenever mail call was announced. And now, since close to 25 percent of his bid had already been served, and since he'd settled in enough to see his chances of surviving prison were better than average (so long as he played by the rules, respecting others and minding his own business), Colin had no choice but to use his energy for something that might pay off now or, at least, in the near future.

If you can't do the time, don't do the crime, was the bitter, after-the-fact, jailhouse saying. And Colin knew damned well that he had done the crime; maybe not to the extent that he'd been convicted for, but a crime nonetheless.

Now in a different state of mind, Colin swiftly shifted gears. He read just as relentlessly as he wrote. He did his best to stay on top of current events—his effort not to become institutionalized, dependent and complacent with that easily adopted prison mentality. A state that keeps grown men fighting over the use of the television, board games, the telephone and other government-owned property, such as extension cords for floor machines, brooms, mops and even hot water. Colin swore he had seen it all. And since he did, he also knew how to stay trouble-free—"sucka-free," they called it.

But still, there was always some asshole; some disrespectful, inpatient, ignorant imbecile, who made it a point to throw a monkey wrench into doing "good time." And this meant that some fights just couldn't be avoided. After all, it wasn't the time that was difficult, since to exist was a reality that you exercised whether you did it in jail or on the street. It was *other people* who made time difficult.

Even though the answer to doing time might be to stay away from others, you still had to cohabitate, communicate and cooperate. Be it cultural differences, lifestyle differences; whether you were wealthy or impoverished; whether you were someone who had been places in life, or if you were one of many who never left your small town, these were all men that the prison experience made into a tossed salad. These were the men Colin would have to deal with for the length of his residency.

Just as Colin observed and experimented with the worst examples of humanity, those surrounding him taught him about who he *didn't* want to be like as well as who he *did*. It helped him to formulate a standard of living, a lifestyle. He unconsciously studied those who exemplified a balance of sound mind and body; men who took expert care of themselves, and who respected others. He learned some of humanity's most essential virtues: compassion, self-awareness and hard work.

He met Cliff, and from him, Colin absorbed a hunger for wisdom. He met Sonny, and from him, Colin learned discipline and how to develop physical power. Chris was a financial wizard. Rasheed had been all around the world. Young Kim, a Korean who was as much Korean as he was American, exhibited great integrity and character, and so did some of the Mafioso, the Africans and the Chinese. There were also patterns. Colin could understand the poverty-consciousness of blacks, and he was easily offended by the better-than-thou attitude of some Jewish extremists. He saw Dominicans as mostly loud and obnoxious, and Rastafarians as hell-bent on expressing themselves through rich beliefs, a fiery attitude and, of course, the rebel dreadlocks.

Of course these were merely isolated opinions, based on cult groups—just a percentage of what the real world was like. Still, they were Colin's truths nonetheless. He had to live with these men day after day, and he could only see it in his own unique way.

Beyond Colin's thorough education on human nature, there were administrative controls in place. Periodically, counselors reviewed his institutional adjustment. And so, it was inevitable that with good behavior, his custody level would drop. When points dropped, convicts were transferred to more appropriate facilities in order to pressure institutional safety. From Illinois, Colin was sent to Allenwood Penitentiary in Pennsylvania. He stayed there for 16 months and then was transferred again to Fairton FCI, a medium-security facility where prisoners were called inmates instead of convicts.

In Fairton, the climate was overcrowded and stressful,

only there weren't as many stabbings or fights as there were in the penitentiary, otherwise known as the "big house." In any of the big houses, especially in the lower custody facilities, the highest priority might be to avoid or confront troublemakers while still making the most of the time.

One adjustment after another, Colin hoped finally that Fairton would be one of the last, if not the last transfer he'd be subjected to. He could get a lot done here.

All inmates were required to have a work assignment, jobs that in one way or another served in the upkeep of the institution. Colin assumed a clerk's position at the institution library, enabling himself enough leisure time—even his hours at work were leisurely—to focus on his writing. After more than five years with old-head Lee's box of paperwork in tow, Colin was able to construct four full-length books, which according to those around him were "guaranteed" to be successful.

Naturally, being so accustomed to the types of spins, mind games and confidence schemes of jail, Colin couldn't allow everyone to read his work. So for the most part, when he wrote it was for the purpose of amusing himself. His belief was that if it earned his interest . . . if it made him smile or gave him satisfaction, then it would do the same for others. Maybe many others. Lee's spirit would live on through Colin.

"Williams, they got mail for you up in the unit office," said Carter, an inmate from Colin's unit—a muscular, six-foot-tall man, with skin a few shades darker than Colin, the color of whole wheat bread, and a 50-year prison term to serve.

"Really? Probably junk mail. *Vibe* magazine tryin' to get my money again."

"Naw. I think it's legal."

Colin couldn't imagine what that might be. And just the thought of it being from court, or a lawyer, caused him writer's block. He packed up his notebooks and took aggressive steps across the prison compound to his housing unit.

"Yo, C.O., you had mail for me?"

The correctional officer had a small pile of mail on his desk that would require little effort to pick through. Everyone knew of Williams, the author, so the officer didn't need to ask his name, even in a housing unit of 300 men.

"Here ya go, Williams. Good luck."

"Thanks," Colin replied and disappeared with his head and eyes focused on the letter. It was from the Court of Appeals. He couldn't wait to open it.

Order

This matter having come before the court on the petition of Colin Williams for relief pursuant to 28 U. S. C. 2255; and the government having moved to dismiss the petition pursuant to Federal Rule of Civil Procedure ("Rule 12 6"); and this court having carefully considered the arguments submitted in support of, and in opposition to, the petition; and for the reasons expressed in my opinion issued this same day; IT IS ON THIS DAY ORDERED that COLIN WILLIAMS' petition to vacate, set aside or correct the sentence imposed is hereby, GRANTED; it is also ordered that the government's motion to dismiss Colin Williams' petition is hereby DENIED.

Hon. Judge Berikow

Colin's eyes did a double-take. He'd seen enough of other appeals to know what this letter meant. In the days to come, he'd expect information about a hearing that would have him resentenced or retried.

But there were other concerns.

Prison was a place where bad news made you one of the crowd, and where good news made you an outcast. Bad news fed the wheels and gears of the misery machine. Good news provoked jealousy, envy and even hate.

Colin's time amongst men had shown him an occasion where one twenty-year-old's news from the court made another convict so upset that the good news never saw the light of day. The twenty-year-old never made it to his court appearance. He never lived to see age twenty-one. Another occasion of good news provoked an argument and subsequent stabbing. The court date was delayed but for the prisoner's extended stay in the prison hospital.

Colin stuffed the letter from the court in his back pocket when the knock came at his cell door. (The FCI had doors with small windows as opposed to the gates and bars of the pen.)

"Come in," Colin called out, already seeing Carter's big head through the mirror before him.

"Hey. Good news?" he asked. "I don't mean *my* good news, I mean, did *you* get good news?"

"Ain't nothin'. More back-and-forth shit on the appeal. You know the story."

"You wouldn't just up and disappear on a nigga, would you, son?"

"Come on, Carter. You's my dog. We doin' this thing together, ya dig?" Colin put his fist out for a pound.

"Dig it. Wassup wit' yo girl? How was the visit?"

Colin was accustomed to these conversations, the trite ones in search of a glimmer of hope. News about a good visit, a good letter from home or even a money slip coming in was something that was within reach regardless of one man's plight with the justice system. Even a new trial was okay news, in that it wasn't a promise of freedom.

The only promise of freedom that a comisserator would find acceptable was an M.R. date. Mandatory Release meant the very last date a man could be incarcerated. It was the very end of the sentence. You paid your dues. All else was but false hope, a frequent non-event that prisoners either grew callous toward or fooled by. Carter's M.R. date was close to 40 years away. And that was only because he'd already served ten on the fifty.

"To tell you the truth, it's startin' to burn out. That girl been comin' to see me for years . . . sends me money, cards, all that. She done explained to me every sex act that she's ever done and ever will do to me, and . . . it's played out, dog."

"Yo—but you about halfway done with your bid. Might

as well hang on to her till you get home. Twist it out, nah-mean?" Carter chuckled as he said this.

"You need Jesus, man," Colin said jokingly. "But, for real . . . I've been thinkin' about my wife and daughter. Man, I've done missed half of her childhood. See, that's what really matters. Kitty? She ain't nothin' but somethin' to get me by. But my daughter? Even though I ain't see her for half a decade, she's still my blood. My eyes. My ears. All that. I'll love Lady till the day I die—no matter where she lays her head."

"What about Toy?" Carter asked. He was one of the few people who was privileged to hear the whole of Colin's life story. He was the only one who was so much into the details; Colin knew that the painful sentence forced Carter to stop and smell the roses. Wherever they were.

"Well . . . we're still husband and wife. Even though I guess I want to see her once more . . . you know, to at least tie up loose ends. I loved her when I was out there."

"But she dissed you, dog. She lost faith."

"Yeah, but a woman's always gonna be emotional. You never know why she makes one decision or the next. Sometimes I think it has to do with which way the wind blows."

"Dig that. I don't know how my girl does it. All that time I got. She's all devoted, sends me all these intimate photos, visits all the time . . . money slips . . ."

"Face it, dog, you got a solider with you."

"More like a missionary," Carter said, knowing he was blessed.

"I wish I had that," Colin said. "I *wish* . . . I had that."

Colin was kept in the dark about when he'd be picked up—a writ, they called it—and bussed back to court for the hearings. The Bureau of Prisons always went out of the way to hold back on those details; an effort to throw off any attempt at an ambush. The only thing Colin had to go by was the court date. A date that was eventually postponed once, twice and even a third time. That was nothing new in a world where men were numbers, and where liberty was merely a shoulder shrug from reality.

The only sure thing was how he was living now. The writing kept him unconcerned with dates. The only thing that mattered was how much time was left in a day, and what could be accomplished during that time. "Readers are leaders," a quote said. And if that was the case, Colin figured on being a leader.

"Williams! R&D," the correctional officer announced over the unit loudspeaker.

An R&D call meant that he'd be packing up to leave soon. *Great. Now it's all out in the open,* he thought. Colin responded to the call as if it was news to him; that way those around him wouldn't feel slighted or that he was attempting to sneak off without saying anything.

"I just want you to know that I ain't no fool, dog. I knew you was headed out. I didn't know when, but I knew," Carter later told Colin in a friendly way.

"Yeah, but I didn't really want to rub it all in your face. You my man, ya know? And it's hard to deal with getting to know you so well, and then knowing I'd have to leave you behind with all this bullshit."

"Don't sweat that, man. Just go in front of that judge and give 'em hell. Make 'em let you up out of here . . . and when you get to the bricks, live for the both of us. Do the right thing so you ain't never gotta be back here. It may sound crazy, but I don't ever wanna see your face again. Except in photos."

It was painful for Colin to smile. He could easily see himself in Carter's shoes, stuck in an environment of men who had mostly set out to do the best they knew how just to accumulate life's resources—in many cases, to feed their families. Colin could see that these men were the scapegoats of society. Some deserved what they got . . . if life's universal balance was the rule. But in another sense, Colin knew that these men did no different than men who had killed other men to call America their own. They were no different than moonshiners who broke the law enough to eventually capitalize on the entire liquor industry they'd eventually control. These men did nothing different than the U.S. government did, selling arms to other nations and regimes, or selling drugs for one reason or another. In Colin's eyes, the greatest institutions had committed the world's greatest crimes, yet they were powerful and financially able enough to hold themselves above the same consequences that they imposed on those men who tried and even succeeded in a lesser manner in the way of financial ability. In a world so proud to author what or who is right or wrong, it was still impossible to know who or what indeed had the authority to make such claims.

The morning after Colin packed his belongings, he was handcuffed, shackled and set on a bus headed for the Bergen County Jail, where he'd be held for this and that court appearance. Nobody back in Fort Lee, not in Vince Reed's organization, and not even Kitty, knew of Colin's whereabouts, or that he faced possible release.

At the jail, federal prisoners were treated differently from others. They were separated from local offenders with their assaults, moving violations, domestic crimes and other misdemeanors. They were kept in segregated rooms, locked down for 23 hours a day. The guards were insensitive to the needs of federal prisoners as opposed to the locals who they even knew as neighbors outside of the jail. Colin recognized the bias immediately, how some guards knew prisoners on a first-name or nickname basis, with that whole long-time-no-see acquaintance between them.

Meals were carted to the tiers where the segregated prisoners were held and passed through an opening in the door. The regular prisoners, those who were residents of the jail, served as orderlies, assisting the guards with the menial tasks such as food service. Beyond meals, the orderlies swept and mopped the tiers. When the guards weren't watching they'd slip notes back and forth between cells, make arrangements for cigarettes and cater to other prisoners' needs, such as toilet paper, pinkie-sized pencils, toothbrushes and toothpaste or soap.

"Ay, yo . . ." An orderly was close to Colin's window, pushing a broom and faking out the guards down at the desk on the main floor. "Psssst!"

"What up?" Colin asked, finally waking to the orderly's signal. "Yo . . . dude down the way says he knows you. Says his name is Brinton."

"Brinton?" Colin tried to recall the name. "I don't know anybody by that name."

"Aiight . . . cool. Just passin' the message, dog."

"Yo—ask him where he knows me from. Maybe that'll help."

The orderly pushed his broom along the tier, making a convenient stop about ten cells away. A moment passed and he went farther, made a U-turn and headed back to Colin's cell.

"He says he used to work for Reed. Wants to know if you can take your hour break at five." He pushed the broom a little farther. "I'll talk to the guard. Don't worry."

"Thanks."

Between 4 and 9 P.M., three inmates were let out of their cells during each hour. It was time used to make collect phone calls, to take showers or to simply sit and watch television or talk.

Colin immediately recognized the face of the prisoner who said he'd worked for Reed. He was the same short and stocky cat Colin had first observed years earlier in Club Jaguar, asking that woman at the bar if she could guess which $20 bill was real and which was fake. The same one who'd introduced Colin to Reed for the first time.

"Damn, man. Seeing you is like seeing a ghost! How long's it been?"

"Six years."

"Man. A lot been happenin' in six years," Brinton said. "Dude's operation went *nuclear*! Remember the deal he had on scrap paper from the Treasury Department?"

"In Philly?"

"Yup. Well, as soon as that started comin' in . . . after it was recycled n' shit, things started kickin' off *major*! I figure the whole operation was doin' over a hundred, maybe two hundred mill a month. Truckloads of bills was shipped to like every fuckin' state on the East Coast."

"Oh yeah?"

"Yup. We started bringin' in more associates on the low and midlevels and—"

"You know anything about my trial?" Colin interrupted.

"Yo! That shit was crazy what you did, man! You's the most stand-up ma-fucka I ever knew."

"How's that?"

"I'm talkin' about how you took the fall for Reed so the business would be allowed to move to the next level."

"What?"

"Well . . . you were the one, right? I mean, you took—"

"Listen, Brinton. Where'd you hear all of this?"

"It was a few nights after the big raid at Club Jaguar. Reed had this big meeting with all his associates. We toasted you and everything. He called you the hero. Said you'd put on an act through trial and all that, just so the feds would ease up on the investigation and eventually close the case."

"Goddamn."

"He even hired a lawyer for you to play along. At least that's what I heard. I wasn't a big dog . . . just movin' bills, ya know?"

Colin felt funny inside. "So why are you here?"

"They caught me spendin' a twenty. They arrested me and said I'd be here till I told where I got it. But I know I'ma get out in a few days. Ain't shit."

Colin charged Brinton's words to naivety, even if his inside information was 100 percent on point. "You ever met a woman named Toy from Jersey City?"

"Of course! That's *Reed's* bitch. He had that ass whipped nice, hangin' on his arm at the clubs, at the restaurants, all that. I saw a video this freak did for him—a porno joint! Yo! The bitch was doin' another woman . . ."

Colin was livid! His lips pursed tight. His toes curled in the blue skips he'd been issued, and his stomach felt knotted up with a three-day hunger.

"And she was all tied up with duct tape over her mouth . . . and Reed was fuckin' her too!" Brinton said.

"Stop-stop-stop. Are you sure her name is Toy?"

"Looks like that Miss America chick—the one who was thrown out for the lesbian pics."

"Vanessa Williams."

"Yeah! Yo! But Vanessa came off! Albums, videos, movies. She made it big-time . . ."

Colin's mind was somewhere in outer space. He was beyond the confines of the jail . . .

"But Toy? Yeah, sexy motha—"

"And this is Reed's girl?"

"I ain't seen her in the past few months, but yeah, I guess."

Colin's head was flooded with imagery. "But didn't the orderly say you *used* to work for Reed?"

"Yeah. There's . . . well, one of his mid-level women is doin' her own thing. Some trick named Kitty."

"Don't tell me: white girl. Pretty. Straight blondish-red hair?"

"Yup. She started her own thing. Just a piece of the action. But Reed don't know about it."

"And she's *still* working with Reed?"

"I dunno—maybe. Maybe not. Hard to tell with this trick. She got a lotta game with her."

"Hmmm. I bet."

Back in the isolation of his jail cell, Colin tried to sleep himself away from the reality. But he could only lie there with his eyes open, thinking about all that had happened to him, all the many changes that were once his life back home. He wondered how Toy could fall so deep so fast. He wondered about his daughter. And when he was angry enough to want to let go of the horrors he imagined about Toy, he began to think of himself. How did all of these revelations figure into his future? What would happen if he was released?

Colin had so much rage built up inside. So much fire in his heart when he thought of Vince Reed . . . when he pictured the man's face. There came a point when he decided that it wouldn't matter what happened in the courtroom. Hold him or let him go—if it took a lifetime, Reed would answer for destroying his life.

CHAPTER

30

Toy still had the letter in her purse. She just didn't know where to send it. She didn't know where he was. Kitty said she'd help Toy find out where her husband was being held, in what prison, but it had been a while since she'd seen Kitty. The only thing Toy could do to remember Colin was to read the letter to herself. It was her way of justifying all that had happened.

Hi husband,

I'm sorry, sorry, sorry for not being there for you. Just remember there is no love lost. Since you left us, my life has been one big roller coaster of confusion. And as the days, weeks, months and years pass, I am feeling guilty about everything that's going on in my life. Guilty for not being a mother instead of letting other people raise our daughter. Guilty for not going to college when I first met you, to start a career. Guilty for sleeping with other men.

I hate you, and love you at the same time. Please don't tell me it's okay either, because it's not. Regardless of what I am going through, I find it very hard to communicate with you, and thinking like that should never cross my mind. I feel guilty for going on with my life. You've been gone for longer than I've known you, and I feel trapped. You said to have faith and eventually things would be okay. I would really like to trust you on that. But that's easier said than done. I miss you, but I'm also dying every day without you . . . without my husband . . . without the father of my child.

Please respect about other men. As I said, things have been confusing . . . and I have to be honest about the other men.

I was with Reed. It was good at the start. He was paying all the bills and even Lady's tuition when she started school. He bought me an Expedition. He covered the rent for the penthouse. He did so, so much, Colin. And when you were sentenced, he was the shoulder I cried on.

But it turned sour. I won't get into the details, but I'm stronger because of the experience. A stronger woman.

I went back to work, Colin. I'm back at Nuts & Screws. Mr. Harris said I still got what it takes to do the job: tits and ass. He's not disrespectful, he just keeps it real, ya know?

Now I'm seeing this other man. It's another strange situation that I won't get into details about, but again, it's paying the bills.

WHERE HAVE YOU BEEN?

I used to write you and get your letters every day. But then you wrote that nasty letter, telling me to get lost, telling me to leave you alone. And I even heard you had someone else. What was I supposed to do? You never called when I gave the lawyer my new phone number. I couldn't believe you! After we committed to one another. I would've been with you regardless of the 14 years. Regardless!

I'm still in the penthouse, Colin. And you know the address too. So I hope to hear from you one way or another. By the way, Lady is doing great. This was supposed to be a short note to share my feelings with

*you. But no matter what happens in the years to come,
I will always be in love with you.*

*Your wife,
Toy Williams*

"It's good to have you back, Toy. How long's it been? Like
five years? When you decide to bite the bullet, *let me know*.
That's the day I'ma quit, 'cuz with you out there on stage,
the game is gonna get shut down," joked N'Tasha.

Toy giggled and left the bathroom feeling a lot better, despite her burdens.

Donald Berkshire's nickname at Nuts & Screws was
Donny. It was as secretive as he chose to be about who he
was. If anyone asked what his field of business was, he'd
usually say pharmaceuticals, which wasn't at all a lie, but a
boring conversation in a titty bar.

Toy was coming back to tend bar now—T, he called
her—looking incredible in a money-green chiffon dress with
white polka dots. She also had a matching scarf, which she
used to tie her hair back in a bouncing ponytail. She wore
black leather sandals with wooden heels. Her toenails were
painted emerald green as well.

Donald couldn't stand when Toy had to leave the bar for
this reason or that, but at the same time, their conversation
was good. He wanted to see her today and until now he had
been gathering up enough nerve. It was just that Toy was so
striking, so authoritative. She mesmerized him like his wife
never had.

"Can I get a kick, precious?"

"Anything for you, Donny," Toy replied and turned to the
stock of liquors, swaying her ass in a way she was sure
would excite him. Donny was more than just a "regular" to
Toy. He was her bread and butter.

Before they really got to know each other, he merely made
light conversation when he showed up once or twice a week.
But in the past year, ever since Toy's return, Donny came by

five to six times a week. Toy was now familiar with his dapper style, his tweed-suited business attire. Most times, he had his shirt and tie fixed to the nines. His idea of hanging loose was a loosened tie and his top dress shirt button undone.

Their dialogue touched on everything from the civil rights era, to racism in America, to the various terrorist acts around the globe. Today, it might be a discussion about a news item: someone going postal on their former boss, a group of police officers assassinating an innocent man or a young boy who got back at a bully with his father's assault rifle. Tomorrow the two might talk about this dancer or that, and how the patrons in the club were so diverse. They'd talk about the lyrics in some of the music playing on the jukebox. Nelly. Missy Elliot. Jay-Z and Madonna. Yesterday had been a different story altogether.

Donny came in with his tie loosened, shirt button undone, and he had a few shots of Captain Morgan's Spiced Rum. He'd brought a handful of $20s and $100s (real money), and urged Toy to say things that she might do with him if he was 40 years younger—a college boy.

Toy had done this quite a few times already with Donny, and could always look forward to being paid well for her innuendos. So today, the day after, Toy knew Donny was *hot*. She knew that he'd gone home frustrated and that he'd be back today for something more. Her knowing this was almost like inside information on a hot stock pick, one that would shoot to the sky in a hurry.

Toy poured Donny another "kick" of Malibu Rum, his choice drink of the day, and leaned over the bar with folded arms. Her cleavage was only two feet from his beak. "You all right?" she asked, her interest not being anywhere near the compassion in her words.

"Oh—sure. I was . . . I was just wondering if I could see you today."

"After work?" she asked.

Donny nodded and took a swig of the rum at the same time. A shamed man's answer.

"I'm not sure. There's the babysitter, ya know?"

"No problem," he muttered abruptly.

"And, uh, my rent?"

"Got that in my pocket. Three thousand, right?"

"Mmm . . . I don't know, Donny. Can you respect me for doing this with you—what is it—a half a dozen times now?"

"Oh, T, I respect you more than you can know. The feelings you give me are out of this world. With you, I don't *ever* need Viagra to—you know—make me happy."

Donny was turning pink in the face, and Toy knew he was embarrassed. She knews she was doing her job. As Mr. Harris would say: "It's all about tits and ass."

"Throw in the payment for the Expedition and it's a go."

"You just tell me how much, precious. Whatever you want."

Donald Berkshire, the number two man at Pfeister Pharmaceuticals, was *loaded*. Toy knew it, even if she pretended not to care. He told her about his position at Pfeister, a Fortune 500 company, many times. He'd explained how the corporation serviced hospitals throughout the world with medical supplies and the base products with which pharmacists made prescriptions drugs.

But Toy shrugged at all the yadda-yadda. She could care less. All she was interested in was some conversation that challenged her, something more than the ordinary shit that patrons came to the counter with.

However, once she and a friend surfed the Internet and Googled Pfeister, things changed. She saw Donald Berkshire, the CEO. Donald Berkshire, the happily married husband and father of four. Donald Berkshire, the well respected member of the Pharmacists of America's board of directors. He was a noted philanthropist. Toy, however, knew the Donald that the world didn't know. She knew how he lusted after the dancers and made eyes at Toy more than a few times. Toy knew Donny, the philanderer.

Toy encouraged him. She stood by to hear his woes and peeves.

Where Toy was deserted by her husband, Donny felt imprisoned by his wife. Where Toy had her whole life ahead of her, Donny wanted to preserve whatever possible was left in his.

She had first thought Donny nauseating to look at, deserving of no more than the average attention span between bartender and patron. He had pink blemishes freckling his white skin and wrinkles about his forehead and all over the backs of his hands. His lids hooded over his blue eyes, their whites blotched by time. The lines at his cheeks and at the sides of his mouth were deep, and his lips were hardly visible. The skin under Donny's neck and chin hung and wagged at the slightest movement. His nose was warted and reddened. And his white and gray hair was pulled across like a wayward toupee so as to hide the obvious bald spot at his crown. Donny made no bones about his looks. In fact, he joked about them from time to time, saying that Toy should look so good at sixty. And he'd claim to have jogged ten miles just before he came by. All kinds of silly things he'd say just to pass the time. To make Toy smile.

And she smiled. She tolerated Donny's old age and his opinion just to get to where she was now. In his pockets.

Toy and N'Tasha strutted out of the club together that night. They split up (with kisses) at the curb; N'Tasha went for the nearest of the waiting taxicabs, and Toy went to the silver Cadillac Deville.

"Chicken shit, did you say?" Toy cut a devil's smile at N'Tasha as she reached for the door handle.

It was 8 P.M. Showtime.

"Whooo-eee . . . what a day," Toy said. She shut the door and leaned over to kiss Donny's cheek. Always the cheek. "Take me to Riverside," she directed.

Donny had made it clear how he liked Toy being authoritative. It was a drastic difference from what he was accustomed to on a day-to-day basis at Pfeister and at home.

"Yes, precious."

"And don't call me precious so much. It irritates me."

"Sorry."

The two went directly to the Riverside Restaurant, on the bank of the Hudson, where they had window seats that offered a brilliant view of Manhattan's twinkling skyline.

While Toy looked over the menu, Donald got out his cell phone. Toy lowered the menu to cast a scornful gaze at him. The waitress was standing by in the meantime, her eyes darting back and forth as if at a tennis match.

"Just activating the voice mail," Donny said, knowing he'd done wrong.

"You could've done that earlier," Toy said. "Would you excuse us for a moment," she asked the waitress, jumping from one extreme to the next with her salty tone.

The waitress walked away, feeling both embarrassed and disciplined.

"Let me tell you something, Mr. Big. You don't do business when we're out at a restaurant, I don't care if you *are* playing with your voice mail." Toy put her hand out. "Hand it over," she ordered. *"Now!"*

Donny hesitated, but inevitably his cell phone wound up in Toy's palm. She was using the cell phone as a pointer now.

"You need to have a little more respect for a woman. What—do you think I'm your little push-around?" People began staring from their nearby tables. Toy didn't care. "I just finished a long day's work. I'm hungry, I'm stressed and I need a freakin' shower."

The polka dot dress came to life as Toy got up with the cell phone in hand. She strutted a few feet away to the giant fish tank and dramatically dropped it in the bubbling water, frightening the fish. Just as easily, she strutted back to the table and cradled Donny's chin in her hand. "Now get some food in my body and let's get on with this."

Dinner was expensive. Toy picked the most exquisite dish she could find on the menu. Lobster tails and crab legs. She had Donny pick the wine because he was good at that sort of thing. When dinner was through, Toy told the waitress to bag everything. Ghetto. Then, when she returned, Toy told Donny to pay her a $100 tip. The waitress rejected it at first, but Donny beckoned her as though his life depended on it, and she went ahead and took it.

"The Motor Inn . . . near the G.W.," Toy said once they were back in the Cadillac. Then she put her head back against the seat, and closed her eyes. "I want quiet so I can rest. It might be a long night," she told him, already into some shut-eye.

Toy eased her eyelids open once the car door closed. Next thing she knew Donny was loping across the motel parking lot toward the office. It was a relief that he had left her alone, and it was nerve-racking to keep up this act. This wasn't her. He wanted bold, aggressive and bitchy—something that Toy figured was N'Tasha's speed—yet Toy was just the opposite; laid-back, quiet and kindhearted.

Next to the nervousness, Toy had other things on her mind. For one, there was Lady, under someone else's watchful eye while Mommy was out with her new sugar daddy. And second, there was this cloud that she kept with her, one that was ready to reveal how this was too good to be true. The fast money. Getting something for doing nothing. All of the above. She just wanted to finish this and get home.

"Keep your mind on the money," she told herself. "Pretend he's a dog," she remembered N'Tasha saying.

"All set," he said upon returning to the car.

"Did you get what I asked for?" Toy asked.

"I did. It's in the trunk. Just a moment . . ."

He came back with a gift box with LORD & TAYLOR printed on its face and a giant bow.

"For you," he said, watching for her reaction after he passed it over.

Toy pulled the bow off as though it was life's greatest hindrance, and lifted the top off to reveal red tissue. She dug in and pulled up a silky black outfit—a bra and thong set that played against the skin of her hand as diamonds would to the eyes. Toy tried to hold her excitement in, but couldn't. He'd gotten just what she'd asked for. Spared no expense. She smiled. But just as she did she noticed the price tags still on the lingerie. Toy already knew that the bra retailed at $500, and the thong at $190. But in a snap decision, seeing the price tags was enough to trigger her, enough to have her keep up with the performance.

"What is this?" she asked, instantly switching her smile to a frown—her eyes from stars to flames.

"I'm sorry?" Donny's face turned crimson red.

"The price tags, mister. You left the price tags on! What is that, like evidence that this is expensive? That you paid big money for it? Well, I'll tell ya what, you old fool . . . you can take your five-hundred-dollar bra"—Toy took the bra and affixed it around his head and face—"and you can take your two-hundred-dollar thong"—now she pulled the thong over his head so that the crotch was fitted over his forehead and nose—"and you can stuff 'em both up your ass! Now take me home! Deal's off!"

She turned her head toward the window, away from Donny, with the neon motel sign looking at her from the other end of the lot.

"I . . . I'm . . . T, I didn't . . ."

"Yeah, yeah, yeah, you didn't . . . you *didn't* think, asshole. Now do as you're *told*. Take me home!"

Donny blinked his reddened eyes; stretching them open wide at Toy's sudden outrageousness. He began to get out of the car.

"Where you goin'?"

"To return the keys to the room," Donny said, thinking he was doing right.

"Do it after you bring me home."

Again his eyes widened; he pulled the door closed.

River Road stretched along the back of the Hudson and was lined with newly developed housing complexes, a shopping center and some office buildings, all taking advantage of the view of the water and the city on the other side. The Riverside Restaurant was on River Road. So were a number of roadside rest stops—the infamous lovers' lanes. Toy knew this dark stretch of road from that night more than three or four years earlier when Vince Reed took her from behind.

But while Reed was history (as far as she was concerned), the memory was still with her. And now, on this dark night years later, that memory—however rough it was—excited her. It gave her ideas. "Pull over," she said. "Over there in the rest area."

Donny had been silent for the past ten minutes, completely confused. This made him more confused. He didn't speak. He only did as he was told.

Donald put the Cadillac in park and the motor hummed quietly. He was stuck on what Toy wanted next. Wondering. Curious. Nervous.

"Do you have one of those classical music CDs you told me about?

"Eh . . . sure," he said, and he reached over to the glove compartment.

There was a plastic caddie inside that held a half dozen selections. Toy took one out. It said Moscow Radio Symphony Orchestra. She pushed the CD into the car's CD player and listened to selections until she was satisfied. When she found one, the digital display on the device read: "Piano Concerto Symphony 1." The music began and she turned up the volume until it filled the Cadillac. It was as if the orchestra was a few feet away; not loud, but enough to seize the senses. Enough that her commands could still be heard.

"You're sorry, aren't you?"

"Oh yes, preci—I mean, Toy. I can't imagine what I was thinking. I'm so stupid . . . I wasn't . . ."

"Go on . . . tell me what a fool you are."

"I am . . . oh—I am the biggest fool, Toy. How could I have been so—"

"Dumb?"

"Yes. Yes, I was dumb."

"And arrogant?"

"Yes. I was arrogant. I should've known better."

"And you have shit for brains."

Donald Berkshire, CEO of Pfeister . . . 1,200 employees with locations in New York, Louisiana and Europe . . . the number-two man . . . with children successful enough to raise grandchildren . . . the whole American Dream sitting there in the driver's seat, turning white with shame and answering, "Yes. I have shit for brains."

While he was confirming the labels that she named him, and while the music in the vehicle crept through its violins and cellos and trumpets, all serving their impact alongside the piano's solo, Toy had been undressing Donald's upper body. His chest was bare now. And she fixed him so that his necktie remained with the shirt, its blue and yellow designs a mere gray and white in the gloomy climate of the front seat. Only the moonlight (pieces of it blocked by the trees) provided slight visibility under that darkened sky. Whatever glow did make it through ignited the polka dots on Toy's dress. She fixed the bra and thong back on Donald's head.

"Okay, shit-for-brains." Toy sat away from Donny now, her back to the passenger's side door and window, her legs stretched, one on the floor, and the other lifted to where her heeled foot was flat on his thigh. "Turn around. Face me so I can look at your lame ass."

Donny did as he was told. One leg bent on the seat and the other still in the well under the steering wheel, his back against the driver's side door and window. Now Toy's foot and shoe was wiggling against the older man's thy-will-be-done. Toy would be able to feel his throbbing; as well she guessed that he might do worse . . . he might lose his water and piss his pants.

"Now tell me how sorry you are. Start begging for my forgiveness."

He did. He stuttered when he did.

Toy was amused by the fear he displayed. It empowered her all the more. But still, she wondered why there was no response. *Why isn't his dick getting hard?* The lack of Donny's response gave Toy more fuel. *How dare he not respond!* Her foot worked up Donny's stomach and then his chest, slow like an inchworm. The music continued to drum and drone and climb, its cymbals clashing in teams. Her leg was half-extended now, the heel inches from the man's lips.

"All right, all right . . . stop your whimpering and do what you do best—go on."

Donny knew this part well. He took Toy's calf and ankle in his hands, a position a flutist might assume, and he began licking the shoe's leather straps, the sides and the undersides of the natural wood heel.

"The heel, shit-for-brains . . . suck the heel!" Toy commanded.

Feverishly, he sucked on Toy's shoe heel, his slurping sounds lost in a flurry of flutes, trumpets, bells and bass drums. Just the sight of him and his fetish was a sick, twisted image to see. It fascinated her and called for her pity all at once. And yet, something about this control, *her* control, aroused Toy. She began to touch herself as Donny made progress; the usual. He gave greater attention to the hard skin, the evidence of a working woman, before he concentrated on her toes. Then he did it all over again with the other foot.

There was a point where the piano solo built to a heavy crescendo. Toy's breathing moved with it as Donny's tongue snaked in and out and between her crusty toes. She craved more . . . some end to this longing madness crawling in her chest, her belly, her loins. The madness in her mind. Her fingers worked dutifully in and out of her, and her heart raced with her breathing. She squeezed her eyes and rectum closed simultaneously, still with that image of him in her mind's eye. Donny with the bra strapped around his warted beak. Donny eating at her toes as though there was frosting on them. Or caramel.

All the music began slamming and crashing and thundering at the same time . . . coming to a close. And so did Toy, gushing when she tried not to, fluid pushing out of her when something in her head wanted mercy for the Cadillac leather seats. Finally, Toy let out a vicious scream of satisfaction.

Her eyes rolled back in her head and her body lay limp against the door.

Like a drunk with fuzzy vision, Toy could see through a lazy eye that Donny was readying himself. He was already fiddling with his zipper, waiting for the go-ahead. Toy made a gesture with her hand, the flick of her fingers.

Donny, quick as he could, opened the car door and made a dash to the front of the Cadillac. Its headlights illuminated the elder as he stood there staging the grand whack-off, with his semen spurting onto the hood and fender of his car. He'd done it this way at least three times.

Toy turned away. She cut off the classical music and turned on the car radio. Some smooth operator's voice melted like hot butter on her soul before he played an Angela Windbush tune. It was only then, as it always was, that Toy knew she'd sold a part of herself just to pay the rent. It haunted her, knowing how she had to face the very same responsibilities next month. This liaison, coupled with all the others, was Donny's instant thrill ... something that may have balanced him—that happened. But for Toy, this was the quick fix. A quick fix that would forever leave her with mental scars. Scars that she'd have to live with for the rest of her life.

CHAPTER
31

Kitty Turner was flyin' high. For a Jersey girl hooked on Bruce Springsteen and campfires on the beach, she'd come so far, so fast. By the time she turned eighteen, all kinds of urban influences weighed in on her life. Instead of Jewel or Stone Temple Pilots, Jay-Z, Jadakiss and Eve became fashionable. Missy Elliot and Nelly Furtado were hollering and wheezing about how everyone should "get their freak on." Britney Spears and Christina Aguilera went from Mouseketeer sweethearts to performing like exotic dancers and whores, respectively. That hooker working the streets of Harlem or the South Bronx might be that next inside story on E! Entertainment Television. This was what the world was changing to; one where those creamy-white institutions of government, of finance and of the private business sector, were suddenly multicolored, with skin tones, dialects and cultural practices diverse enough to challenge a bowl of mixed nuts.

Thanks to MTV, BET and the thousands of magazines and Internet websites, mainstream America became flooded with imagery and impressions that history had never seen before. It became more and more acceptable and politically correct to mix with those who were different from you. Generation X; where yesteryear was a climate of all-things-segregated versus tomorrow, unpredictable and diverse.

This was the world Kitty grew up in. A world that, thanks to her being white, she could call her own. What was most unique about Kitty was that she was white *and* incredibly street-smart. She wasn't naive about crime or violence or the ties that bind, just as she wasn't a stranger to what made the world go round. Not money, or love or people. Those were all necessities; they'd be there one way or another. It was sex. Sex made the world go round. The greatest men buckled to what was between a woman's legs, just as women—the majority of them—wanted what a man had between his.

Vince Reed taught Kitty this when he found her at the ripened age of seventeen. He was a few years older; a shoe salesman on Martin Luther King Drive. Kitty and friends had come into the store all giggly and rosy-cheeked. Reed was immediately at them, serving one and all with his firm pitch and smooth hands along their ankles and feet.

Kitty couldn't speak for the others, but she could say herself that Reed's touch made her quiver. It was as if he'd pushed a start button inside of her. Their eyes met, saying things that would never otherwise be said. Kitty kept her feelings to herself and returned to the store alone, flirting with Reed, turning down his offer for lunch. She was too nervous to step right out there and go for it.

But Reed did the unexpected. He ran out of the store after Kitty. He was smooth at first, all out in the open on the busy street. And then he imposed himself, grabbing hold of Kitty's elbow in an almost possessive manner and whispered in her ear, "I don't know what you're thinking or what you're up to, but if I ever get my hands on you I'm gonna twist you inside out." And just like that, he left her on the sidewalk and went back into the store.

By his words alone, Kitty felt as if she'd been penetrated.

Weeks later, Kitty and a girlfriend wanted to change their routine. They grew tired of the same old songs, played by the same old DJ, with the same old Ivy-League jocks, at the same old club they went to every week. O'Mally's. Oh brother.

"Why don't we go to Club Jaguar? I heard the music rocks," said Jacqueline, Kitty's then long-time friend. And when they made it past club security with their fake IDs, Jacqueline spotted Reed. "Isn't that the shoe guy?"

Kitty froze. She could still feel his firm grip on her elbow, his lips near her and his words filling her. She could feel how he'd touched her feet and it almost caused her to quiver like before.

After watching him for half the night as he mingled with what seemed like a dozen others, Kitty got the nerve to face him. "I know you saw me," she said as a greeting. "I'm only like the fourth white girl in here."

"So you caught me. What about it?"

"I dunno. It's my first time here—my friend is over there dancin' her butt off, so I . . . thought I'd come and say hi."

"Well . . . hi, and, uh—get lost."

"What? How you gonna treat me like that? What did I do to you?"

"Short memory. I offered lunch, you said no . . . am I gettin' close?"

"You could make this easy, you know."

"Yeah, and I could make it hard," Reed said. "Something you couldn't handle, Kitty."

She was ready to walk away disgraced until he'd said her name. "How'd you, like, remember my name?"

"You could start by saying I pay attention to details. You could go from there and say that I liked what I saw."

The conversation grew, but Reed continued to be condescending. Kitty wasn't used to that. For all her young life it was her beer-bellied father and her chain-smoking mother vegetating in front of the television, telling her yes to most of what she asked for. Her friends kissed her pretty ass too.

But now, Kitty had this challenge before her: a domineering man, an arrogant man, a black man who expressed interest in her. He told her about herself, despite her being bruised by the truth. He seemed to know what he wanted, where the other boys she'd dated were all about football games, pitchers of beer and the cars they drove. Not Reed.

Reed, in her experience, was a king among the mere studs she knew. He was confident and he acted on the decisions that he made. Meeting Reed changed Kitty's life forever. She made all kinds of excuses not to be home . . . not to *sleep* at home. Eventually, she didn't go home at all.

For three years, Kitty was Vince Reed's homebody. She was impregnated with his forceful teachings and in fear of his raw power. By surrendering her all to him, Kitty learned to like what he liked, live as he wanted and do as he told her to. Indeed, her life had been twisted inside out. Reed had become a powerful man before Kitty's eyes. His needs and desires changed into more excessive ones. He always wanted more of something.

When Kitty was nineteen, Reed taught her what he'd learned about the counterfeit game by the mere activities ongoing in his apartment. She watched, she learned and she kept her mouth shut. Soon, he had Kitty counting his money and pregnant with his child.

There was a bit of drama, in that Kitty feared having an abortion. She believed the pregnancy too far along to terminate, so she wouldn't have to do what scared her the most—killing. The circumstances angered Reed, who at age twenty-two felt he was too young to be responsible for a child. His first reaction was to abandon Kitty as just another knocked-up woman. He even set her up in that garden apartment to begin the process. But inevitably both of them agreed to put the baby up for adoption when it came. The baby never came. Kitty had a miscarriage.

This was good news for Reed. It made him burdenless once more. It brought them close together again, although Kitty was made to live alone—available for Reed's convenience, but also allowing him freedom to use his favorite drugs (women and sex) when and how he pleased.

Kitty never wavered from being the missionary at Reed's every whim. It just felt so comfortable. So familiar. She still came by his place to count money. Still made deliveries and ran errands when he asked. She was still the sleeve in which he could stick his dick when he wanted to.

She accepted Reed's criminal deeds. She didn't object to his side joints, Danielle and Rachelle. She understood the sacrifice of Colin's liberty and keeping him in the dark . . . keeping his wife Toy sedated and docile. Kitty even accepted Reed's manic tirades, his crazed sexual deviancies and the ways he acted after a few swallows of the tiger-bone juice.

What Kitty didn't realize was that *she* would be the one to digress from the you-and-me-against-the-world association. She would outgrow being kept or directed, stifled from becoming her own woman.

At twenty-five years old, eight years after she met Reed, Kitty chose to embark on her own journey . . . her own promises and objectives.

It was about to be a busy day. Kitty's connect, Ralph, the same U.S. Treasury employee who provided Reed with the scrap money green parchment paper, was expected to meet her in Newark, New Jersey. Kitty had a small sports bag full of counterfeit $20s, all neatly packed in sky blue thousand-dollar money bands. The bag was sitting on the floor near her front door. It was a sweet deal she worked out with Ralph, to pay him $200,000 in funny money in exchange for 50 trash bags. Big, bulging, green Hefty bags of scrap paper from the Treasury, all those little slivers and shreds of the same paper they used to print the real McCoy.

Kitty had already done this same transaction twice before with not-as-large loads, taking the scrap paper to Trudy at a private paper recycling plant in East Orange. Days later, the actual paper would be available for pickup. Kitty would take the stock home, and with her personal computer (beefed up to handle the load) and an $8,000 printer, she'd print good-as-new $20 bills.

The phone rang while she was in the bathroom brushing her teeth and admiring her Saturday morning reflection. Her greeting was distorted with foam, her mouth still busy with toothpaste and brush as she carried the cordless back into the bathroom.

"Mmm . . ." Kitty muttered. "Mmm-hmm," was her reply to mean she was getting ready. She took the brush out of her mouth. *"Fifteen minutes,"* she reiterated as if Knuckles was hard of hearing, some toothpaste spitting at the mirror.

She hung up and looked back in the mirror, her eyes saying that everything was in order. Knuckles would be by soon to pick her up. He'd be by her side for most of the day for that big-man support that she required to protect her interest. Once she completed her hygiene, Kitty pulled off the gold teddy she'd worn to bed, her naked body floating across the bone white carpet of her bedroom.

There was another mirror there on the dresser, a big one that she ignored as she bent down to select a bra and panties from a drawer. When she straightened up she was startled by an image in the mirror. She thought she'd seen a ghost, and she jerked as though she'd stuck her finger in an electrical outlet. Immediately, she swung around to see if the reflection was real.

Kitty shrieked. It was more of a high-pitched sound than it was loud. Quick like a referee's whistle.

"Didn't mean to scare you. I thought you'd be *happy* to see me. Ecstatic," the ghost said.

"Ohmigod! How—? When—?"

"Mmm-hmm . . . caught you off guard, didn't I? And look at you . . . all dressed up for the occasion."

"Colin." The name came from Kitty's lips as a last dying breath would. Instinctively, she covered herself.

"In the flesh. Sorry I intruded. I wanted to surprise you so I hopped the wall back there in the garden. You really should be more careful about leaving your patio door unlocked. You never know who might drop in, ya know? Well? Aren't you gonna come and say hello?"

Kitty was beside herself with fear. It was him. It was really him! Colin. She could've melted right there in front of him. Melted or died, one of the two. After all that she'd done to cripple this man. From first identifying him—pointing him out that night of the raid at Club Jaguar—to the phony letters she wrote, pretending to be Toy, to spinning him with her jail visits or during his collect phone calls—even her own typed letters. Kitty had done so much scheming on behalf of Vince Reed that she couldn't remember it all. So much so that the scheming came natural.

Yet, in all that she'd done, she couldn't be sure if Colin

knew. She couldn't be sure if he knew that she'd befriended Toy at the same time just to help Reed with his obsession to control the woman. She *had* to assume that Colin didn't know. She could do no better than to continue pretending. After all, Knuckles would be by shortly.

She put on a happy face and strolled into Colin's waiting arms. This was a moment that she'd promised him, how she'd be waiting for him "butt-naked with erect nipples." Only Kitty never imagined in all of her twenty-five years that it would actually come to pass.

"Aren't you gonna let your friend know you'll be busy for a while?" Colin, the eavesdropper.

"But I have an appointment this morning, baby. It's really— how did you get out? You escape or something?"

"No, baby. I'm a free man. But getting back to your friend and your appointment . . . why don't you give him a ring. I'm sure another fifteen minutes won't hurt. After all, I've been locked up for over six years. It's the least you could do for a desperate man." Colin's way of saying that . . . his imposing will captivated Kitty, there was little she could do. The last thing she wanted to do was disappoint a man whom she'd helped to imprison . . . whose family she'd help to destroy.

"Sure. I'll call him, Colin." Kitty was thinking of taking up her teddy, a robe, something to cover her body. She felt more like a prisoner herself now—not at liberty to make decisions or call the shots. Besides, Colin had his hand on her shoulder, directing her to the cordless handset. *Was he this big before?* Kitty made the call. She dared not pretend or deceive Colin. No question how clever he'd grown through the years. These were sensitive moments. He practically glued himself to her every move, her every word and expression. When she hung up Colin took hold of her. Her arms got caught in the embrace so that they were by her side.

"You don't know how much this moment means to me . . . how much I missed you," Colin said. "All those letters, phone conversations . . . the visits. I had so many dreams. So many fantasies. And here you are. Flesh and blood."

"Yup," Kitty said, her coy expression facing him. "Here I am. Flesh *and* blood." She couldn't help wondering what she'd gotten herself into.

"Remember that promise you made? The first thing you'd do for me once I got home?"

Kitty hesitated before replying, "How could I forget?"

"Well—*damn*." Colin stepped back, exploring her body with his eyes. "Looks like half the job is already done, doesn't it?" He was propped up against the dresser now, arms folded with that expression about him: *what are you waiting for?*

This was a trip. Colin could even *smell* the fear seeping from Kitty's pores. He could sense how she felt forced into this . . . how she'd probably never intended this moment to arrive. Sure she'd made promises and excited Colin beyond compare. Sure she inspired his mind's eye to see his passions and fantasies before they could ever come to pass. But she had been catering to a desperate man. A deprived man. He was stuck, and forced to cope with the hand he was dealt. His only means of expression, of relations with the outside world were filled with Kitty. Kitty this and Kitty that.

However, lightning struck Colin once he met Brinton. His eyes were opened. Now he could see things as they were and as they could be.

Brinton opened Colin's head up with the comments about Toy and the freak video, where she had been bound and gagged. And it cut like a knife to know that Kitty was in the video as well . . . and Reed too.

So many ideas and thoughts were pounding inside of Colin's head at the moment. To know that Kitty was this venomous snake who had played him, and maybe Toy too. To know that she was a part of Vince Reed's game all along. And then to have her standing there before him, the naked and helpless woman at his mercy. It was enough to make him want to explode.

Kitty with that willing expression. Kitty so soft against his body, caressing him with her hands, Kitty on her knees, her hands busy with his zipper, about to please him as she said she would over and again.

As Colin stood over her, he knew that he could do it right now. He could come at her with a stiff death blow, with his hands as a meat cleaver, and she would topple to the floor—all of her schemes and scams with her.

The other heavyweight thought was whether or not he wanted this blowjob from her. Of course he'd been looking forward to it. For years.

But Colin was a bona-fide AIDS-free human being. Bigger than that, Colin had been away for so long, he was practically a virgin again. Kitty on her knees, about to take him in her mouth, was beyond a fantasy fulfilled, it was damn near a dire need.

"Hold it, green-eyes. Don't even budge another inch . . ." The moment Colin said that, his body was overcome with resolve. His mind shut down to thoughts of sex. Kitty was suddenly a living nightmare about to infect him with whatever horrible disease she carried.

"I'm sure that this would be a mind-blowing joyride, but I've got some other things I need to look into . . ." Colin took hold of Kitty's arm, helping her to her feet. "Put something on and have a seat," he told her. And while all the air seemed to be sucked out of her, Kitty obeyed.

CHAPTER

32

Roger Charles was a huge, big-boned, black man to most people who confronted him. Over seven feet tall, thick enough to be a pro wrestler, with a background that was mostly military, from a cadet in military school to an MP in the U.S. Army. Roger now worked for the Justice Department. He was actually a P.I.—a private investigator—when it came down to the bottom line. Except he wanted more empowerment than a mere P.I. had. He wanted governmental backing. He wanted to be able to access Interpol, DMV records, CIA and FBI intelligence and, of course, a man's rap sheet on a whim. Roger wanted access to all of these resources, and now he finally had that, being a private contractor with the Justice Department.

Eight years ago, some U.S. prosecutor (that is, another government-sponsored advocate for justice) came up with the idea to track criminals' finances even after they've been captured, convicted and sent away. The idea had somewhat of a delayed effect, being that cons of any significance were put away for 5, 10 and even 20 years to life, but it was a productive idea nonetheless.

Prosecutors believed that criminals who were in the game for life, who had been in and out of prison or who had evaded further criminal indictments were somehow either living off of the proceeds of their successful crimes or had sound investments under other names, aliases or false representations.

It was the successful criminals like Crazy Ernie (the one with all the audio franchises), like Mark Kennedy (the one who owned the notorious Blue Light Nightclub) and like John Gotti (the Teflon Don) who inspired prosecutors to run post-conviction investigations in search of the further ventures of the criminal mind. Thanks to UCs—undercover agents, who included everybody from ex–police officers and ex–federal agents, to gung-ho private eyes who went out of their way to impress the Justice Department, to incarcerated felons who sought to have their sentences reduced, or even a nosy neighbor—information was always incoming. Always available. Sometimes further investigation revealed that family members and friends controlled and managed the nest eggs many criminals were wise enough to stash away, out from under the scope of major investigations.

Roger's job was to track down money and eventually confiscate it under the umbrella of the all-powerful RICO Act, the findings falling under the definition of a "continuing criminal enterprise." However, his beliefs were the impetus that made him so successful at what he did. Just as there were zealots in religion or in politics, who lobbied for this and that cause, so too were there zealots who fought for and chased after what was right. Roger was such a person.

He was a nuisance when he was a young schoolboy, telling the teacher if a fellow student was cheating on a test or smoking in the boys' bathroom. There were kids from around his Riverside, New Jersey, neighborhood who sold fireworks from their garage, an illegal operation. Roger had that shut down.

Even when he played Little League baseball for Riverside Auto Shop's team, he got wind of parents betting on or against one team or another. It was actually Riverdale Auto's proprietor who ran the gambling scheme. Roger spilled the beans and the operation was shut down, the proprietor and his team ousted from the League.

In college, Roger helped to run the student government, many times dropping notes to the administration, information about this person smoking pot in his room or that person's relationship with a teacher. His information even led to an aspiring track star's elimination for steroid use and a raid on a frat house that facilitated some ungodly and even some illegal activities.

Roger always kept his actions hidden and already felt as though he was the ultimate undercover agent, having never been discovered, so it was only natural for him to play a part in law enforcement. After a two-year stint in the Army, during which he had his first taste of policing as an MP, basically waving in oncoming traffic at the front gate of Fort Bragg, Roger sought more exciting platforms on which he could wield his penchant for weeding out illegal affairs.

Being a private investigator called out to him. It was as official as he cared to be since he'd already served time in military school and the U.S. Army. It was in Roger's first year as a private investigator, while he worked for various criminal defense attorneys, that he became wise to the criminal mind. He not only got to meet them one-on-one, but got to access every record, from grade school through college, from misdemeanors to felonies; he had all of the evidence and records that prosecutors used at trial.

But while prosecutors had the manpower necessary to address and investigate the substantive crimes, and while defense attorneys were merely interested in having their clients found "not guilty," Roger Charles took it to the next level.

He was one of the primary advocates for Operation Crime Pays as a post-conviction proceeding, even after a criminal had been locked up for years.

The Colin Williams case was the fifth such investigation to come Roger's way. Out of the previous four, two were resolved without incident, the ex-cons surrendering a car dealership, a candy store and an $83,000 Cayman Islands bank account in return for a nonconfrontational resolution. A third case was unresolved, the ex-con fleeing the country with a reported $2 million in jewels. And the fourth case was out on the shelf because Mickey Blue Eyes was currently recovering from triple-bypass surgery. Colin Williams was a special case for Roger. Here was a young man who was pinned as a principal of the $1-million-a-month Jersey City counterfeit money ring. Just $1 million in phony bills was in this guy's name; no cars, no homes and no businesses. Not that Roger could find.

All that illegal activity connected to Williams, and yet he needed a public defender—a lawyer hired by the courts—at first. Then a private attorney had taken the case, a $400-an-hour suit whom sources said could've done a lot better to defend his client. He also investigated Mrs. Williams, and asked her about the Expedition (which she said was a gift) and how she was able to afford the penthouse of the Shangrila. To that she replied, "You're the investigator, *you* figure it out."

He tried. All he could see was that Toy worked the day shift at Nuts & Screws, a job he was sure wasn't paying her enough for the rent, the upkeep of her daughter, the babysitter and on and on.

And then one night he thought he'd hit pay dirt. Toy left work and jumped in a brand-new Cadillac. They stopped at a restaurant, then a motel. But the man who checked into the motel—Roger discovered his name to be Donald Berkshire—turned around and left. He didn't return the key until the next day, by messenger.

Roger followed the Cadillac for a mile or so until it pulled over into a service area. He figured that Berkshire was a john and that Toy was turning tricks for a buck. Roger could understand that, considering that she was left as a single parent with expenses to carry. Only, if this wasn't the most peculiar, freaky sight that he'd ever seen: the john eventually got out of the car and . . . *Damn*!

Roger switched gears, certain that Mrs. Williams wasn't in contact with substantial wealth. He did a minimal amount of research and found out that Mr. Williams was currently housed at Fairton FCI in New Jersey. He spoke confidentially with a counselor at the prison who checked the institution's inmate accounts. Records showed that Williams spent $275 a month at the prison commissary—the spending limit for every inmate—and up until six months earlier he had been spending his limit on phone calls as well. Not exactly a poor man.

The prison didn't know where the money orders were sent from. There were more than 1,200 inmates there; with so many more priorities and concerns to see to, the staff could care less about who was spending what from whom. The fact that Williams was "living it up" in prison was all Roger needed to know. It was enough to keep the investigation warm.

Then one day Roger Charles received a call from the counselor he'd spoken with.

"There's some news you might be interested in," the counselor said. "Williams is on the next bus out of here. The court vacated his sentence."

"Vacated? What exactly does that mean?" asked Roger, unfamiliar with courtroom terms outside of "guilty" or "not guilty" or "I plead the Fifth."

"That means he's going home," the counselor confirmed.

The news brought a smile to Roger's face. Not necessarily because he was coming close to stunting a man's finances, but because he was the advocate for what was right. He was the righteous one who kept a watch over life's imbalances. If the bad guy was getting ahead, then Roger wasn't doing his job. So Colin Williams was just another bad guy he needed to shut down. These were times that he anticipated, how following a suspect often led to waiting and more waiting. You had to have patience to be a P.I.

So in preparation for the day Roger purchased a pound of seedless grapes and the latest editions of *Ebony*, *Black Enterprise* and the *Star-Ledger*. Just because black consciousness somehow sympathized with black men who were said to have few options or opportunities in the quest for the American Dream, a position that gave them no other choice but to turn to crime, didn't mean that Roger also had to sympathize.

After a phone call to the clerk of the court where the Williams case would be heard, and then another to the U.S. Marshals' Office in the basement of the Martin Luther King Jr. Building (where the courts were located), Roger got a good enough hint that Williams would be released.

He stuck his head in the courtroom, tinted glasses and all, and once he got a grip on Williams' appearance, he posted himself in he courthouse lobby.

Williams, the victor, emerged from the courtroom at 10:30 in the morning. Roger noticed that he wasn't smiling like a man who'd been released after six years in prison. Maybe he had something important on his mind, like getting hold of some money. Roger closed the *Star-Ledger* and headed for his car. Williams would be traveling by taxi or someone would pick him up, Roger was sure of it, wishing in either event that he were the man behind the wheel disguised as the driver.

The taxi dropped Williams off at the YMCA in downtown Hoboken and he rented a room. Roger played the waiting game, parking in a lot across from the Y before following his target. Williams spent the day wandering up and down Washington Street, where he purchased jeans, a shirt and a Chicago White Sox baseball cap. Roger figured he'd spent less than $100. With his few bags in hand, Williams took a time-out, sitting on a park bench, observing the children, the atmosphere; at one point he pulled up a dandelion and smelled it.

Roger had always wondered what it would be like to follow a man who'd just been released from prison. He was curious about his actions, habits, the things he'd find interest in. So far, Colin Williams didn't exactly live up to Roger's expectations. The day ended at sundown when Williams retreated to the Y and didn't come out again until morning.

And now Roger Charles, private investigator, found himself on River Road, outside of a five-story building. Williams took a taxi at 8 A.M., reached the building at 8:30. After standing out front for a time, he went around back, climbed up on a Dumpster and went over a wall. Finally, Roger knew that things were taking a turn in the grimy direction, something he looked forward to. Illegal activity . . . trespassing . . . maybe breaking and entering . . . or worse. Roger's heartbeat went into overdrive and he pulled the .38 special he kept in his ankle holster. These were mere precautions for a man whose focus was to track down the finances of known criminals. But as Roger would say, never underestimate the power of a man.

CHAPTER

33

"What did you think?" Colin asked Kitty, more or less demanding an answer. "I was gonna *disappear*? Did you think you could pull this off without anyone finding out the truth?"

Even with her robe on, Kitty felt cold and naked. A moment ago she had been on her knees without the robe, at his mercy. Now, having been rejected, she was having a hard time finding relief. This was one of those gray areas where she had to be careful of what she said, and honest, or else.

"To be real with you, Kitty—if that's your *real* name— I'm not here to hurt you. Although I have plenty of reason to do it, violence is not my purpose for being here. My beef isn't with you . . . what I need to know is why. Why did you set me up? And after you tell me that, explain to me why you're in a porn video with my wife." Colin took Kitty's chin in his hand. She was sitting on the bed while he stood just in front of her. "And I want to know the truth."

There was a lot to be said about Colin's eyes. They were sincere. They were uncompromising. They were knowing and they were focused. He knew what he wanted and wouldn't settle for less. Kitty felt as though she was under the power of some truth serum or Wonder Woman's magic lasso. She explained her relationship with Vince Reed from A to Z, how they met, how they grew together and how they parted.

Teary-eyed, she also explained Reed's instructions at the time of the raid. "He was expecting them," Kitty said. "He wasn't sure when, but he knew they were coming. He said it was necessary."

"Necessary?"

"Yes. An arrest would throw off the investigation so that Reed could step to the next level. I don't know if you remember this, but there was a connect he made with . . . well, someone who could get us the exact grade of paper so that the money printed would be exact. Exact texture. Exact smell. The whole bit. These were scraps that he had recycled . . ."

Colin had heard about the idea and said, "Go on."

"Basically, there was just more money. Reed cut off his old supplier and began the whole printing bit on his own. But I swear, he told us that you were okay about taking the fall. But I knew that was a lie when I overheard some things he said to a lawyer, about you not knowing this and not knowing that. He had the lawyer setting you up."

Colin didn't change his expression. He was in shock; the sense of nothingness made him wonder if he'd ever be able to love again.

"When I really found out the truth was when Reed sat me down and explained. He said he had a mission and that some people would be hurt along the way. He said, that's life. Winners and losers and all that sort of stuff. All I wanted to do was what he asked."

"And if he told you to jump off a bridge? You'd do that too?"

"Thinking back? Honestly? I was so fucked up, so much under his control, that I probably would've. I know how stupid I was. But Reed was . . . he was God. I looked up to him. I believed everything he ever said from the time I met him. Remember, I was a teenager then. Didn't know jack-shit."

Colin could see now. He understood well how Kitty was able to do what she did. He understood why. It was like he'd once read in prison, about Moses and the Israelites. Without their leader, without that strong guidance, they wound up turning to a golden calf as their idol. Their god. Colin wondered if Kitty ever had a leader or a god in her life before Reed—the false god—came along and imposed himself. Kitty became Reed's missionary. His soldier. Like so many suicide bombers, Kitty had been brainwashed and spellbound.

It didn't hurt that she also loved Reed and that they'd almost had a child together.

He couldn't help feeling a bit sorry for Kitty. It was either compassion or pity. Her life left her vulnerable at a point when Vince Reed swooped in and captivated her common sense.

"I don't know what I can do now to help fix things, Colin, but if it means anything to you, I'll help you any way I can. Anything—"

The doorbell rang.

"Oh . . . that's Knuckles. He's supposed to pick me up. My appointment. I'll tell him to wait a few more minutes."

Colin braced himself, wondering if Kitty was lying about this too. It was difficult to know what was real and what wasn't with her—even after so thorough a testimony. Colin would have to see it before he believed it, especially when it came to Kitty. He overheard Kitty say, "Just give me a few more minutes. No, there's no problems whatsoever. Wait in the car."

Kitty came back with the faux winded expression. "Hired help . . . I tell ya. Okay, Colin. Back to you." She seemed more confident now, the tears behind her. Determination in her eyes. "Tell me what you want me to do. I owe you, big-time."

"I want details. Where does Reed operate? Where does he live? And as best you can, tell me about his security . . . his hired guns. And there's one more thing I need."

"What's that? Anything, you name it."

"I need a car. I need to go and see my wife and daughter before I do anything else."

Kitty didn't deliberate in the least. "No problem," she said.

Colin didn't have far to drive, just a mile's worth of tree-lined streets in middle-class neighborhoods. It wasn't as if he'd forgotten where he once lived, the Shangrila. However, his mind had traveled far from the lavish penthouse. For one thing, Toy's letters—the ones that Kitty or Reed actually wrote—mentioned that she was moving. The letters didn't say where she was going, just that Colin should move on like she was. "Colin, let it go," the words read.

The other thing was that Colin had forced himself to put Toy out of his mind. He even had to ask Carter, his buddy back in prison, not to bring up Toy's name. Colin figured he'd lost it all. No sense in holding on to something outside of his control. But he discovered that being abandoned made him stronger. More self-reliant, with the fortitude to fine-tune his character. Colin was no different than a castaway left on an island to make the best of what he had right where he was.

Colin had other things on his mind as he approached the Shangrila. Would Toy be angry or overjoyed? How would she and Lady look? Was there another man with them? Someone taking Colin's place?

At the same time, he considered what to do about Reed. There was so much heat and fire and desire for revenge in his heart that he had to suppress it in every waking moment and with every step he took. His head was a pressure cooker full of conflicting ideas. Too much to be organized or put in proper persective.

On one hand, he hoped his daughter would run up to him shouting, "DADDY! DADDY! DADDY!" On the other hand, he was flashing back to how he got revenge on his bosses back in Los Angeles, and thinking of doing the same to Reed's house. He seethed about having been set up, but he also had the jitters in anticipation of seeing his family. His mind was a big football stadium with spectators, fans and announcers all fighting to be heard.

"You don't remember me, do you?" Colin asked the doorman at the Shangrila. "I mean . . . I don't blame you if you don't. It's only been six years."

The doorman made a funny face, like he was trying to come up with the $25,000 answer on a game show. "Sorry . . . can't say I do."

"Okay. Lemme help you. I always gave you a hundred-dollar tip at Christmas . . ."

The doorman still didn't get it.

"Winston! It's me, man! Colin Williams, from the penthouse?" Colin said this as though he himself had a hard time believing it.

"Oh! Hello, Mr. Williams. Wow! Long time! You . . . you got so *big*. You go on vacation? The army?"

Colin smirked, thinking, *Sure . . . vacations.* "Close, Winston. Real close. How you been doin'?"

Colin with his hand firm on Winston's shoulder, the other shaking Winston's hand.

"Fine. I'm real fine, sir."

"Tell me . . . have you seen Mrs. Williams? Or Lady, my daughter?"

"Uh . . . well . . . the missus hasn't been here for a few hours, probably at work, ya know. But I know the lil' one is home. The babysitter just came back with her from the park."

Colin thought briefly, then said, "Kimberly, right?"

"Of course."

"Well, I'm gonna head up. Don't bother to announce me. This is a surprise."

"Oh, you bet, Mr. Williams. Sure good to see you again."

"Same here, Winston."

The elevator ride, as smooth as it was, felt like a time machine passing Colin from one warped world to the next. Everything up until now was today's world. When those doors slid open, it would be the past suddenly hitting him in a head-on collision. If there were an easier way to do this, he wanted that right now.

The doorbell quickly tugged at Colin's memory. It was the second half of the ding-dong sound ringing five times over and fading with each progression. Colin looked himself over once more for a quick inspection before he heard soft footfalls near the other side of the door. He sensed Kimberly's eye in the peephole.

"Who?" she said, short and sweet.

"Kimberly?"

There was no answer, as though Colin had startled her.

"It's me. Mr. Williams. Lady's father?" It felt strange to speak this way, as if he didn't belong. As if he questioned his own existence and title as Lady's father.

Colin thought he heard a gasp, a "whoa" drifting, falling away from the door.

"Kimberly?"

Still no answer.

"I always looked out for you, Kim . . . make this easy for me, would you? I just want to see—"

The door opened. It was an older Kimberly. Black hair looping into big curls just above the shoulders. John Lennon glasses. A tube top and paisley printed bellbottom pants. She was barefooted.

"Wow, Kimberly. What're you, twenty? Twenty-one now?"

Her mouth was still open, captured by Colin's presence.

"Kim-berly," a young voice called out in a singsong tone.

Kimberly turned and Colin looked at the young girl strolling into the entry hall only ten or so feet from where he stood.

"Lady?" Colin said the name, another strange sound coming from his lips. His daughter was about seven years old and tall; she was thin in her white T-shirt and jeans and her hair was braided in zigzags about her head and then hanging down in extensions fanning over her shoulders. Colin could easily see his eyes, ears, nose and light-coffee skin tone in Lady; all of her characteristics serving as affirmations of his rightful place as her father.

"Do you remember me?"

Lady effortlessly molded to Kimberly's side. Kimberly comforted her with a hand on her upper back. Colin looked at the sitter, almost begging for her help.

"Lady?" the sitter said.

"Yes, Kimberly?"

Kimberly bent down and whispered into Lady's ear. Colin watched with pure delight as Lady's eyes lit up. Her lips graduated into a smile. A big smile.

"Daddy? Oh my *God*! Daddy!" Lady exclaimed in a sigh

and then a burst of joy. She immediately glided toward Colin. He quickly squatted to receive her. Lady practically dived for her father. He fell back on his ass with her on top of him.

"DADDY-DADDY-DADDY!"

"LADY-LADY-LADY!" Colin had her in his protective embrace, rolling on the floor in the foyer.

Kimberly's eyes were already wet with tears that outdid Colin's own.

"Daddy, where have you been all my life? I prayed and prayed and prayed that you would come home to us, but God never answers me. All I get is rain."

"Oh God, Lady." Colin pulled her to him, as much to hold her as to hide his sobs. "You don't know how much I missed you . . . how much I've thought about you."

"Me too, Daddy. Me too. *Daddy . . . you're crying.*"

"No, no . . . just something in my eyes," Colin lied, feverishly pulling his arms across his eyes.

Kimberly carried on as silently as she could, her sniffles serving as a distant reminder of her presence.

"I can't believe you're home, Daddy. I have so much to tell you. You know I'm in the fifth grade now and I got four A's and two B's on my last report card, and—*Daddy?* Are you okay? Why you starin' like that?"

Colin pulled Lady into him again. He didn't want to let her go. Ever.

Every moment that Colin spent with his daughter was a jubilant one. He felt all crazy inside and didn't know what to do with himself. The feeling reminded him of even happier times when Lady was born, when she said "Daddy" and "Mommy" for the first time, and when she took her first steps. Those were times Colin shared with Toy. They'd commemorate each occasion by making love. Colin couldn't help thinking of Toy now. He wanted to see her. He wanted to hear her voice and to say things to her.

"Kimberly, where's Toy?" Colin asked as he watched Lady show him a little dance routine. He had already done a walk-through of the penthouse.

"She's at *work*," Kimberly said, emphasizing that Lady was unaware of her mother's job.

"Oh yeah?"

"Yeah, Daddy," Lady said, suddenly at ease with her dance steps. "One day I'm gonna work a lot too, just like Mommy."

"Really? You *are*?"

"Of course! Do you know Mommy works at the club? Where women get undressed and dance?"

"Oh really," Colin said, sharing a surprised expression with the babysitter. The sitter, speechless, shrugged and wagged her head simultaneously. It was clear that Colin needed to see Toy and that there were some things to discuss.

Kimberly didn't know what to make of Lady's knowledge. All she could say, once she got Colin alone, was, "Lady is as sharp as a tack. Almost nothing gets by her."

Colin asked Kimberly where Toy was working. "No. Let me guess," Colin said. "Nuts and Screws."

Kimberly said, "Yes." She was apprehensive, as though she might be violating her confidence with Toy.

But Colin said, "Don't worry, Kimberly. I'm back. Things are gonna shape up around here, but quick."

Kimberly smiled and breathed easier as Colin went to kiss Lady. And then, just as suddenly as he had appeared, he was gone again.

The car that Kitty gave Colin to get around in was one of the blue Honda Civics, the compact cars that Reed used to transport a million dollars at a time, the counterfeit bills kept in a safe welded in the floor. Colin didn't pick up on it, didn't remember until he found toll receipts in the glove compartment. Apparently, from the looks of things, Reed had accomplished a lot in six years. He used a lot of people, too.

Colin was still considering how Reed would pay; that is, if he'd be able to pay for all the pain and damage he caused. And then again, maybe *Colin* would be the one to do the paying. Paying back. Payback.

Nuts & Screws hadn't changed a bit. Still in the same

location, next door to the car wash, with the Chinese fast
food restaurant on its other side. Except, just like most
things Colin observed upon his return, everything seemed
smaller. Smaller, and in many cases, irrelevant. Everything
seemed like a hustle for a person's dollar, or for a person's
attention. Colin's fresh overview of things made it easy to
spot foolishness, deceit and insincerity. It was as if he had
different eyes. He could see more clearly. He could see
through things.

"Wan' we watch y'car?" a dreadlocked Rastafarian asked.

Colin's mind suddenly returned to the images in prison.
Some Rastafarians were well groomed and took good care
of themselves. Others were ashy and unkempt, like this man.

Colin had a pocket full of money, thanks to Kitty. He
took out his bills and pulled off a ten. "And there's more for
you when I get back," Colin said.

"For dis? I'll wash y'car too, mon!"

Colin snickered under his breath, feeling compassion for
the man, hoping that his two cents would help, but knowing
that the man needed a whole lot more than ten dollars. He
needed direction.

The club was pitch-dark inside in contrast to the atmosphere outside. It was rush hour—after 4 P.M.—and the busi-
nessmen had the club halfway filled to capacity. Prince was
singing from the DJ booth, proclaiming that she didn't have
to be rich to be his girl, or cruel to rule his world. He just
wanted some extra time and her . . . kiss. Meanwhile, an
Asian dancer was up on stage behind the bar, her back to a
pole as she sank and rose against it. Her expression was
saucy as she played with her one-piece thong bodysuit—it
was one those Day-Glo orange pieces, like an elastic V that
was super-thin but could at least cover her nipples and pubic
area. Still, there was little left to the imagination.

Colin's eyes shifted from the dancer on the pole to another seated on the bar, a customer facing her on a stool with
his hands smooth along her thighs. The girl was wiggling
there in front of him counting her money and smacking on

gum. There were up to a dozen or so other girls throughout
the small club, all of them preying on the desires of working-
class men, both blue and white collar.

Still, Colin couldn't find Toy.

Years ago, when he had met her, she was tending the bar.
But Colin knew things had changed. He was ready for almost anything now; maybe Toy naked, descending from the
ceiling, riding a 12-foot, 200-pound plastic penis. No . . .
even that wouldn't surprise Colin, considering the things
he'd heard.

"Can I get you a drink, playboy?"

"Oh . . . of course," Colin said to the bartender. "A Pepsi
will do."

"Pepsi and rum? Pepsi and vodka?"

"Just Pepsi. Pepsi and Pepsi," Colin said with his boyish
smile peeking through. "Do you know a woman named
Toy?"

"Of course. You tryin' to get with her?"

Colin was thrown by the inquiry. Was this woman a
salesperson or a broker of some kind? Was Toy somehow
up for grabs? "Ah . . . well, you could say that," he said. He
didn't come right out and say he was her husband, but he
wanted to.

"Well, I took over for her. She might be around here. See
that girl over there? The chick with the curls and the leopard
thong?" Colin nodded. "That's N'Tasha. She could help you.
I ain't seen Toy in a minute."

"Thanks," Colin said. He offered a curt smile, paid the
woman and approached N'Tasha. She was wedged between
two men in business attire on stools. N'Tasha's back was to
the bar with the stage show going on above and behind her.
Colin could easily see through N'Tasha's practiced presence:
the sultry eyes, the pouted lips and the laid-back attention
she required. She was sending a message to her audience of
two: *I don't need your money, but go on and look anyway—
and tip me while you're at it.*

Colin stood out of the way, waiting for the dancer to notice him, hoping at some point she'd become restless. When she did look Colin's way, he made the signal with his free hand. *I'd like to talk to you.*

Eventually, N'Tasha excused herself when she realized that Colin wouldn't lay off. The wayward man usually would. And she approached him. "I hope you make this worth my while. You see I'm busy."

"Sorry to interrupt your, ah, corporate merger, but I'm told you can help me. I'm looking for Toy."

N'Tasha gave Colin a look and said, "Is that why you got me over here? For another bitch?" She rolled her head as she said this. Colin couldn't help noticing how more of her cleavage showed while she worked the attitude.

He took hold of her elbow before she could turn away. "N'Tasha," Colin said.

She stared at Colin's hand, expressing how he had to be crazy for touching her.

"Sorry . . . I really need to see Toy. This isn't a game and I'm not a john lookin' for a trick."

"Well, then what do you want with her?"

"I . . . I'm her husband."

N'Tasha froze. Her lips parted to the degree that Colin could see her tongue ring—a bead of silver that glistened behind her teeth. "Oooooooo—" N'Tasha's response was what a child would say after spilling a pitcher's worth of purple Kool-Aid on white carpet, expecting that there was gonna be trouble. "You mean . . . you're Colin?"

"Oh . . ." Colin sort of chuckled. "You know about me?"

"Do I?" N'Tasha gave Colin that quick head-to-toe examination. Then she was eye-to-eye with him again. "I can't believe you're actually here. Home. In the flesh."

"In the flesh," Colin said, feeling like a broken recorder.

N'Tasha suddenly swung her head left and right. She said, "Wait a minute." She pulled Colin into a dark corner. "Are they lookin' for you? Did you break out?" The way N'Tasha said that made Colin want to laugh. She turned into a criminal all of a sudden, the accomplice willing to harbor a fugitive with her sneaky ways.

"No, N'Tasha. I didn't escape. I'm not a wanted man. It's all on the up-and-up. I was released once and for all. The sentence was vacated."

"Wow. Everybody thought you were gone forever. Like you were never comin' back. Dang!"

"Well—*surprise*. So fill me in, N'Tasha. You good friends with Toy?"

"Sorta. Since she came back, a year or so, we've been kickin' it a lot. Yeah . . . I guess you could say we're friends." N'Tasha explained a lot about Toy and what she'd been up to, to the best of her knowledge. She was a mere outsider to Toy's world, but at least she knew about Colin, about Lady and about the few men who came into the picture when Colin went to prison.

She was discreet enough and had mercy enough to omit things that might upset Colin, but she was also witty enough to drop clues that might inspire and encourage Colin to act. Things that might trigger him to put things back in working order.

"So where is she now?" Colin asked again, realizing that N'Tasha had rambled past the first time he made the inquiry.

"She's . . ." N'Tasha took a deep breath, about to violate a trust among friends. "She's with a man . . . his name is Donny. Some big-time dude who owns some pharmacy or somethin'. They just left for dinner. But you ain't heard it from me."

"Of course not. Where's the restaurant, N'Tasha?"

"River Road. It's called the Riverside Restaurant. They always go there."

"Always," Colin said, hoping to misunderstand her.

N'Tasha wagged her head, not happy with the news she was relaying. "You gotta go get her, Colin." She grabbed hold of Colin's arm and went to whisper into his ear. "You gotta go and *get your wife back*," she said with a certain importance in her tone.

CHAPTER

34

He had to remember three things as he cruised down River Road: Riverside Restaurant. Silver Cadillac Deville. And Donny. Was that her new man? Did the expensive car and his ownership of a business mean that he was well-to-do? Rich?

N'Tasha had explained briefly that this "Donny" was a bespectacled, older white man. "Older" to Colin meant somewhat out of shape. And bespectacled could've meant partially blind. Either way, for some reason, Colin wasn't intimidated or as concerned about a physical threat. But did the man have a gun? Did he know that Toy was married and had a child waiting for her at home?

It was moving on eight in the evening when Colin pulled into the parking lot of the Riverside Restaurant. Vehicles of every expensive taste were set up like a car dealership's top-of-the-line picks—maybe 50 of them all reflecting the moonlight and the lantern lighting that was dropped about the perimeter of the property.

"You dining, sir?"

"Ah, yes and no. Could you—or would you remember a Cadillac Deville, a silver one, pulling in here anytime within the past hour?"

The parking attendant made an exhausted sigh and said, "I can't say. There's a lotta cars in here, chief."

"How 'bout now?" Colin asked, a folded bill in hand.

"Now that you mention it." The attendant took the money. "Thank you . . . there might've been a silver one a few minutes ago. Pretty girl in there too."

"Where'd you park it?"

"I didn't. They said they'd do it themselves—the guy did. I ain't seen 'em come in the restaurant yet." The attendant was leaning in now, more attentive.

"Point it out. Please," said Colin, dizzy with adrenaline.

"Over near the benches . . . close to the water."

Colin directed the Honda around a bend in a crawl as he observed the different cars. Mercedes. Lexus. Land Cruiser. Another Mercedes. Porsche. Jaguar. Humvee. Saab. BMW. Mercedes. Cadillac . . . silver. He hit the brakes and threw the car into park. He didn't turn it off. Just left the engine running and hopped out. The weather was gorgeous. No wind. Not a cloud to hide the stars. Not a degree too hot or too cold. There was that familiar scent of herb in the air. It was seeping from the Cadillac's passenger side window.

Colin quickly thought up a plan. He circled to the driver's side of the car and rapped at the window. Colin still wore his wedding band, so his rapping sounded more like a key. The man inside began to lower his window. More of the weed smoke escaped the vehicle's cabin.

"Can I help you?"

"Yes, I'll need you to step out of the car, sir." Colin flipped open his wallet quickly, a fake-out to pretend he was an authority of some kind. He could see that Toy was in the passenger's seat, her legs folded under her. He was sure that she hadn't seen him. "You'll need to step this way, sir . . . around to the rear of the car, please."

Colin was careful not to allow a visual through the rear window and kept the man's body in position to obstruct Toy's view. Colin began to pat the man down.

"Any weapons, sir?"

"No. Of course not . . . young man, I assure you—"

"Quiet, please."

"This is preposterous!"

Colin had the man's wallet in hand, a business card in the other. "Mmm . . . so you're Donald Berkshire, huh. CEO at . . . what is this, Pfeister Pharmaceuticals?"

"We're a pharmaceutical company," the man said.

"Who's the girl in the car? I bet your, uh, wife might be

interested in her, wouldn't she, wise guy?" Colin with the family photo.

"Listen . . . I'm sure we can fix this. I have a lot of money—"

"Do I sound like I give a fuck about your money?" Colin noticed that Toy was moving in the Cadillac, maybe cleaning house, tossing the weed. "Turn around, Mr. Pfeister Don. I wanna have a word with you. Eye-to-eye."

Berkshire turned around. Colin handed him his wallet.

"I've got news for you, Berkshire. Now that I know who you are, let me introduce myself. The woman inside that car? Her name is Toy, isn't it?"

"Yes, but how—?"

"You need to know that the woman in there, the one who you've been doing God knows what with? That's my wife. Toy Williams. My name is Colin Williams."

"But—"

"Shhh! Don't say a word. I want you to listen to me. I'm an angry, bitter man right now. I've been locked up for six years of my life. My wife, my daughter, my everything has been stripped from me during that time. Now that may not be your fault; maybe you didn't even know about me. Or maybe you did. But guess what? I can be a reasonable man. Now I'm gonna ask you a favor . . ."

Toy was scared out of her wits. The last thing she wanted was to be arrested for weed. Locked up like her husband was, or end up like so many other horror stories she'd heard about. She hustled to toss the stick of weed out of the window and lowered the other windows to air out the Cadillac. She figured the ounce bag of marijuana she had might get her and Donny in trouble and that it was too large to just toss out the window. So she opened the car door and quickly emptied it on the ground, hoping it would get lost in the dirt and gravel.

"Hey! You! Stay in the car!" the cop-agent-*whoever* shouted at Toy with his deep voice.

"Oh God!" Toy gasped and shut the door as fast as she

could. For the next couple of minutes she squeezed real hard so she wouldn't pee herself. Next thing she knew, her door was pulled open. It was Donny.

"Is everything all right?" she asked.

"Not quite. Somebody wants to talk to you. I think you should get up. And bring your things."

Toy made a face and took up her shoulder bag as she got out the car and walked toward the cop. "What's happening? Did the cop—?" She stopped midsentence, then she said, "Ya know, I swear, this weed must be some real good shit, Donny, 'cause I swear, I'm seeing—Donny?" She looked back over her shoulder. As she did, the Cadillac backed out of its parking space, kicking up gravel as it sped off. "Donny?" She turned to the apparition before her.

"You're not seeing things, Toy. It's me. Colin."

Toy's vision became foggy, then she saw stars and the moonlit sky turning, winding overhead as she lost consciousness, falling toward the gravel.

CHAPTER

35

For once, Roger Charles wished he had some popcorn instead of the box of doughnuts there in the seat beside him. "This is better than the movies!" he said out loud in the isolation of the pickup truck.

From Colin Williams being released in court, to his hopping the wall to somebody's garden apartment, to him getting the blue Honda to drive home, to Nuts & Screws and then to the Riverside Restaurant where he impersonated an officer . . . wow! This was getting better by the moment. Roger couldn't stand it. He craved more. He was shaking like a rattlesnake and at the same time, feeling very privileged to see it all unfolding right there in the privacy of his pickup truck. His eyes bugged out when Williams confronted his wife for what Roger guessed was the first time in a long while.

He was at the edge of his seat when she fainted and commended her husband with a private hand clap for hurrying to catch her before she hit the ground.

Colin took his wife back to the Shangrila in that blue Honda, at which time he carried her up into their penthouse, leaving Roger out of the picture once again. Roger was determined to wait, knowing for sure that there would be a point when Williams would reach out for his money. Money that Roger was sure was buried someplace or stashed in a safe-deposit box somewhere. But Roger knew that it might be a while, since Williams and his wife were probably consummating their reunion.

* * *

"Good," Colin said, when Kimberly told him that Lady was fast asleep. It was almost 9:30. Way past her bedtime. He didn't want her to see Mommy this way. Colin had Toy in his arms, carrying her over the threshhold, past Kimberly.

"Is she sleeping?" she asked as she closed the door behind them.

"Sort of," Colin replied. "Get me a washcloth and a bowl of cool water. Hurry," he said, setting Toy on the nearest couch. "Don't worry, baby. Daddy's home," he said softly into Toy's unconscious ears.

It was another seven minutes before Toy came to semi-consciousness, her eyes fluttering from her own darkness to the lamplight of the penthouse.

"Kimberly," she said with a moan. "Lady."

"Kimberly went home. I paid for her. And Lady is sound asleep."

"It's you," Toy said with a sigh. "My God. It's really you."

Colin touched the damp washcloth to Toy's brow once more before setting it aside. His other hand had been stroking her hair. Combing his fingers through it. "It's me, baby. Yes . . . it's really me."

"How—?"

"Shhh . . . the details aren't so important now. Just relax. I'm a free man and I'm back to take care of my wife and daughter."

"But . . . Donny . . . you're not mad?"

"How can I be mad at you? Would you tell me that? How can anybody be mad at someone as beautiful as you? This is the Toy I married, isn't it? The one with the loving heart? The one with the brave heart?"

"Love. I forgot what that was the day they took you from me. I don't know how I'll ever be the same. So much has—"

Colin touched his forefinger to Toy's lips. "Toy. I promise to forget the past—whatever it is—if you promise to focus on the future. You're healthy, Lady is healthy and smart as a tack. That's all that matters to me. Truly, that's what counts."

Toy smiled and cried at the same time. She cuddled her head against Colin's waist and reached around to hold him at the same time. She still found it hard to believe, not expecting to see Colin ever again. Toy closed her eyes, hoping it wasn't a dream.

Both Colin and Toy remained still for some time, as ten turned to eleven and eleven turned to twelve, both of them having difficulty with letting go. Toy had the scars of abuse on her mind. Reed. She had the immediate memories of living out a rich man's perverted fantasies. Colin had six years of pain. Torture. Separation. On top of that, he felt Toy's pain as his own. He realized that Toy had gone through some things. He didn't want to know what things, however. What he didn't know wouldn't hurt him.

Sometime around midnight, Toy woke in Colin's arms. He prepared a bath to relax her and usher her back to sound mind and body. After the bath, Toy went out into the living room where Colin had a bottle of champagne waiting on ice. He apparently had had flowers delivered as well, the bouquet sitting to the side of the champagne glasses. If she hadn't been surprised or overwhelmed earlier, then she was now.

The two sat side by side on the couch, Toy in a pair of silk shorts and a T-shirt that boldly read BABE, Colin barechested in his day-old jeans.

"To a fresh start with new memories," Colin suggested, raising a glass half-filled with bubbly.

"And to my knight in shining armor," Toy responded, tapping her glass to his.

They locked elbows and sipped, closer than they'd been in more than six years. Colin inhaled everything about Toy's essence, from the fragrance of her hair to the perfume she wore to the fresh sent of her flesh. It was a refreshing boost to his senses, opening his mind as if welcoming a morning sun, a wave of cold air during blistering heat or a rush of warm air during the bitter cold. Experiencing Toy was all of these sensations at once. It was enough to make a man shiver with delight, or else rejoice for all the world to hear.

"Colin." Toy uttered his name somewhat breathlessly.

Colin answered her call, bending forward to kiss her. Both of them closing their eyes. Both of them wanting this to be the first, the best and the most memorable. Toy put her hand flat against Colin's face and said, "I'm so happy I don't know what to do with myself."

"If it makes you feel any better, I've been waiting for this moment for years. You can't be happier than me."

"Oh, baby," Toy said, kissing him more affectionately, more aggressively. This went on nonstop, their hands beginning to touch and fondle and relearn one another. Their lips parted with a sucking sound, like they had been underwater and in dire need of air.

"I want to put it on you, Colin. I mean really, really put it on you . . . help you get rid of all that anxiety and tension, ya know? But I don't know how you'll look at me. You're my husband . . . and . . . well, I'm your wife. So that's my job, to make you feel good. But I also don't want you to see me as a freak."

"Shut up already," Colin said, and the two attacked each other. They exhausted themselves and each other. They were selfish and giving as far as passion could take them, until it was hard to breathe.

"Well, well, well . . . I wouldn't believe it if I didn't see it myself. If it isn't the two lovebirds, all cozy n' shit." The voice shook Colin from his sleep. He jumped out of his embrace with Toy, but just as he was about to heave off the bed, someone wopped him across the left side of his skull, knocking him back to the bed with a gash and a growing lump.

Toy took in a mouthful of air, about to scream at the top of her lungs. But that was impossible now, as another man covered her lips with his thick calloused palm.

"Go easy on her, J.J., I might need her later," Reed said, sucking on a cigarette. He raised his booted foot and planted it on the sheets. His elbow went to his knee, his chin to his hand; the thinking man's position. "You'll have to excuse Benny here; he can get a little aggressive at times. Your best bet is not to make any sudden moves. He's just as good with the left hook as he is with the right.

Colin?" Reed touched Colin's naked calf with the burning end of his Newport.

"Aaahhh!" Colin shouted.

"Oh. Okay. I was wonderin' if you were alive."

"What the hell do you want?" Colin growled.

"Now, shit, Colin, after six years that's how you greet me?"

Benny was cocked, ready to pop Colin with another shot, but Reed gestured for him to hold back.

"I heard you were back home, dog. And I, uh, well, let's just say I needed to holler atcha."

"What the fuck for? Couldn't you use the phone?"

"I'm afraid not, convict. The element of surprise is what works in this case. Ya see, I heard you were over at the YMCA . . . got a room, didn't ya . . ." Colin said nothing. "Oh, that's okay; I wasn't looking for an answer. I already *know* you got a room, isn't that right, J.J.?"

Colin looked toward the man with his grip over Toy's mouth. He was well over 300 pounds; his hair was unkempt and thin at the crown of his head. His eyes were beady, inset within his face. His forehead was prominent.

"See, I got soldiers everywhere, Colin. I know everything that goes down even before it goes down." Reed pulled out a slip of paper, unfolded it and tossed it on the bed. "Look familiar?"

Colin was still recovering, or trying to, from the blow to his head. "It's from your room at the Y." Reed made a tsk-tsk sound. "I wasn't so concerned about the first two things on the list—must see Kitty, must see Toy. I'd expect you to want to get your weed whacked. The more the merrier, right?"

Colin looked at Toy, at the confusion showing in her frightened eyes.

"It's the third goal that bothered me, Colin. I couldn't get any sleep tonight, ya know? What's that mean, must see Reed? See me about what?"

Colin was still stumped from the information that Fatso broke into his room, invaded his privacy.

"What you need to see me for, Colin? Huh? You wanna get at me for what I done to you? Huh? For what I done to your bitch? You wanna get at me for that?" Reed twirled a key ring on his finger.

Colin's stupefied expression turned to stone, fiery eyes within the slits under his furrowed brow.

"Guess what? I don't have no regret for shit I done. Shit don't get done to people who don't *let* shit happen to them— feel me? You got shitted on, dog. If it wasn't you, it woulda been somebody else. That's life. Shoulda kept yo' ass in the slow lane. You get in the fast lane and close your eyes, ya gets run over."

"Words from a scholar, huh?" Colin said.

"Scholar? Yeah. Why not. I guess you could call me that. I've been everything else. Right, Toy?" Colin had had just about all that he could stand. Sure he was outnumbered, and all three men probably weighed four or five times as much as he did. But Colin had the one thing that the three of them were likely lacking. Heart.

Benny's punch didn't hurt Colin like he was pretending. It stunned him, that's all. And all the while that Reed was talking, Colin was calculating. First, he'd have to protect Toy. And then somehow he'd have to throw off Reed, so far the only one that Colin could see with a gun in his waistband. But a fellow prisoner had once told Colin that you only brought a gun to a fight to use it. And so far Reed hadn't used it. *Fake thug*, Colin thought.

Colin shifted his weight and swung his body as a gymnast would on his pommel horse or a break-dancer on a cardboard box. In that instant, Colin hooked his left foot into Fat Boy's chin. Still in motion, Colin rolled on the bed, over Toy, snatching her to the floor with him. Fatso was on the floor holding his chin.

"Run," Colin told her, and then he hoisted the entire bed by its side, frame, mattress, box spring and all. He did this swiftly enough to catch both Reed and Benny off guard.

As Colin thrust the bed into the intruders he heard a gunshot. Then another. Also, Fat Boy had made a quick recovery and was charging at him. Colin had had this happen once before in prison, and as he'd done then, he threw his weight into a low side kick to the knee. Fat Boy instantly buckled, hollering, "He broke my leg! My leg!"

Colin bolted through the bedroom door and saw that Toy had their sleepy-eyed daughter in her arms. "GO! GO! GO!" he ordered, nearly pushing both through the front door.

"Colin! Come with us! Where are you goin'?"

"Nobody's chasin' us out of our house, Toy. Let me handle this." Colin closed the front door. He turned around to see Vince Reed and his two straggling henchmen. Vince was the only one with a weapon in hand.

Toy reached the lobby and cried for help. The doorman immediately came to her aid.

"What's wrong, Mrs. Williams?"

"Two men—three—upstairs. Guns. Call the police! Now!" Toy was saying this all at record speech while bouncing her crying daughter in her arms. "Shhh . . . it's gonna be all right, baby. Daddy's gonna be fine."

Roger Charles had his eyes set for any sudden activity, especially since those thuggy fellas stepped into the Shangrila. He could tell that they were men of evil intention by the looks on their faces and their aggressive steps. Besides that, it was almost one in the morning. What a time for a friendly visit.

When he spotted a hysterical Toy Williams rush out of the elevator into the glass-enclosed lobby, he jumped into action. Inside the lobby, Roger hustled toward Toy and the doorman. "Something wrong?"

"Yes! We need the police!" Toy yelled.

The doorman was already on with the 911 operator.

"There's men upstairs shooting at my *husband*!"

Toy forgot that she'd already met Roger—he could see that. It was of little importance now. There was nothing more to say. Roger was on a mission, not about money, but about saving lives. He hurried into the elevator and hit P—penthouse.

"Okay, so you got me," Colin said with his hands up. "You got me locked up as your scapegoat. You turned out my wife, and now you've got me under the gun. So what's left? Go on and shoot. Go ahead, shoot me!"

He was moving off of the penthouse entry hall and down into the sunken living room where Reed and his thugs were. It was clear that his words took them all by surprise.

"Don't come any closer, boy! I'll shoot."

"Why ain't you shot me already? Huh? What? The money too good? Killin' is too thugged-out for your rich taste?"

"I swear, I'll—"

"I bet you could do the time too. They'll put you in Marion Penitentiary where I was . . . oh, they'll be waitin' for you over there. As soon as it gets around about Reed! The man who set up one of his boys . . . they'll have a nice welcome for you . . ." Colin was a few feet from Reed now. "So go ahead. Shoot. Here, I'll help you." He lifted Reed's hand, gun and all, so that the barrel was at his forehead.

"Go ahead. It's only life in prison. Shoot! Shoot! Shoot me, motha-fucka!"

Reed was shook. His eyes were watering.

"Hmmm . . . just as I thought," Colin said, halfway turning. His turn was only so that he could get a good swing. Like Reed's cheek was lunchmeat, Colin slammed a right hook into him. Reed went spilling back toward the fireplace. The gun skidded a few feet across the white marble floor.

"Bitch-ass, scared-ass motha-fucka," Colin said. "Get your men up out of my house. And no. Ain't shit I gotta see you about now. I'm a better man for what I went through. If you wanna know the truth, I was gonna stop by to thank you. I don't care how many millions of dollars you push on the street, one thing you'll never have is integrity." Colin turned and went for the front door, expecting that they were preparing to leave.

A man was at the front door when he opened it, a puzzled look about him.

Roger pushed Colin aside the instant he saw danger. At the same time, he had his .44 Magnum out, firing at the bald-headed man with the gun. The first and second shots went off in rapid-fire progression, both hitting the gunman. Reed lay motionless on the marble floor in his own blood. The two henchmen stood still as statues, their hands reaching high.

Colin and Toy Williams moved out of their penthouse to rural Clinton, North Carolina.

Mrs. Malcolm Lee-Bryant, sister of Nathanial Lee—Colin's late prison buddy—owned a large home down the way. It had once belonged to slaveholders and included a large farm that provided corn, cotton and tobacco to traders far and wide.

Currently, the farm was producing an average of 1,000 bales of cotton twice per year, and netted the Lee-Bryant family financial freedoms that a Fortune 500 might envy.

Colin, following up on some of the personal papers Lee left with him, contacted Mrs. Lee-Bryant to mail or ship Lee's works to her. She asked him to personally deliver the property. Colin ended up striking a business venture with the family and he, Toy and Lady wound up making a good, honest, *legal* life for themselves. They never returned to Jersey City again.

*Stay alert for
part 2, the continuation
of the* Sugar Daddy
trilogy.

TURN THE PAGE FOR
A SNEAK PEEK AT

SEEMS LIKE
YOU'RE READY

COMING SOON FROM
ST. MARTIN'S PAPERBACKS

THE People's Choice Awards was the usual, confused, celebrity-packed event that I've grown so accustomed to. Mother told me that whenever I meet someone, even if I've never seen their work, I should smile and act like I have. Be diplomatic, she'd tell me.

"I love your work" is tattooed on the inside of my forehead, ready to be shared with everybody who even looks like a celeb. Even though Mother may have had something there, and it may even grow a nice appreciation for me, I'm not too happy with the idea. It's so cheesy and fake. I go to these shows and after-parties almost every week, and the praise seems to run out of gas sometimes. And it gets obvious, like I *obviously* don't mean it. I mean, I might as well open up a phone book, make mad calls, and tell everyone how marvelous their work is. So what if they hate their job cleaning up dog shit? Mother told me to say it.

Sincere was so cool. He even decided not to give out autographs for the night so that he could focus on me. I was flattered. Really. The limo took us to Roscoe's Chicken n' Waffles, and I felt more comfortable with more of our folks around. Even though I was too formal in my sequined gown, people understood. Lots of rappers, singers, and actors filed into the place after us. I even saw Mike Tyson, Busta Rhymes, Eve, Redman, Method Man, and that actor, Wesley Snipes. Tyson and Wesley looked like they had some kind of disagreement over a girl. And they even disappeared for some time toward the men's room. *Oh well,* I thought to myself. None of that mattered, 'cause Sincere was finally alone, with me. We held hands in our booth, fed each other chicken wings, and toasted the future over some milkshakes. I felt so honored to have him all to myself when half the world would've bent over backwards for his time. But here he was, interested in *me*.

"Hold my table," he suddenly told the waitress. Then he led me out through the back way to a passage that said "Employees Only." When we reached the back of the restaurant, nobody was there, and he spun me around and nudged me against the wall.

"I couldn't wait anymore, Angel." Sincere said this right before he pressed up to me and gave me the sweetest kiss. I counted all ten seconds. I was feeling weak and in need of air, but I liked it. I put my arms around him—maybe so I wouldn't fall—and I kissed him back. Tongue and all. I immediately felt the pressure of having to show him I knew what to do. I mean, Rory and I had done a little kissing, but Sincere had been all over the world. Probably with dozens of the most beautiful women begging him to kiss them. So I fed the frenzy and got as sloppy as I could until I really *did* need a chance to breathe. My eyes were still closed, and all I could think of was the birds in Minnie Ripperton's song— "Loving You." My body was soft and my head was woozy. For the first time in a long time, I didn't know what to do. I felt naked, like my clothes were still in the limo, my body was still in the fourth row at the PCAs, and my mind was one hour into the future. I was floating, drifting away on a stream of incredible feelings. He kissed me again, and my eyes stayed closed, revisiting that warm sensation—and then I was shook. A tremor rattled my bones the second Sincere felt me up. His hand was pulling my gown up over my hips until it grabbed my behind. Actually that wasn't the bad part. It was how he went behind and between my legs, slipped his fingers straight under my panties. That's when I lost it. I pushed him away from me. I mean, I didn't even know I was that strong to send him back up against the wall. That's when I ran back inside of Roscoe's and into the ladies' room. I didn't bother to fix my dress, I just felt it fall back into place. In the bathroom, I was a wreck. I was shivering like a freeze pop. My hands covering my face, talking to myself, "I can't believe he . . . I can't believe I . . . *Oh my . . .*"

I was beside myself. Humiliated and embarrassed. Afraid and alone. I didn't want to see him. My whole vision of him was distorted now and I couldn't imagine how it could ever be the same again.

"Angel . . ." Sincere was knocking on the bathroom door. My safe haven changed into a cage. He kept knocking. I just ignored it, though. I wanted him, me, and the world to disappear. The knocking stopped, but not inside of my chest. I realized I was tense, squeezing my butt cheeks together like I was trying to stop something from gettin' up in there. Something, like *him!*

"Hey, girl. One of them Nubian dudes is out there askin' about you."

Oh no . . . now I got the girl from *A Different World* all up in my face and my business. Lookin' at me like *"Whatchu' gonna do?"*

Now why did she suddenly look like a backstabbin' ho who wouldn't mind taking my place? Her hand on her hips-n-stuff. That got me goin'. I didn't know *what* I was gonna do or say, but I *did* know that I had to get out of *her* face.

"What? . . . Baby . . . where you goin'?" Sincere's voice was just behind me, trying to keep up as I strutted out of the bathroom and through the restaurant with an agenda. I didn't care who saw me, or if I was keeping proper etiquette or not. I just wanted *out.*

"Take me home," I demanded when I got to the limo driver. He looked at me like I'd just stabbed him, but he opened the door anyway. Sincere gave me space—I gotta give it to him for that, 'cause I don't know what I woulda done had he gotten in the limo with me. I waited as the limo driver and Sincere had a few words, then the car engine started up. I was taking one of those so-so-deep breaths when the window lowered. Sincere peeked in.

I turned my head, cussing the driver under my breath.

"Sorry, babe. I'll let him take you home." I let my lids flutter until they closed.

"Can I call you later?" Sincere, my dethroned Prince Charming,

But my lips were sealed. Next thing I knew, the limo was moving. And I didn't look back. I had mad questions when I got home.

How long do I have to be a virgin? Everybody's doin' it but me. I know what goes where thanks to Biology at Central High. So when can I get down . . . when can I get this monkey off my back? If I made the move, wouldn't today have been different? Was he makin' the right moves, and was I making the wrong ones?

Funny thing about mirrors; they're just like dolls. They don't talk back. I swear I stayed in the bath for an hour and a half. Sincere called my private line so many times I had to adjust the answering machine to pick up on the first ring. Between his calls and Rory's before him—because I was steadily erasing everything—the machine was doing double-time. I was afraid it was gonna break and I wouldn't be able to retrieve my business calls.

I focused a lot more on my ever-growing singing career after the Roscoe's fiasco. We did a video for "Like That" and I became a popular image on BET and MTV. They played the song to death on the radio. My producer, Jingle, taught me a lot about the behind-the-scenes business, like the Sound Scan numbers, the Billboard charts, and how I can make more money writing my own songs. I figured I better buckle down, since (it seemed) the world was putting me on this God-almighty pedestal. While I traveled on the major promo tour, taking trains and limos to stations from L.A. to Texas, to Florida and up the East Coast to New York, I began to write down my ideas for songs. Jingle gave me a formula to work with. He told me if there's a song I like by Whitney, Luther, or even Stevie Wonder, I should keep the melody in my head and just put my own words in place of the original lyrics. So I would hum "The Greatest Love of All," but I would write: "Whenever I'm Away." When I hummed the melody for "A House Is Not a Home," I would instead write: "Your Dreams Are Safe with Me."

I called Jingle while I was on the road, shared a few of my lines with him, and he assured me that I had good songs. I don't know if he was just pumpin' my head up or what, but I stayed excited. One thing Jingle told me, and which I never forgot was, "You're in a good place in the industry, Angel. Your music is being played on the R&B *and* pop formats. MTV, VH-1 *and* BET. Not many performers can claim that type of crossover appeal. Just keep doin' what you're doin'," he told me.

The publicist from Artistic was Lianne. She was nice to put up with me for the whole tour, but I could see she thought I was wasting my time writing. Some of the radio personalities were real funny on the morning shows. My favorites were Doug Banks and Olivia Fox, Dr. Dre & Ed Lover, and Wendy Williams in New York. She keeps it ghetto. The local video shows were everything from cheesy to broadcast quality, but it seemed like there were public access shows forever. Like, anybody who wanted to start a video show could do it just by raising their hands. *"Ooh . . . I'm a video producer!"* And everybody's supposed to go *woo-woo-woo,* and bow down to them. I just kept Mother's words in mind. *"Diplomacy, darling. Remember your diplomacy."*

I was excited when we reached New York. It was the end of the tour, plus I'd only been to New York once when the single was getting a buzz in certain markets. After the morning shows on WBLS, Hot 97, KTU, Power 105 & Z100, I had lunch with one of the labels' vice presidents. It was a whole big deal at the Russian Tea Room, where we discussed my future and how I had to maintain a *certain image* to satisfy my fan base. I got the idea that he was caught up in all the hoopla about Sincere and me. Those damn fan magazines never stop with the gossip. The instant that I thought about Sincere again, I caught a chill below my stomach. It felt like a cramp, really like my period was coming around again.

After lunch there were more video shows. Lianne scheduled interviews in half hour segments, all to be done in the conference room at Artistic headquarters. Some of the hosts were weird, and I learned to appreciate them because they broke up the usual humdrum questions I got from the ignorant hosts. I know I'm supposed to think diplomacy, but it's pretty hard when these folks are just plain ignorant. They sound like children sometimes, running the same ole questions. You'd think that my fans already knew how I got started and that they studied the same answer every time they turned the station or looked on my website.